The voice was male; deep and powerful, it seemed to come right out of the misty air. Dawn shivered on her perch on top of the gate.

"Who's there?" she asked the empty air. A wisp of fog drifted past her eyes. "Who is it?" She could hear the shrillness of fear in her voice. "I'm not trespassing."

A man stepped suddenly out from the trees. He moved as silently as the fog. "Now you're lying as well as trespassing," he said.

"Who are you?" she asked.

"The owner of the gate you're sitting on."

If that was true, Dawn thought, this was the famous Jacob Barr. The person she'd come all this way to investigate.

He wore frontier-style buckskins, complete with fringe and a touch of beading at the shoulder. He had the lean yet muscular build of an unaffected athlete and outdoorsman. He was definitely good-looking. Not what she'd expected to find here in the West Virginian wilderness.

Her reporter's instincts took over. Jacob Barr was too intriguing a man to ignore....

Dear Reader,

The setting for *The West Virginian* is, of course, West Virginia. I was drawn to the location because my eldest son lives there. In addition to his professional work, Greg does historical reenactments at an eighteenth-century fort just outside of town, and it was from this place that I conceived Jacob's Well. I visited the area in February, which explains the wintry weather that dominates the story. This is no time-travel venture, but an attempt to show how our past can enhance our present—and our future. So don your buckskins or your gingham gown and journey with me to this colorful setting that uniquely blends with the modern world.

Sharon Brondos

Books by Sharon Brondos

HARLEQUIN SUPERROMANCE

505—EAST OF THE MOON
527—SOUTHERN REASON, WESTERN RHYME
554—THE MARRIAGE TICKET
588—LUCK OF THE IRISH

HARLEQUIN CRYSTAL CREEK

4—WHITE LIGHTNING

Don't miss any of our special offers. Write to us at the following address for information on our newest releases.

Harlequin Reader Service
U.S.: 3010 Walden Ave., P.O. Box 1325, Buffalo, NY 14269
Canadian: P.O. Box 609, Fort Erie, Ont. L2A 5X3

Sharon Brondos

The West Virginian

Harlequin Books

TORONTO • NEW YORK • LONDON
AMSTERDAM • PARIS • SYDNEY • HAMBURG
STOCKHOLM • ATHENS • TOKYO • MILAN
MADRID • WARSAW • BUDAPEST • AUCKLAND

ISBN 0-373-70657-X

THE WEST VIRGINIAN

To Greg and Kristin, for the ideas,
the place and the love.

CHAPTER ONE

THE NARROW MOUNTAIN road had turned into a dirt nightmare a few miles back, but it was still a shock to Dawn Sutton when the high iron gate appeared out of the early-October morning fog, blocking the way. She slowed her car and stopped.

The gate loomed ahead, filling the view from her windshield. On either side, the thick West Virginia oak and pine forest seemed to move closer, shutting her into a capsule of car, dirt road and mist.

Dawn sat for a moment, contemplating the scene. She had suspected it wouldn't be easy. Had figured it would be more complicated than simply taking a half-day's drive into the mountains to get her story. The story was likely to be a good one, and because of that alone, she should have known the barriers would be up. One of the prime laws of investigative journalism: if it was worth getting, it was going to be hard to get. With an air of resignation, she set the parking brake and got out.

The air was cold and damp. It chilled her instantly after the dry heater warmth of her reliable old Saab. She jammed her bare hands into her coat pockets and walked up to the gate.

She studied it. Eight feet wide, easily that high or higher, attached at the sides to a sturdy barbed-wire fence that ran in both directions into the woods. The gleaming bars were solid and flecked only here and there with rust. Someone obviously had taken good care of the metal, oiling it against the damp cold. Checking to make sure there were no warning signs about possible electrocution, Dawn gave the gate a push.

It was locked. Big surprise.

"Hey!" she called. "Anyone here?"

Her voice was swallowed up by the trees.

"Hello!"

Nothing. She walked back to her car, leaned against the hood and stared skyward. Heaven was a blank, gray canopy. No answers there. Had she come all this way, only to be stopped by a gate? The gloomy sky seemed to mock her. Dawn closed her eyes.

It was her own fault.

She'd driven out here on an anonymous telephone tip. Had not taken the time to check out the possibility of obstacles in the form of barely passable dirt roads, gates and fences. The tip had seemed so hot and timely that she hadn't bothered to check much of anything. She could just hear her editor fuss at her for her lack of preparation. David would chew her out up one side and down the other.

And he would be correct.

She hadn't done her homework. She might well be wasting valuable time. Maybe nothing the caller said was factual.

But somehow, deep down, she *knew* the tip was a good one. Whether or not all the accusations the caller made were true, the subject itself was going to be valuable to her. Somewhere behind this imposing gate lay Jacob's Well, a secluded community of scientists, marketing specialists and other professionals who had chosen to abandon their pasts and live here in the middle of nowhere. Most of them worked for nothing except the pleasure of accomplishment.

And what accomplishments! Here, under the direction of a biochemist, Dr. Jacob Barr, they produced a line of personal-care products that had taken the retail world by storm.

It was a unique and fascinating economic community structure that could serve as a prototype for other industries. The more Dawn had thought about the concept, the more excited she'd become.

The phone call to her office at the magazine had come late last night, while she was alone putting the finishing touches on next month's lead article. The caller—a woman—had sounded calm and determined as she explained that she'd chosen to contact Dawn after reading her previous investigative work. Jacob Barr was running a slave camp of psychologically indentured workers, the woman continued in the same emotionless voice. And he was about to commit insurance fraud that would bring a swift and dramatic end to Jacob's Well. As well, the caller added, when it came to insurance scams, Jacob Barr was no novice. Before Dawn could respond, the woman quickly provided directions to the place and hung up.

It was the sort of stuff an investigative business reporter could not resist. The accusations might not be accurate, but they begged exploration.

So Dawn had done a little reading—probably too little—in the news files before taking off for the wilderness. If something rotten was going on, she wanted to be the first reporter to expose it. Not only would the story earn her kudos at the magazine, it might pro-

vide information about the community she could use
for her long-delayed Ph.D. thesis. Two for one.

She looked up at the gate.

Or none for none.

The gate stayed in the center of her vision, stolid,
unmoving, unopenable. Suddenly, Dawn felt something twist deep inside, and her level of determina-
tion rose. She would not give up without an effort. She
wanted this story.

She drew in a deep breath, and exhaled twin plumes
of vapor into the cold air. She reassessed the gate. It
wasn't all that high. She'd climbed more difficult
fences in her time.

She shrugged out of her long wool coat. It was
warm enough but not styled for fence climbing. She
put the garment in the car, grabbed her backpack and
locked the Saab. She turned to face the gate.

Her clothes—jeans, running shoes and a heavy wool
sweater with a cotton turtleneck underneath—could
take some punishment. She rubbed her hands together. Too bad she hadn't worn gloves. Oh, well. No
help for that now. She slipped the backpack on,
walked over to the gate, gripped the bars and set one
foot against the iron. It was ice-cold and slippery. But
with effort and concentration, it was climbable.

It took a lot of effort and concentration but after a
few minutes of struggling, she was straddling the top
bar, balanced precariously on a few inches of frigid
iron. Her breath came in short, smoky puffs, and in
spite of the chill, she was sweating.

She looked down, planning her descent. The ground
was far, far away. Tendrils of fog curled around the
base of the gate. The mist hung in the trees and en-
cased the surrounding area in a cottony aura. A car-

pet of dead leaves covered the road that extended behind the gate. Evidently, no one had driven a motor vehicle on it for a long time. That was odd. Surely a community the size of Jacob's Well, not to mention a fully operational factory, would require vehicles. Dawn hesitated.

Was she in the right place?

She had to be. Her anonymous contact had given excellent directions, except for neglecting to mention the gate. This was the way to Jacob's Well, all right. Dawn swung her legs over and hung, ready to drop to the leaf-carpet below. She paused for a moment.

And was extremely glad she had.

Without a sound of warning, three huge dogs hurled themselves out of the fog-shrouded woods and lunged, snarling, at her dangling feet. Dawn screamed and scrambled back to her perch on top of the gate. Her backpack fell to the ground in front of the dogs, and the three beasts turned their attention to it, growling and barking and worrying the object with their paws and teeth.

"Stop it!" Dawn yelled. "Quit it! Don't touch that! I've got a camera and tape recorder in there! Hey! Stop! Stop it right now!"

To her amazement, the three black monsters backed off, sat down on their furry haunches and gazed up at her. Their combined stares were solemn and curious, but oddly not really threatening.

Dawn considered. Maybe she could deal with them. She'd always gotten along with dogs. She eased forward a few inches. "Hello there, fellas," she said to the Labradors, making her voice high and friendly. "I'm..."

Her words trailed off. They weren't paying her a bit of attention. The dogs were staring at the forest. In a moment, Dawn saw why. An elf peeked shyly out from behind a tree.

Dawn nearly fell from her roost. The slender form was dressed entirely in green. Fair hair, short pixie-style. Heart-shaped face with big green eyes that stared up at her. Boy or girl, it was impossible to tell, but the face was so wonderfully pretty that Dawn let out an "Oh!" of admiration and astonishment.

The elf disappeared.

Dawn blinked.

Of course it wasn't an elf, she told herself. Elves didn't exist except in imagination and legend.

On the other hand, despite the fact that the woods were thick and the air was foggy, there was no way a human being could have vanished so quickly. She shivered. Iron gates, black dogs and now green-clad elves. What next? Maybe she ought to just get back in her car and forget the whole thing.

One of the dogs barked, stood and paced off into the trees, disappearing almost as silently as the elf.

Like a big black ghost.

Dawn shivered again. Eerie to see such a huge animal move so silently. She shook her head. The "elf" was probably a child. The dog was just a dog. She returned her attention back to the two remaining animals. They were real enough. Black hides, white teeth, red tongues... "Okay, fellas," she said. "Look. I'm—"

"Trespassing."

The voice was male, deep and seemed to come right out of the misty air. Deep and powerful. Not the voice of an elf. No indeed! But the owner was not visible. Another ghost?

No. Not with that voice.

Dawn's heartbeat went into overdrive. "Who's there?" she asked the empty air. A wisp of fog drifted past her eyes. "Who is it?" she added, hearing the shrillness of fear in her own voice. "I'm not trespassing!"

A man appeared, stepping out from the trees. He moved as silently as the fog. But his physical presence was too striking for him to be an illusion or a spirit. He went over to stand by the dogs. "Now you're lying as well as trespassing," he said evenly. "What should I do about that?"

Relieved to be dealing with a real person, Dawn was nevertheless speechless. First, hounds from hell, then an elf, ghosts and now this! This...

This *man*.

He wore frontier-style buckskins, complete with fringe and a touch of decorative beading at the shoulder. His feet were shod with soft moccasins, and he held a long rifle with an ease that indicated great familiarity with the weapon. He had the lean, nonbulky yet muscular build of an athlete and outdoorsman. His expression was pleasant enough for the moment, although something about the dangerous glint in his green eyes made her shiver again. This could be *real* trouble. She studied her adversary carefully.

He looked to be in his mid-thirties, a few years older than she, but something about his face bespoke a man who'd been through a lot. He looked wary, with an almost-predatory manner about him. His light brown hair was flecked with droplets of moisture from the fog, giving it a silvery sheen. Perhaps some real gray in it, too. His features were cleanly formed and just a shade shy of being too handsome. He was definitely good-looking enough to pose in a magazine ad. Not at all what she had expected to find up here in the West Virginia wilderness. Not at all.

"Who are you?" she asked.

"The owner of the gate you're sitting on," he replied. With one hand, he patted one of the dogs. With the other, he shifted the rifle to a more threatening position, almost pointed right at her. The dog looked up at him, adoration in its eyes.

Dawn eased herself toward the outside of the gate, ready to jump and run for her car, wishing she hadn't locked it. "You can't own this gate," she said. "It's on a public road."

"No, miss, it's not," he said. "I do own it. Don't think of trying to drop and run, please. I can have the gate open and my dogs at you before you get to your car. They won't hurt you, but they will stop you cold, if I tell them to."

"You're *threatening* me?"

"No." He smiled. "Just making a strong suggestion." The tip of the rifle moved a millimeter in her direction. "Come on down now. On this side."

"I don't trust you." She gripped the bar tightly and eyed the two dogs. "How do I know you won't sic them on me once I hit the ground?"

"You have my word. As for trust, it's not *me* intruding on your territory."

"There's no trespassing notice."

"Not needed. The gate speaks for itself. To most folks, that is," he added. He lowered the rifle. "Look, I'm not going to hurt you, and I won't sic my dogs on you. So come on down and let's sort this out before one of us does or says something foolish.''

Dawn considered what he'd said. She had a job to do and it lay on his side of the gate. She'd known there'd be risks. She could hardly stay up here forever. Her legs and hands were starting to cramp. He didn't look mad. In fact, his handsome face had more than a trace of kindness on it now. The hunter-predator look was gone.

Furthermore, he sounded reasonable.

''Okay,'' she said. ''Stand back.'' She swung over the side and dropped, the air shooshing out of her as she hit the ground hard. Her left ankle gave way, and she sat down swiftly, yelping with pain.

A hand reached down and grasped hers. ''Try to stand. Are you hurt?''

Dawn stood, holding his hand, feeling the strong sure support he gave. She tested her ankle, putting a little weight on it. She felt a twinge, but nothing unbearable. ''No,'' she said, looking down at the ankle. ''The joint's just a little weak there. I broke it when I was small. Climbing trees when I was told not to. Thanks.'' She released his hand and looked up.

And, for a moment, she was lost.

His eyes were greener than the dark pines flanking the road. She felt the breath catch in her throat again, but this time not from falling. Something electric zinged in the air between them, then faded to a gentle tingling that encompassed her.

''I'm sorry to have scared you,'' he said, unwittingly breaking the spell. ''Sure you're all right?''

She nodded. ''Y-yes,'' she said haltingly, feeling the tingling fade and reality reassert itself. ''If you do own all this as you claim, you must be Jacob Barr.''

"I'm Jake Barr. You have the advantage, miss."
The gentle expression left his face, and he looked
tough once more. "This is a private road, private land,
and no trespassers are allowed. None. So why are you
here?"

Part of the truth will do, Dawn told herself.

"I'm a graduate student," she said. "I'm working
on my Ph.D. in economics. My thesis is about small
American communities that are bound together by
single, successful economic enterprises. Like the
nineteenth-century attempts at Utopian groups or the
modern Israeli kibbutz. Your place, Jacob's Well, really fits the pattern from what I've read. I want to
study it. That's why I'm here." *There, that wasn't a
lie.* Just a few details left out.

He looked at her. One eyebrow went upward.

"Really," she said, defending herself. "I've got
proof. You can call my thesis adviser at Georgetown.
She'll confirm what I said."

He stepped back, away from her, resting the butt of
the long rifle on the ground near his foot. "I'm sure
you have someone to back you up, but why should I
believe her? I caught you trying to sneak in. If you
want to look around, why didn't you call me and make
an appointment?"

Good question. She looked down, pretending to be
embarrassed. "I acted on impulse, Dr. Barr. Sorry,
but that's the truth."

"Hmm."

"It is!" She looked right into his eyes. To her
amazement, they still had an electric effect on her. The
something hit her again, but she kept her emotions
under control. He was gorgeous, but he was in her
way. "Why should I lie to you?" she asked. "You

have the dogs and the gun. All I've got is my dependence on your goodwill and generosity.''

''Then you are in trouble, miss.''

''And so are you.'' She crossed her arms and glared at him. ''You wouldn't dare harm me. I have lots of close friends. They all know where I am!''

''I'm *sure* they do.'' After putting a gently sarcastic emphasis on the words, Jake studied the woman. He believed her about having close friends, but somehow he doubted they knew what she was up to at the moment. She had the air of a woman who worked and lived alone.

Although, he had to admit she was too darned attractive to be alone for long. Not just physically. It ran deeper. The sheer energy of her personality would draw others to her. Her winsome appeal formed a pleasing aura around her. An aura she was completely unaware of, he was willing to bet.

He had already appreciatively studied her figure while she'd been balancing on the gate, but close up he found her even more pleasing to the eye. She was small and pretty with a fresh-scrubbed face and a headful of tangled dark brown curls.

Her clothing looked comfortable and well worn, but of good quality, and the Saab outside the gate indicated a person of some substance, even if the car was an older model. It looked clean and well-cared for.

He found himself admiring her control during what was, as far as she knew, a dangerous confrontation with a stranger. Yes, indeed. She was clearly very sure of herself, even though it was obvious she wasn't telling the truth. At least not all of it.

Obviously she hadn't come seeking shelter at the Well. She was on some sort of self-serving and self-directed mission. The steady gaze she gave him out of her blue eyes told him that she'd seen trouble before.

Seen it and dealt with it.

Or caused it.

Jake made a decision. She might be any number of things, but one thing for sure, she was here and he would do well to keep close tabs on her until he was certain who she was and what she was up to. Although she didn't know it, her timing could be both an advantage and disadvantage to her. But he'd tackle that dilemma later. "You know who I am, but I have no idea who you are. What's your name?"

"Dawn Sutton."

"All right, Dawn Sutton. Maybe I'm making a mistake, but I'll make a deal with you. I'll take you to the Well, but I want to see what you write about it before you submit it for your thesis."

She shook her head, the dark curls haloing her face. "No deal. If you show me your community, you'll just have to trust me that I'll write about it truthfully."

He laughed, amazed at her audacity. "Trust you? After you tried to sneak into my turf?"

"I made a mistake doing that, and I apologize. I promise only to tell the truth about your setup."

"Sure you will."

"My academic reputation depends on my veracity!" Her blue eyes were blazing now. "I *have* to be reliable."

"And temperamental?"

She settled down. "You pushed a few buttons. Sorry."

"Is that sorrow genuine?" He barely kept from smiling. Her annoyance with him was almost palpable and, oddly, it pleased him that he could affect her this much even if it was only to make her mad. "Or are you just trying to soften me up?"

Now she smiled. "I doubt if I could do that, Dr. Barr." She uncrossed her arms. "Look, I know what I tried to do was wrong. I ought to have called and made an appointment. But I'm here. Please. Won't you show me your place?" Her smile increased in wattage and her blue eyes shone. She held out her hands in a pleading gesture.

How could he resist that? Jake signaled the two dogs, noting that Jasper had taken off, doing his job looking after Sophie. "All right," he said, looking back at her. "You have a point. You *are* here. I'll take you to the Well. The community itself has no secrets, and you're welcome to look around and talk to people." He turned and started to walk into the woods. The dogs barked and romped into the trees ahead of him.

Dawn followed. "If the community has no secrets, where are they, then?" she asked. She ran a little to catch up. "What dark things go on here in the woods?"

Jake found himself laughing again. "You really are one big nerve, Dawn Sutton," he said. "You trespass, make demands and now you want to know my darkest secrets."

"Well, the woods seem full of them." She fell into step beside him. "When I was up on the gate, I thought I saw an elf or a wood nymph."

"What?"

"Really. A small person, wearing a green outfit. I said something, and it disappeared. I mean, vanished! One of your dogs took off after it, I think."

"You think you saw an elf?"

The amusement in his tone was audible enough, but when Dawn glanced sideways at him, she could see he was doing his level best not to laugh at her once more.

"Okay, what do you think I saw? No kid would be running around out here in the middle of nowhere."

"Oh yes, that kid would be. You saw my eleven-year-old daughter, Sophie."

"Your daughter?" Somehow, he didn't strike her as the married type. Then the resemblance hit her. The elf's green eyes were the same color as the man's. "Oh."

"You sound disappointed. Prefer it to have been a wood nymph?"

"Maybe. I just didn't know kids stayed at your community." She had read enough about Jacob's Well last night to know that it was a working community of highly trained, career-oriented adults. Single folk, not families.

"Not ordinarily," he said, something in his voice telling her that she had touched a very sore spot. "Families usually don't come here. Just individuals. Sophie is an exception. She's the only young one here."

"But doesn't the child get lonely out here in the middle of the forest with no other kids to play with?"

He stopped and looked at her. "You really are a nosy person, Ms. Sutton."

"Sorry again. I'm just relieved I wasn't seeing things that don't exist."

"Who says elves don't exist?"

"But you said—"

"I said you saw Sophie. I think. This time."

"You're pulling my leg, aren't you?"

"Ms. Sutton, this forest is very old. Ancient, in fact. Who knows what lives here besides us?"

"Very funny." She tried without success to detect a teasing glint in his eyes.

There was none.

He started walking again, striding along as if he was in a hurry. Dawn jogged to catch up. "Slow down, please," she complained. "Your legs are twice as long as mine."

"We have a good ways to go." He didn't slow.

"How far?"

"About five miles."

"Five? Miles?"

"Want to go back?"

"No. I came a long way to see this. And if I have to run, I will."

"All right." He slowed a bit.

They moved along in silence for a while. Leaves crunched under Dawn's running shoes. The dogs raced around, crashing through the undergrowth, seeking unseen prey. Once they treed a squirrel that sat on the end of a high branch and chittered curses down at them. The dogs barked joyously, clearly enjoying the exchange.

Only Jake Barr moved silently. Silently and very quickly. Much too quickly.

Finally Dawn stopped, bent over and put her hands on her knees, her breath puffing like steam in the cold air. "I can't keep this up. I'm a city woman, and my lungs miss the pollution," she told him. "I have to catch my breath for a few minutes."

Ten paces ahead of her, he stopped. "Okay," he said. "I don't mean to desert you, but I'm going to move on and check out a few things, including my daughter. I expect she went home with the other dog, but I'd like to be sure. The Well's not too far ahead. You really can't miss it. Just follow the path."

"Path?" she asked, staring down at the tangle of dark undergrowth, dirt and dead leaves at her feet. "What path?"

No answer.

When she looked up, he was gone. Disappeared like smoke.

Like a ghost.

"Dr. Barr?" She walked forward, listening. "Jake?"

The forest was deathly quiet.

Dawn felt rising panic. "Jake!"

Nothing. He was gone.

She was alone. She was lost.

Overhead, something moved in the trees. She heard a sound behind her. A disturbance in the underbrush. Off in the distance, a crow called raucously. Through the overhanging branches, she got a glimpse of leaden sky. It looked gray and close, as if it were ready to press down on her.

Another rustling sound.

Dawn turned in a circle. "Who's there?"

No answer.

Okay. She was abandoned, but she needed to keep moving. He had pointed out the way. And he didn't strike her as the type who would leave her if doing so was dangerous. He didn't seem the type to leave a defenseless city woman out in the middle of nowhere to die of starvation or exposure.

So the noises meant nothing.

Even silence meant nothing. All she had to do was put one foot in front of the other and move in the direction he had shown her.

She could do that, couldn't she?

CHAPTER TWO

JAKE BARR RETURNED to the Well quickly, loping along at a ground-eating pace with the two dogs running beside him. Although he had some qualms about leaving Dawn Sutton out in the woods alone, he was confident the woman would be able to negotiate the rest of the way unescorted. She seemed capable. And he had good reason to want to be ahead of her. Sophie was not really his concern at the moment. Dawn Sutton was.

He needed some time to check her out. Everyone who showed up at the Well these days was suspect. No, that wasn't exactly accurate, he thought with regret. Everyone *at* the Well was suspect.

Sabotage was a problem any small industry had to be aware of, but out here at the Well, the situation was complicated by the fact that no outsider could enter the grounds without being noticed. So the sabotage attempts that Jake had uncovered and dismantled so far had to have been made by someone on the inside. Someone he trusted.

The realization was extremely painful to him, but it was the only possible explanation.

That didn't mean, however, that the saboteur had no outside connection. Could Dawn Sutton be that connection? Coming to check on why the attempts at subversion had failed?

Coming here to accomplish what one or more of his once-trusted people had not succeeded in doing?

Unlikely. She would have come up with a more conventional way to get inside if she was involved in a conspiracy; sneaking in over the gate only made her look guilty.

Still, he couldn't be too careful. As yet, nothing and no one had been harmed, because he had been on the alert. He needed to stay that way. His future and the futures of all the people at the Well depended on his checking everything. Over and over again, until at times he was so weary, he thought he could lie down and sleep for a week! Jake couldn't remember when he'd last slept peacefully through an entire night.

But rest would come when he had made his place safe once more. Until then, he had to keep pushing himself. First, he made sure Sophie was back. Then he entered the main building and headed for his office. There, he set his rifle against the wall and sat down at his desk. The computer screen danced with a colorful program Sophie had developed the other day. Jake changed directories and went into the system that accessed the Internet, thinking not for the first time, how grateful he was for the ease with which he could gain information on any subject. It certainly made his job a lot easier. He began to hunt.

Ten minutes later, he knew who Dawn Sutton was. And why she was here.

Then, because he'd seen all the signs in the sky this morning, he checked the regional weather report. It confirmed what he already knew.

FOR WHAT SEEMED like forever, Dawn walked through the silent, cold forest, cursing Jake Barr with what little energy and emotion she had to spare. She hoped she was going in the direction he'd indicated, but as far as she could tell, there was no path, no clear way, no signs that anyone had walked this way since the beginning of time. The tree and brush branches seemed to grab at her clothing, and her feet slid and skidded on the slippery carpet of pine needles. Finally she gave up and stopped.

She was lost. Hopelessly. She listened, straining to hear any sound that would help guide her out of this maze.

"It's just a little farther."

Dawn jumped, then settled down. This time, the disembodied voice was female. An adult female who sounded friendly. "Who's there?" she cried out.

A woman stepped from the trees and stood in front of Dawn. Except for the parka, jeans and flannel shirt she wore, she could have walked right off the page of a fashion magazine. She had long blond hair and a perfect complexion unaided by any makeup.

"Hi," the woman said. "I'm Laurie Tanner. When you didn't show up right away, Jake sent me to check on you." She held out her hand in greeting.

Dawn shook it. "Hi, I'm Dawn Sutton," she said. "I got lost. I'm really glad to see you. Are you Jake's wife?"

Laurie laughed. "No. I'm just one of Jake's refugee-from-the-outside-world employees. He's divorced. Has been for a long time. His ex-wife wouldn't be caught dead around here!"

"Oh. I thought . . . I mean, I saw his daughter and I assumed that his wife was here, too."

"You saw Sophie?"

"She was dressed in green and she peeked out at me through the trees. For a moment I thought she was an elf."

More laughter. "That I can understand. The girl is special and more than a little strange when she chooses to be. As for your being lost, the compound's right over there. You would have reached it in a few minutes if you'd just kept on going."

"I had no idea. I thought I was completely off track."

"Jake didn't give you directions?"

"Not so I could tell. He said to follow the path. I couldn't see one to save my life."

"That's just like him. He knows these woods so well, it's hard for him to imagine anyone else not being able to find their way around as easily as he does. Come on. I'll walk with you the rest of the way."

"Thanks. I was getting close to panic."

"No need. Just remember when you think you're lost around here, stop moving. Stay still, and someone will eventually find you."

"Eventually?" Dawn gave an exaggerated shiver. "I'd be frozen by then. It's really getting cold."

"Yes, it is. Early in the season for it, but I see your point."

They walked on for a few minutes, chatting. Dawn noted with some satisfaction that Laurie made as much noise moving through the brush as she did. "Tell me, is Jake some kind of woods expert?" she asked. "He didn't even make footprints when he was walking with me."

"He's an expert in lots of things," Laurie replied, quite seriously. "He was born nearby and has lived out here for a long while. Some of the more superstitious

locals claim he's really an old West Virginia frontiers-
man come back to life. They act like they're joking,
but I'm not sure they believe it.''

"The buckskins? The rifle?''

"It adds to the legend,'' Laurie replied. ''But I think
he uses that gear only because he likes it, and it's
comfortable for trekking in the woods.''

"He can do whatever he likes out here, I guess,''
Dawn commented. This was a perfect opportunity to
draw out one of Jake's people. ''He's like a king. I
mean, who would interfere?''

Laurie stopped. ''What kind of a thing is that to
say?'' she asked, her tone and expression indignant.
''You make him sound like some sort of dictator.'' She
paused for a moment. ''Who exactly are you?'' she
said finally.

"I'm Dawn Sutton.'' She was taken aback by the
sudden hostility. ''I told you...''

"No. I mean, who are you and why are you here? I
thought you were coming to the Well.''

"I am, but—''

"But you didn't come to get away from the outside. You aren't one of us. I can sense that! Tell me
right now what you want with Jake, or I swear I'll lead
you out into the woods and leave you there for bear
bait!''

Dawn took a deep breath. The woman was completely serious. ''I'm a graduate student at Georgetown,'' she said. ''My thesis is on communities like
Jacob's Well, so I—''

"You're a student?'' Laurie looked embarrassed.
''Gosh, I'm sorry, Dawn. I didn't mean to...''

"It's all right. I should have explained.''

"No, really. I'm sorry. Jake's been having some personal problems lately and I...I guess we're all feeling more than a little protective of him."

"Personal problems?"

Laurie started walking again. "Let's change the subject," she said. "I'd rather not talk about Jake's private business."

Dawn moved beside her. "Fine. I have no intention of using anything personal in my thesis. I'm concentrating on the community as a whole, not on individuals."

Laurie glanced at her. "But that's what the community is. Individuals. How can you...?" She stopped and held up a hand.

Dawn also stopped moving. Something large was looming on the path ahead of them. A bear?

"What's the matter, ladies?" Jake stepped into view. "Did you both get lost?" His expression showed concern. "Laurie, I thought you knew the way."

"We were talking, and I wasn't paying attention. Are we off track?" Laurie asked.

"About a hundred and eighty degrees." He pointed. "Home is back that way."

"How did you do that?" Dawn asked.

"What?"

"Find us. Sneak up on us."

Jake frowned. "I wasn't sneaking, and I heard your voices. Just followed the sound."

"You heard us? We weren't talking loudly. Not much above a whisper."

"He has radar for ears," Laurie declared. "He can hear a mouse burp."

Dawn laughed.

Neither of the other two did. An awkward silence settled upon the trio.

Laurie broke it. "I think I'll head back," she said. "See you at the Well, Dawn."

"Okay." Dawn was reluctant to see the woman leave. The idea of being alone in the woods with Jake Barr was not adding to her much-eroded sense of security.

He waited until Laurie was out of sight and the sounds of her moving along the forest path were almost gone. The entire time, which must have been only minutes but seemed like hours, he stared at Dawn, his green eyes strange, piercing and . . .

And utterly disconcerting. She held his gaze, but with great difficulty.

"I'm rescinding my invitation. You have to leave," he said. "There's a bad storm coming. I want to get you back to your car and see you're on your way before it hits."

This was the last thing she'd expected to hear. "No," she told him. "I'm not leaving! There's no storm. You're just afraid to let me see—"

"Dawn, don't be stubborn. I really don't care if you come and camp in the middle of the Well. But you'll be doing it in five or six feet of snow by tomorrow."

"Not true. I checked the weather before I left Washington. It's supposed to rain, but that's it."

"It's going to snow." He turned away. "But, all right. Suit yourself." He started to walk into the trees, seeming to fade from sight even as she watched. The bare branches of deciduous trees and the boughs of evergreens seemed to embrace him and cover him from view.

"Don't do that!"

He looked back at her. "Don't do what?"

"Don't leave me, Jake," she said. "Please."

He stopped. "Sorry. I thought you were right behind me."

"You're like a ghost. How could I follow you?"

"What do you mean?"

"I . . . I'm not sure. You move so quickly and silently. Just don't leave me alone. I came all the way out here to see your place. Why don't you want me to?"

He moved back to face her. "You tell me. Is there a reason I should be concerned about showing you the Well?"

He was confronting her. She felt his stare all the way to her soul. The trees seemed to stand closer, too. Waiting. Listening to her heart.

Truth time.

"I guess I sort of lied to you," she said. "I'm not here just for my thesis research. I'm working on an article for a magazine. I'm a business-news reporter."

Jake Barr nodded. "That's what I hoped you'd say. All right. Come on, follow me." He reached out and took her hand. "I won't let you get lost again."

"Don't you want to know why . . . ?"

"It's going to snow, and I already know," he said. Then, without another word of explanation, he led her into the woods.

Too overwhelmed to speak, Dawn walked beside him in silence. She had the feeling that only when Jake Barr was good and ready would he let her know exactly what he knew, how he'd found it out and what he thought about it.

A few minutes later, they were at the edge of the forest, looking out on a wide, open meadow.

And on Jacob's Well.

"It's a fort!" Dawn declared, staring at the high wooden palisades surrounding the place. The logs were easily fifteen feet high and pointed at the top. In each corner, a square watchtower rose even higher. The vantage point from them had to take in miles and miles of the surrounding terrain, she realized. No one could sneak up on Jake Barr!

"Is it real?" she asked, turning to look at the owner of the fort. "It's magnificent."

"Thanks," he said. His expression showed the pride he had in the place. "It's real, authentic, but not original. It's a reproduction of a revolutionary-era frontier fort. When I bought the land, I investigated the history of the area and found out that a fortification like this one was set right about here over two hundred years ago."

"So you put up a new one?"

"It seemed fitting."

"Like wearing buckskins?"

He gave her a long look. "Welcome to the club of folks who think I have a screw loose."

"Oh, I didn't mean..."

"Sure you did." He turned his attention back to the fort. "But it doesn't matter. What matters is that I'm happy with all this, and my work is going well. People who come here find something good for themselves. On top of everything, we manage to put out a good line of products."

"That's true. I've used some of them."

"So you know about it. Maybe when you get to know more about me, you'll understand and appreciate my eccentricities."

"Maybe," she said, doubting it. But then she glanced at him and caught the full power of his gaze.

Once more it was a breathtaking experience.

He didn't reply to her comment, nor seem to notice the effect he had on her. He led her out across the field and up the hill to the gate of the fort. Walking beside him, Dawn wondered what she was getting herself into. The dead autumn grass crunched underfoot, the stalks made brittle by late-morning hoarfrost. Not enough sunlight had broken through the heavy clouds to melt away the spiky frost.

A wind blew across the open space, and she felt the cold right through to her bones. Jake might be right about snow, she thought. It was far too early in the year, but they were certainly in high Appalachian country. Snow came up here long before hitting the lower lands nearer the coast. As they walked through the open gate, she heard the moan and sigh of the wind in the tall pine trees behind them.

Like a warning.

But once inside, she saw nothing alarming. The interior space formed a huge rectangle. The fort area covered the hill, as she had seen from outside, but it continued onward to the north and dipped back into the trees beyond. No real defensive fortification would have done that, she thought.

So, this was more than a historic reproduction. The architecture was geared to the purpose of the builder: production not protection. Although the surrounding high fence was constructed of rough log and looked authentic, some of the buildings inside the compound were modern in design and material. Glass, concrete and steel instead of wood.

"You can tell where we do the work," Jake said, pointing to the modern edifices and confirming her guess. "Those buildings are completely outfitted and up-to-date. Air-conditioned, a LAN computer system that interconnects all the computers at the Well. In there, you'd never think you were out in the middle of the West Virginia wilderness."

"But you sure know it out here," she commented. The central area was an open, grassy space, autumn-brown now. To her immediate left and right were two large long buildings made of logs.

"True. These are called the main buildings, for lack of a better title," he said. "They're all-purpose. Offices, guest rooms, dorm section, dining area, meeting rooms, auditorium. Heated and lit by electricity, too. While we live in a pretend version of the eighteenth century, most of us would balk at having to survive without modern conveniences."

Dawn gave him a look.

Jake smiled at her. "Including me," he admitted.

"I have to say I'm relieved to hear that," she replied.

"Would you like to hear why I've decided to let you in even though I know who and what you really are?"

"S-sure." She was shivering from the cold. She'd been standing still, and her body warmth had fled quickly.

"Then let's get inside, and I'll tell you." He took her past the long building on the right to an area where several dozen smaller log buildings stood apart. They were replicas of authentic log cabins with wooden steps leading to short front porches. He took her up the stairs to the front door of the first one.

"This is my home," he said, opening the door. "Welcome."

Dawn went in.

Home.

The room enfolded her. Golden wood floor, polished by feet and time. A multicolored oval rag rug lay in front of a couch covered in blue-and-red plaid. Along the wall to her right was a large bookcase. One of the big black dogs lay on another rug in front of a fireplace. The dog's tail thumped the floor in greeting. Coals glowed warmly and blazed to fire when Jake went over to stir them and add a fresh log.

Dawn breathed in the smells of wood smoke, coffee, cinnamon and leather and gun oil...and the tang of maleness. This was definitely a man's home. Jake really lived here. The very air was imbued with his essence.

"Sit down," he said, indicating the sofa. "I'll get us some coffee."

"Okay."

"Then we can talk," he added. Jake left the room and went into the kitchen. While he prepared the coffee, he thought about Dawn Sutton.

It was easy to do. As he'd noticed when he met her, she was most definitely attractive, and he realized that he was already responding to that fact. While his brain was dealing with her intellectually, the rest of him was reacting to her in a far more basic manner. He set the coffeepot on the stove and smiled wryly at his own male foolishness. It had been a while since a woman had touched off the old masculine triggers in him, and so he would be wise to be wary of his vulnerability.

On the other hand, if she proved to be harmless in other ways, maybe being vulnerable to her feminine charms wasn't such a bad thing. Suddenly he recognized that he could use a touch of romance in his life right now. If he didn't let it get to the point where it was a real distraction, pleasure might counteract the stress and tension that chewed at him night and day. His smile broadened as he stoked wood into the stove and felt the warmth of the flames on his skin. If Ms. Sutton wasn't the one to provide such an outlet, he still owed her for making him aware he needed it.

WHILE HE WAS OUT in the kitchen, Dawn removed the tape recorder from her backpack. She left the camera inside. Time for pictures later. She had started out on the wrong foot with Jacob Barr and needed to retrace her steps carefully until she had the right foot ahead. That meant not pushing her welcome or her luck.

He returned after a few minutes. He had changed out of his buckskins and was wearing jeans and a gray sweatshirt. "I put the coffee on to perk," he said, sitting down on the sofa near her. "It'll be ready shortly."

"No microwave?"

"I like mine the old-fashioned way."

"No surprise there." She placed the recorder on the rough wooden table in front of the sofa. "Now that my secret is out, I might as well be professional about this. Would you mind if I recorded the interview?"

"Interview?" He sat back, lounging into the cushions. "Is that what you came to do? Interview me?"

"Well, not exactly."

"Exactly what, then?"

She debated a second. "Jake, how did you find out who I am? My name's not a household word yet."

"But you hope it will be?"

"As the reporter in the room, I'm supposed to be the one asking the questions."

He regarded her for a minute. "Okay. I ran your profile down by using the Internet. I got into the Georgetown system and simply looked for your name. Since you'd said you were affiliated there, I knew if you were telling the truth, I'd find you."

Dawn groaned. "And my job with the *Wilmont Times* is listed in my bio."

"Yes."

"Jake, I admit it was dumb not to tell you right away, but you really did catch me off guard. I was—"

"Why did you come here?"

Dawn thought about the phone call. Should she tell him? Not yet, she decided. She didn't know him, and there was the possibility he was involved in something legally shaky. Until she cleared him in her own mind, he was not to know about the phone call! Perhaps not even then, since telling him might compromise a news source. "Curiosity. Interest. The usual motives," she said.

He seemed to consider her words. Dawn wondered if he believed her. She couldn't tell.

"I'm going to ask you something," he said. "It might seem strange, but I have good reasons."

"Ask away."

"Will you be willing not to tell anyone else you're working for a magazine?"

"Why?"

"I have my reasons."

Dawn hesitated. "Well, I suppose I ought to respect them since you're letting me have a look. Okay, no reporter talk. Just a Ph.D. candidate looking for material to flesh out her dissertation."

His expression told her that her answer was satisfactory.

"Is your interest in the Well or in me?" he asked.

"I believe they're connected," she replied, warming to her subject. She was on solid ground here. "Most enterprises like Jacob's Well depend on leadership and vision. I don't think this community is an exception."

"Flattery?"

She smiled. "Sometimes it works."

He gazed at her without speaking. She returned his stare without wavering.

And waited. He would speak first, she decided. If he did, that would mean he was willing to cooperate with her.

He did. "I'm a biochemist," he said. "My academic and professional background is available through public records." He stood up and went over to stir the fire. The dog raised its head for a pat. Jake complied. "But what isn't public knowledge is why I went into the field in the first place." He turned and gestured at the recorder. "You might find this information worthwhile."

Dawn turned on the small machine.

"I was born and raised in these mountains," Jake said, still standing, back to the fire. "My parents are educated people. Both were teachers."

"They live here?"

"Not here. Over in Fairway. It's a small coal mining town just over the hill."

"Hill?"

He smiled and sat down. "Well...a mountain. Around here, they're all called hills. We walk them as if they were hills, anyway."

"So you're a local boy made good?"

"You could say that. I grew up in a strangely mixed environment," he said, staring into the fire now, not looking at her. "My mom and dad were considered the intellectual elite of Fairway. They were the only ones in the area with education beyond high school. In fact, most local folks never made it past eighth grade."

Dawn thought of her own childhood. All of her parents' friends were college-educated. Most held postgraduate degrees. "So, your mother and father were the only schoolteachers?"

He nodded. "They retired a few years ago. My cousin, Harper Barr, is there now. She's Sophie's teacher."

"Your daughter?"

"She has to go to some kind of school. Fairway's nearest."

"But it's over a mountain from here."

"She gets there by foot, on horseback or by snowmobile, if the weather warrants. It takes about an hour to walk it, much less on horseback."

"But it's still so long, so far..."

"No longer than many people commute by car, or kids ride buses. Think about it. The only difference is that she's out in the woods, while the others are on highways and roads."

"She goes alone?"

"No, of course not." He turned. "I take her to school and pick her up. We were on our way back when I found you. I'd decided to let her miss school because of the weather. I knew it was going to snow, and I was afraid she'd be stuck in Fairway. She could stay with her grandparents, of course, but I'd rather she be here with me."

"Oh. Go on."

"So, as I was saying, I learned the value of formal education from my parents. But someone else taught me what I needed to know to make Jacob's Well."

"Who?" Dawn leaned forward, resting her elbows on her knees. He'd managed to fascinate her with his talk. He was, she realized, a natural storyteller.

A natural interviewee. This would translate beautifully to paper.

"My great-grandpa. He taught me to love and understand the fruits of the earth, how to harvest them without harming the environment and how to use them to help people feel better. He was a natural biochemist. A healer who was taught by the very plants he used." He stood up. "Coffee's ready. I'll tell you the rest later."

She was suddenly aware of the aroma. "It smells wonderful!" She clicked off the recorder. "I really could use a cup."

"Into the kitchen, then. Maybe you'd like something to eat, too."

"Sure. If it's not any trouble."

Jake smiled. "None. I'm kind of hungry, myself."

A few minutes later, Dawn swallowed hot, fresh coffee and ate a sandwich piled with tomatoes, lettuce, cold meat and cheese. The bread was obviously homemade. "This is all delicious," she said between mouthfuls. "I had no idea I was so hungry until I started eating."

Jake ate, as well. "Exercise makes a person hungry, and I guess you had yours climbing my gate then taking the hike to get here."

Dawn looked around as Jake resumed eating. The cabinets were polished gold oak. The table was a long plank with place mats in the shape of miniature oval rag rugs, made of brown, rust and orange cloth. The wood-burning stove and oven unit was iron.

And on the stove sat an old, battered blue-and-white speckled coffeepot. The lighting overhead was electric, but on wooden shelves against the wall she saw kerosene lamps, ready and waiting for use. This house would be cozy and safe, no matter what was happening outside its walls.

"This all seems so rustic and simple, it's difficult for me to imagine it's the heart of a major economic endeavor. How did you start running this place as a business?" she asked. "Did you intend that from the beginning?"

"No." He looked down at his coffee mug. "I wasn't sure what would happen here. I just knew I wanted to try an experiment in different working conditions for myself and a few other scientists. The business angle has grown rather haphazardly. Success sort of came by accident. There was no master plan—or what you business experts call a 'mission statement.' How about you?" he asked. "Have you ever actually managed an enterprise? Run a real business? Not on paper, but in the marketplace?"

"Sure. It was part of my training. I took over a small operation in Wilmont two years ago. Stationery products specifically designed for computer use."

"Was it a success?"

"Yes." She smiled at the memory. "I sold it for enough profit to pay for my car, a condo and to support myself while I finished grad school. The magazine pay is not enough to live on, even though I love doing it."

"I see." He looked thoughtful.

What was he thinking? she wondered.

Neither of them spoke for a few minutes.

Finally, Dawn's curiosity couldn't be contained. "Tell me more about your great-grandfather," she prompted.

Jake took a sip of his coffee. "Great-grandpa was a strange man, made stranger by his fate," he said. "He started out as a miner when he was twelve. Back then, a boy big enough went into the mines, no matter what his age. He worked the coal for two decades before his luck ran out."

"What do you mean?"

Another smile. "He's dead now," he continued, not answering her question. "But he lived to be well over a hundred. Lived long enough so I knew him. Knew him better than I know most people today."

"Then, what—" Dawn's question was cut off by the sound of barking and shouting from the front of the cabin. The screen door slammed, and someone stomped boots on the floor of the living room.

"Daaaad!" a child's voice shouted. "Where are you?"

"Kitchen," Jake called. "We have company." He looked at Dawn. "Sophie's home," he said. "Ready or not, here she comes."

CHAPTER THREE

THE "ELF" ENTERED the kitchen. Sophie was small and finely formed, with short dark gold hair, green eyes and a tight expression that indicated unpleased surprise at seeing Dawn in her kitchen. The child was still dressed in a green outfit made of a thick cotton material that Dawn was now able to identify as a kind of woodsy camouflage garb. Nothing all that odd really—just pants and a heavy sweater.

"You're the person on the gate," the elf declared. "Dad didn't shoot you?"

"Sophie," her father said. "This is Ms. Sutton. And no, I didn't shoot her."

"Hello, Sophie," Dawn said. She wasn't sure what to do next. The child just stared at her.

"Better change, Soph," Jake said. "We won't be going anywhere else today."

"It's going to snow," Sophie said, directing her comment to Dawn. "Snow a lot. So I won't have to go to school."

That made Dawn smile. "I remember the few times it snowed when I was a kid and we didn't have to go to school. I really liked that."

"Where was that?"

"Chapel Hill, North Carolina. My parents both work at the university."

"Oh." Sophie seemed unimpressed.

"Go change, Soph," her father said. "You want a sandwich?"

"Sure." Until she turned and left the room, Sophie didn't stop staring at Dawn.

Jake got up and started to put together another sandwich. "Your folks teach at the university?" he asked, wanting to know some more personal details about this woman.

"Not anymore. They're both professors but they've moved into the academic stratosphere. They administrate and publish."

"Are they happy with that?" He slathered mayonnaise on the bread.

"I think so."

"You aren't real close?" He set the sandwich on a plate and added a handful of potato chips.

"No." Dawn pushed the remains of her meal around on her plate. "Not really."

Silence.

Jake put his daughter's lunch down on the table and poured a large glass of milk. He set the glass next to the plate. "Excuse me for a few minutes," he said. "I need to check on the dogs. Sophie takes Jasper, the older male, with her wherever she goes outside the fort, but once they're back inside, my pets tend to become friendly bums, making pests of themselves with other residents. Especially anyone who'll feed them. I'll be right back."

"Take your time."

He left. She heard him talking to the dog that had been sleeping in front of the fireplace. "Come on, Pearl." Clapping his hands. Male laughter, a doggy *woof* and the clicking noise of claws on the hardwood floor. Then, the front door slammed.

From the living room came the soft, solid sound of a clock chiming the hour.

Sophie came back into the kitchen. She wore a pair of blue jeans and a white turtleneck shirt. Moccasins like her dad's on her feet. She slipped into her chair and grabbed the sandwich.

She kept her eyes on Dawn as she ate.

After a few bites, she put the sandwich down. "Why did you try to sneak into my dad's place?" she asked.

"Um, I didn't know it was his place out at the gate. I thought it was still a public road. So I wasn't sneaking. Not exactly."

"You saw the gate. It was locked."

"Yes, but . . ."

"So you decided to climb over and sneak in."

"I had a job to do. I wasn't sneaking."

"You sneaked." Sophie picked up the sandwich again and took a big bite. After chewing, she announced, "I think Daddy should have shot you."

Okay. . . If this was how the kid wanted it, so be it. "Well, I don't," Dawn replied. "And neither do you. Shooting people is wrong."

Sophie ate in silence for a few minutes. She didn't look at Dawn. "What's your job?" she asked finally.

"Last year I was a teaching assistant at Georgetown. I'm working on my postgraduate doctoral thesis. So I'm in school too."

"No kidding?"

"No kidding."

Sophie pondered that. This time she actually looked impressed. Her blond eyebrows drew upward and together, giving her an oddly aged appearance. "I wish I were in college or had a job," she declared. "Something interesting. School's really boring. I get sleepy and daydream most of the time."

Dawn eased back in her chair. She'd made contact! "I remember doing that," she said. "Most of the time I didn't listen to what was going on. I told myself stories or stared out the window."

"Did you get in trouble?"

"Yes."

"Actually, Miss Harper's not so bad," Sophie said, rubbing a potato chip in a drop of mayonnaise. "She makes things seem interesting even when they aren't. But my old school! Boy, was that boring! I hope I don't have to go back."

"How many kids in your school here?"

"Just me right now."

"Just you? And your father trucks you clear across the mountain every day so your... cousin can tutor you?"

Sophie shrugged. "I have to go to school. It's the law."

"Yes, but..."

"Why don't you teach me?"

"What?"

"Yeah. You said you were a teacher. So you know how. You could teach me while it's snowing. Then Dad won't be mad at you anymore."

"Sophie, he's not mad at me, and I couldn't teach you. I taught economics, not subtraction and addition or spelling."

"That's okay. I know all that other stuff. I'll learn economics. You can teach me."

"Honey, I don't think it would work, even though I might like—" A commotion at the front door interrupted Dawn.

A moment later Jake and the three dogs entered the kitchen. The animals bounded across the room and sniffed at Dawn, then left her alone as they clustered around their master who was opening a huge sack of dry dog food. "Sorry to take so long," he said, pouring kibble into three big plastic bowls set against the wall on the far side of the room. "Onyx was up to his puppy tricks and wouldn't come to me right away. Definitely needs more training."

"Onyx?" Dawn asked. "Jasper, Pearl and . . . ?"

"They're black and valuable. The names seemed to fit. Old Pearl's the mom. Jasper is out of her first litter, Onyx from her last." He finished loading the animals' dishes. The dogs sat, waiting, tails thumping against the floor. When Jake stepped back and said, "Chow time," they bolted for their bowls and chomped happily, tails still swinging widely.

"They all seem pretty well trained to me," Dawn commented. "Especially when they had me trapped on the gate."

"They have their moments." He started to return the food sack to the cupboard.

"Dawn's going to be my new teacher," Sophie announced. "I won't have to go back to school. I'm going to learn about economics."

Jake spilled some of the dog-food pellets onto the floor. Without a word, he began to clean up.

Dawn went over to help, scooping the kibble with her hands. "I tried to explain that I could only teach college level," she said. "But she doesn't seem to understand."

He started to say something to that, but a knock at the back door interrupted him. Jake got up. "You wanted to see the Well," he said, "so I arranged for a guided tour. Remember what we talked about," he added quietly, regarding her intently. "No magazine."

Dawn nodded, glancing at Sophie. The girl didn't seem to have overheard.

Jake opened the door.

Laurie entered, followed by two young men wearing long white lab coats.

"You met Laurie already, of course," Jake said. "She coordinates with marketing on the outside. These two guys work in chemistry. Todd Beckman and Farley Wold. Gentlemen, this is Dawn Sutton. She's here to study us."

"Hi," Farley said. "Hope it's not for anything serious! We're pretty dull." He was thin and blond with a slightly worried expression on his pale face. If he put on a little weight, Dawn thought, he'd be rather handsome.

"No, it's for my thesis," she said, shaking his hand. "I'm trying to fill in some blanks in my dissertation."

"Chemistry?" Todd asked, extending his hand. "I can show you some amazing events over at the lab," he added. He was heavier than Farley, with dark hair and an intense manner. Something about the expression on his face warned her that his friendly behavior wasn't a real reflection of his inner attitude. Dawn was reminded of a politician seeking votes from an electorate he secretly despised.

She put a smile on her face and replied carefully. "No. Economics. I know nothing at all about other sciences. But I'd like to learn."

Jake finished scooping up the dog food and put the bag away. "Ms. Sutton is here to get an overview of how we operate as a community," he said, dusting off his hands. "Let's give her a general tour first, then she can specify what she needs in depth." He turned to Sophie. "Honey, will you please clean up for me after you've finished and let the dogs out?"

"Sure, Dad." She glanced at Dawn speculatively, but said nothing more about teaching.

Which Dawn found a relief.

Jake excused himself for a moment and returned with a gray rough wool jacket, which he offered to Dawn. "This'll be much too big for you," he said, "but it'll keep the chill off."

"Thanks." She shrugged into the garment and quickly rolled up the sleeves, which hung inches past her fingertips. She placed her small tape recorder into one of the pockets.

The four adults went outside through the kitchen door. It was blustery and colder than before, but they were protected from the full brunt of the wind by the buildings and by trees planted within the palisade. They walked down a neat rock-lined dirt path toward the three concrete-and-glass buildings at the other end of the compound. Other people passed by, greeting them, then moving on to whatever tasks they had. Todd led, acting as tour guide by speaking in an instructional manner as he walked along.

"Each of these buildings has a specific function," he explained. "We'll start with administration and planning, move on to production and finally to the finishing area. What you need to understand, Ms. Sutton," he said, taking off his glasses and polishing them on his lab coat, "is that we have a unique professional situation at the Well."

"Nothing else quite like it," Farley added. He had fallen to the rear of the group and was walking along with Laurie. "We have a work force consisting of brains and labor, all members of it highly skilled in their fields or tasks."

"Extremely qualified people work here," Todd continued, going on as if Farley had not spoken. "Companies on the outside would likely kill to get the kind of people Jake gets."

"So why do they come?" Dawn asked, curious to see what sort of answer she would get from each of her companions.

"For the freedom," Todd said.

"For the healing," Laurie added.

Jake spoke. "They come because, like me, they want to get away for a while."

"I read something about that last night before I drove up here," Dawn said. "That this is a kind of refuge."

"It is," Laurie stated, her tone clear and strong. "If it hadn't been available to me, I don't know what I would have done."

"You'd have been fine," Farley said to her, his voice pitched so that the conversation between them suddenly became personal and private. "You're strong. You could have coped."

"Thanks, but I don't think so, Farl," she answered. "I really don't think so."

Something about the way she said that piqued Dawn's curiosity. Laurie had a story worth hearing. Probably everyone here did. It was likely an entire thesis could be written based on the backgrounds of the people who lived here. A thesis or even a book.

Now there was an idea!

"Individuals respond to this place in an individual manner, as I'm sure you'll discover, Ms. Sutton,"

Todd said, clearly ignoring the personal exchange between his colleagues. He brought the group to a fork in the path and turned toward a one-story modern building. "Let's go over to the planning building and have a short briefing in the meeting room."

Dawn glanced back at Jake. He seemed content to let the other man do the talking and leading. In fact, Jake didn't look as if he was really with them at all. He had a faraway cast to his eyes. What was he thinking about? Was he pondering something she had said? Or was his mind completely off her and onto one of his own problems? He certainly seemed to have enough of them.

They entered the first building through wide, half-glass doors and then walked down a hallway into a room set up for meetings. Todd excused himself to get the presentation material, and the others chose chairs at the horseshoe-shaped table that faced a lectern in front of a blackboard. A screen for slides and films was rolled up above the board, and a wide-screen television set stood to one side. It looked like a modern classroom.

"Todd's going to give you the standard lecture that newcomers get," Laurie explained. "That way, you'll see exactly how the Well is structured and how we—"

A knock at the door. "Excuse me . . . Jake?"

A man stood in the doorway. He was slender and balding and wore glasses. He had a worried expression on his face. Like Todd and Farley, he wore a long lab coat. "Jake, I have to speak to you immediately," he said.

Jake unfolded himself from his chair. "Problem, Fred? Can it wait?"

"Afraid not. I need to talk to you right now."

"All right." Jake turned to Dawn. "I won't be too long. Enjoy the tour. Sorry about this."

"It's okay. You have a business to run. I'm imposing, as it is."

He didn't reply to that, but his wry smile indicated he tended to agree. He left, and as Dawn glanced out the window, she saw a few flakes of snow falling.

Just a fluke, she thought, returning her attention to the matter at hand. It might snow just a little, but she'd be out of here and home by late evening. No way was it going to storm so heavily this time of year that she'd be stranded.

No way.

Todd came back with an armful of boxes and set them down on the table at the back of the room.

"Do you want the slide show?" Laurie asked. "It comes with the lecture."

"Sure," Dawn replied. "I'm here to learn. Show me everything, please."

Farley stood, set up the screen then went to the back of the room to deal with the slide projector. Laurie left her seat and turned the shades on the windows so that very little light entered the room.

Todd Beckman began to lecture. As he spoke, he clicked a button set on the lectern, and slides appeared on the screen, illustrating his discussion points. Watching and listening, her tape recorder catching every word, Dawn slowly revised her negative initial impression of the man. He was tense but not really unpleasant. Just a personality that gave off prickly vibes. No crime in that, certainly.

"Jacob's Well Ltd. was founded eight years ago by Jacob McClarin Barr, Ph.D. Dr. Barr purchased the land and had the present facility constructed." *A slide of a younger Jake, standing on top of a bare hill. No fort in evidence.* Another three slides showed the building process.

It was impressive. The modern structures were put in first, then the fort constructed around them. Like a protective shell around a precious and vulnerable center.

Todd went on. "Then he invited several of his professional colleagues to join him." *Jake with eight other people, five men and three women.* The scene was set inside, in a laboratory. The nine scientists, including Jake, looked self-conscious but eager.

"The agreement was that the scientists would work here for no pay, but would have lodging, food and other amenities provided in an isolated, restful locale where they would be allowed to move at their own pace and be as innovative as possible." *Interior shots of comfortable-looking rooms, a large dining hall, a library. A group of people sitting in front of a fireplace, laughing and talking.*

"Using formulas, or I should say recipes, collected from his family, particularly from his great-grandfather, Dr. Barr and his friends produced the first of the now-famous Jacob's Well personal-care products."

"Excuse me," Dawn said. "But what was that about his great-grandfather? Jake started to tell me, but he never finished."

"It was from that worthy old individual that Dr. Barr acquired his initial interest in herbals," Todd explained. "Of course, over the years, as a young person, he interviewed many elderly folk living in the West Virginia hills and mountains and collected remedies and recipes from them."

"But he's a biochemist. How could folk remedies be of any interest to him now?"

Laurie spoke. "Because they work," she said. "Look, Dawn, I'm a marketing expert, not a scientist, so I can't speak with any authority, like Todd and Farley, but I do know that if something works like it's supposed to, it's successful. All Jake did was use the information he got from those wonderful old people and translate it into products he could take to market."

"He applied the most advanced biochemical knowledge and techniques to material produced in nature," Todd said.

"But he's done much more than that," Farley added. "The eight friends who started this place with him eventually left and went on with their lives. But they told other scientists about the place, about Jake and what he was trying to do here."

"And more came," Laurie said. "More scientists, more people with other areas of expertise. Lots more people."

Farley stood up and started pacing in front of Todd. "See, Dawn, what Jake was doing not only gave biochemists like us interesting work, but it preserved much of the folk-remedy legacy of the people of this area. He gave this part of West Virginia a new sense of pride in its past. So he had locals lined up at the gate, wanting to help, to work, to offer the recipes for remedies their relatives had used."

"Many of the support workers you'll meet are young hill people who started out here waiting tables or cleaning rooms as a part-time job," Laurie said.

"How many people live here?" Dawn asked. This was far more interesting than she had ever anticipated. And horrifying at the same time. If her anonymous caller was right and Jake Barr was planning to upset his own applecart in order to profit from an insurance payout, he would be betraying many people. Not just the ones at the Well now, but all those who had so willingly participated in the past and had contributed to its present success.

It made no sense. No sense at all.

So far, she had seen and felt nothing that made her think Jake was the kind of man who would do such a thing. This was quickly becoming far more complex than she had imagined. One day of looking around was not going to be enough. She had to decide how important this story was to her.

She had to decide if, snowstorm or no snowstorm, she could figure out a way to stay longer.

Then Todd answered her question about population after consulting some notes. "At the moment the Well itself has a population of thirty-seven professionals, including people like Laurie who does marketing, and the veterinarian, Johnny Wilson. We have a doctor and a nurse who live on-site. Of the thirty-seven, eleven are actually biochemists."

"How many support personnel?"

Todd looked at Laurie and Farley. "I'm not sure," he said. "I don't have figures on that with me. Do either of you two know?"

"Fifty-six," Laurie answered. "That's down to the cook's helpers and the lab bottle-washers."

"So there are ninety-three people living here?" Dawn asked.

"Actually, ninety-six, counting Jake, Sophie and you," Laurie replied.

"Me? I don't live here."

"You do now," Laurie said, pointing at the window. She had opened the blinds to let in daylight.

Dawn looked. It was snowing. Snowing hard.

"WHAT IS IT, Fred?" Jake asked as he and the chief chemist walked down the hall toward the Deep Lab section. "What's wrong that couldn't wait?" *Not more sabotage,* he prayed.

"One of the new structures is decaying," Fred said, beads of perspiration forming on his forehead. "I don't know why and I can't seem to stop it. I've been working on it for hours. When I heard you were in the building, I decided to quit banging my head against the wall and let you have a shot at it."

Relief filled Jake. No sabotage, just an ordinary crisis. "It's still in the computer?" he asked. "Not into production yet?"

"No, of course not. You designed the system. You know how many tests we put these things through before we try them out. It's still in the damn computer and dying, even as we speak."

They arrived at the elevator, punched in their individual security codes and silently rode down to the secret underground section of the Well. Neither spoke as the doors swooshed open and they stepped out, producing plastic identity cards for the slot in the thick steel door that separated them from the lab. The door swung slowly open, admitting them.

Once inside, Fred led the way to the central workstation. They sat in front of the computer monitor. Both had connected keyboards in front of them.

"Okay," Fred said. "Just watch the screen. You can see it happen." He began to tap keys.

Jake watched the colors dance on the monitor. In a moment, the molecular structure of his latest and best discovery began to form. It was a new blending of natural products, aimed at developing a better moisture cream than the one they were currently making.

It was a great idea. When he'd tried the structure on this same computer just a few weeks ago, it had set up like a charm. It had seemed to be a natural.

He watched. A natural, all right. A natural disaster!

Not only wasn't it working, the way it looked right now, the product could be acidic enough to damage the user, causing slow but sure burning and eroding of healthy tissue. The diabolical thing was that the harm might not be immediately noticeable. Not until it was far too late to make repairs or amends. This should not have happened, given the nature of the original structure.

Could he really have been that far off base?

Or had some intelligent saboteur doctored the formula?

Damn. He was getting paranoid! No one could get into his program and foul things up like this.

"Let me try," he said to Fred. The chemist sat back.

Jake touched a key, observed the result. Touched another.

Something began to happen. He was aware of Fred, sitting beside him, sighing with relief. "Don't get excited," Jake said. "Not sure what's going on here." He touched two more keys.

And the decay process reversed.

"Yes!" Fred cheered.

"Don't break out the champagne yet," Jake cautioned, continuing to tap the keys. But he knew things were looking better. He stopped and pushed his sleeves up. He fiddled in a drawer under the counter where he kept a spare pair of half-glasses. Putting them on, he blinked and the monitor became much clearer to him. Once more, he began to type.

Minutes later, Jake Barr was apparently unaware of anything but the dance of molecules on the monitor.

Dr. Fred Turner smiled and left the station. Jake Barr was at work. Nobody needed to worry now.

CHAPTER FOUR

THE TOUR CONTINUED.

"Think of all this as a single organism," Todd Beckman said as they walked through a series of large rooms, subdivided into smaller workstations. About half the spaces were occupied. "Here you have the brain and nerve center of the Well."

Dawn nodded, noting the relaxed but intent demeanor of those designated as "the brain." One and all they looked as if they were having a good time. This was her first look at actual operations after sitting through Todd's presentation. It had been interesting enough, but this!

This was what she had come to see.

"So this is where the planning is done?" she asked.

"Some of it," Todd answered. "These people are involved in the actual scientific study and testing phase. Planning occurs at all levels, however. For instance, Laurie and her marketing group are situated over in the Finishing Building at the art center. That's where marketing strategies are developed. Advertising, packaging, distribution."

"And the actual physical production area is in the middle building," Farley said. "So you have planning, production and finishing. With subdivisions, of course."

"Sounds like it's been well thought out."

"It has. Jake's a genius," Farley said.

"So what's he like to work for?"

"Wonderful, but we're not really working for him," Laurie replied. "We're working for ourselves and one another."

"He just gave us the setup," Farley added. "We can do with it what we like."

"Jake's a great guy," Todd said. "But he does lack a certain vision."

Laurie laughed. "What Todd means is that the Well products are so good, they could be sold for twice, even four times what they're priced at now."

"Why doesn't Jake increase the prices?" Dawn was sure she knew the answer to that question before she asked it.

"Because it would be wrong," Farley said. "He won't let prices go any higher than they have to in order for the Well to make enough profit to support the people who live here. He's not out for the bucks."

"He's out for himself and for us," Laurie said. "He's no saint, giving up everything for others. Jake likes the things that money can buy just like most people do. But his priorities are—"

"Screwed up," Todd said. "I have no problem with not wanting to gouge the consumer, but a little price increase wouldn't hurt anyone."

"That's your opinion," Farley said.

For the first time, Todd smiled. "It is," he replied. "And I stand by it."

Dawn shivered a little. The chemist's smile was grim. Clearly, there was a difference of opinion between Todd and Jake. All was not harmony and good feelings here.

They went outside and on to the next building, walking along another neatly marked path. The two men in their lab coats hurried forward against the wind. Dawn and Laurie wore jackets and were therefore more comfortable. The conversation continued in spite of the weather. As it did, Dawn decided Todd was the odd man out. The other two seemed to like the way Jake managed things.

"Working here helps bring out the best in a person," Laurie said.

"It's amazing," Farley added. "I, myself, was on the verge of jumping off the edge of a deep depression when a good friend drove me out here and dumped me on Jake's doorstep."

"And?" Dawn asked.

"And you see before you a happy man."

Dawn was mystified at this brief confession. "Didn't you try therapy or counseling?"

"I tried everything," Farley assured her. "Only living at the Well worked for me."

"Likewise," Laurie added. "I can't imagine being anywhere else now."

Todd said nothing, and Dawn thought about what she had heard. Were Jake and his Well creating an unhealthy dependence in these people?

Or had they just found a home?

They reached the next building and went inside. The entire area was one open laboratory. Dawn saw stainless-steel and tile counters, overhanging hoods meant to suck out vapors, metal, glass and ceramic beakers, tubes and instruments. Huge covered vats stood along the central aisle. Tubes and hoses led from intake and outtake valves to a wide metal venting system overhead.

The overwhelming impression was the smell. It was like walking into a solid wall of scent. The assault on her nose was so instantaneous and intense that she almost turned and ran back outside.

"I can't take this," she gasped, covering her nose and mouth with her hands. "It's too strong!"

"Here." Laurie went over to a case set to one side of the entry door. She took out a small gas mask and handed it to Dawn. "Use this until you lose your olfactory sensitivity." She took a mask for herself and put it on.

"Thanks!" Grateful, Dawn did the same, testing the air cautiously, then taking a regular breath. It helped, but didn't entirely close out the heavy perfume. "That's better," she said, "but as for losing my sensitivity, that's not likely to happen. I've always had an acute sense of smell."

"We've had other people like you," Farley said. "Some can't ever come in. They get sick or headachy or actually become dizzy and faint. It can be a real handicap to a chemist. Fortunately, I can't smell much of anything." He took a deep breath to demonstrate.

"What is it?" Dawn asked. "I mean, what's it from?"

"Flowers," Todd explained. He was maskless, too. "And herbs. Some wood and tree bark. Anything that's plant material and has a pleasant aroma. This is where they're processed along with the oils and other ingredients."

"Oh."

Though the laboratory was fascinating, they didn't linger out of deference to her nose, which was actually hurting in spite of the mask. She got an overview, however, and was impressed with the quality of the equipment. Everything Jake had installed seemed to be the best and most up-to-date material available. If he was making a profit, he was plowing it right back into the business.

When they went back outside, the snow was coming down even more heavily. Dawn breathed in the fresh air and felt the sting of flakes on her face. "I guess Jake was right," she said. "If I'm going to get out of here before this settles into a real blizzard, I'd probably better leave soon."

"It's too late," Todd said. "You would—"

He never got to finish.

From the planning building they had left just twenty minutes before, came the sound of an explosion. A moment later, smoke billowed from the roof.

JAKE HAD FINISHED his work in Deep Lab and was walking down the first-floor hallway when the blast occurred. It shook the entire building and knocked him off his feet. As he stood up, people spilled into the hall, crying out and asking him what had happened.

"I don't know," he said to no one in particular and everyone in general. "But someone sound the alert!"

Even as he spoke, a siren went off outside. In a few minutes, an emergency squad composed of specially trained Well members would be here.

Jake turned around, trying to determine where the explosion had come from. Dark smoke boiling out of the elevator doors told him.

Deep Lab!

He ran to the doors and felt the metal. It was hot. Fire? It didn't seem *that* hot. Behind him, people were yelling. Someone screamed for everyone to get out of the building.

As the noise from the hall abated, Jake thought he could hear faint screams from the elevator.

Fred was trapped in there!

He tore off his sweatshirt. He used the thick material to protect his hands as he tried to force open the elevator doors. The doors wouldn't budge.

Jake jerked the sweatshirt back over his head. He ran to the stairs that led to the roof. Taking the steps two and three at a time, he was outside and over the safety trap to the elevator shaft in less than a minute. Smoke rose from around the edges of the trap, ascending into the snowy air like a dark intruder. With one hand on the chimney that vented the lab, he tested for heat.

Nothing. The metal was ice-cold.

He squatted and touched the trap.

It was cold, too. This made no sense. If the explosion had taken place in the elevator shaft, surely the metal ought to be hot.

Jake unhooked the latch and lifted the lid. More smoke billowed out, darker black against the snow-white air. It smelled like spilled acid. Jake leaned back to avoid the stinking cloud. Then he bent over the shaft.

"Fred?" he called. "Are you down there and can you hear me?"

"I'm stuck in the elevator! And there's smoke." Fred's voice was thin with fear. "Lots of smoke. Help me, Jake!" Fred coughed, choking, by the sound of it.

"Hang on!" Jake lowered himself over the edge and fell through the shaft. He landed on top of the elevator, feeling the car bounce a little under his weight. Kneeling over the escape hatch, he wrestled with it until the door came loose. He set it to one side and looked down.

Fred, his face grimy from soot and smoke and his eyes wide with fear, stared up at him. "God, Jake," he said, coughing again to clear his lungs. "What happened?"

Jake reached down. "Give me your hand and let's get out of here. We can analyze later."

Fred seemed to agree with that plan. His body was slim enough to fit through the escape hatch with little trouble. "What now?" he asked as they stood on the elevator. "How do we get out?"

Jake pointed. From above, a flexible ladder snaked down to them. Several faces with anxious expressions appeared in the roof trap. "The rescue squad's here," he said, helping Fred to mount the ladder. "Up you go!"

Fred lost no time in scrambling to the top. But when the men above called down for Jake to follow, he waved them off. "Wait a minute," he said, kneeling and feeling the walls of the shaft. "I want to check something."

"Jake! Come on!" a voice urged.

"Don't do anything! Wait for the fire guys!" another voice exhorted.

Jake ignored them and lowered himself into the elevator. It was a far tighter fit for him than Fred, and it occurred to him he ought to worry about getting back out.

But if his suspicions were correct, he wouldn't have to.

Taking off his sweatshirt again, he worked at the doors until he'd managed to open them a crack.

No smoke, just a foul stink. If the shaft was on fire from an explosion, there ought to be a choking cloud smothering him right now.

Jake strained, pulling at both doors until he got a wider opening. Then he wedged himself between them and pushed until the doors were parted all the way.

He was between floors, but the lip of the exit for the first floor was right at eye level. Gingerly, remembering how hot the metal had felt, he touched the upper doors.

Warm, but not hot. Definitely cooler than they had been less than ten minutes before. He reached out and ran his hands around the wall of the elevator shaft. It didn't take long to find where the smoke bomb had been placed on the bare concrete. Jake drew back. His arms and shoulders were too big to get at the device. He would wait until someone could help him.

Someone he could trust . . .

Whoever the hell *that* might be!

Cold anger began to replace the fear he had felt for his people. More sabotage. A smoke bomb that made a ferocious first impression—lots of smoke and a terrible smell—but no real damage. This had been worse than anything so far. It was calculated industrial terrorism, pure and simple! Designed to scare and harass. The perpetrator had only wanted to induce fright, not death.

Not death. Not yet.

With a savage oath, he put his hand on the outer doors and ripped them open.

Dawn Sutton was kneeling on the floor, staring down at him. She held out her arms, reaching down to help him. "Jake! Come up out of there!" she said.

"Not just yet." Jake made a quick decision, one he prayed he wouldn't regret later. "I need your help, Dawn," he said. "Will you please go up to the roof and get a tool kit from one of the guys?"

"Jake, a bomb went off! You have to—"

"It wasn't a bomb. It only looked and felt like one. Please. Just do as I ask."

To his relief and surprise, she nodded, stood up and vanished from sight. Jake settled back in the elevator to wait.

Dawn raced up the stairs and out onto the roof. A group of men huddled around an open trapdoor. She saw a toolbox and went over to pick it up.

"Hey!" one of the men said. He was stocky with a bald head and a big, bushy brown beard. "Who're you and what do you think you're doing?"

"I'm taking this down to Jake," Dawn replied. "He asked me..."

"Any of you guys know her?"

No one did.

"Give me those tools, lady," Bushybeard demanded.

"I'm new," Dawn declared, backing away, toolbox clutched to her chest. "Please, don't try to stop me. Jake's down in that elevator and he—"

Bushybeard made a grab for her and the toolbox.

Dawn eluded him and ran for the stairs. She made it down and raced to the elevator just feet from capture. When she reached Jake, she jumped into the elevator and huddled in a corner. Bushybeard stopped at the edge.

The elevator car dipped and settled.

"Hold it, Johnny!" Jake yelled. "Don't jump! Your weight will be too much. We'll all end up at the bottom of the shaft!"

"I wasn't gonna jump." Scowling, Bushybeard pointed at Dawn. "Who's she?"

Jake took a deep breath. "She's okay, Johnny. I sent her to get some tools. Now, do you want to help?"

Johnny looked chagrined. "Yes, of course. Sorry. She's a stranger, and I just didn't know. When she took the box, I—"

"Johnny Wilson meet Dawn Sutton."

Dawn stood up gingerly. The car rocked a little. "Hi," she said.

Jake went over and took the toolbox. "Johnny's the vet," he said. "Takes care of the animals at the fort." He set the box on the floor, opened it and rummaged around. "And he's kind of protective of things," he added, selecting several items.

"Nice to meet you, Johnny. Sorry I didn't take the time to explain things to you." She turned to Jake. "Is this thing going to crash?"

"No," Jake replied. "But don't go skipping rope, please. The cable's askew. That's why the car's unstable. Just keep still and we'll be fine."

"What are you going to do?"

"With a little luck," Jake said, "I'll get the device that caused all this furor and see if I can retrieve some fingerprints."

The car shuddered.

"Jake, you two really ought to get out of there," Johnny cautioned. "No telling if the cable will hold."

"It'll hold."

"Why is the car jiggling, then?" Dawn asked.

Jake handed her a pair of metal tongs. "Because when it stopped here, there was an automatic shutoff below. That set the cable so the car can't be used. The elevator's rigged to prevent any unauthorized entrance into the underground lab. The rocking is just a reminder that we can't go anywhere in the car until I reset the security."

"Can Joan do it?" Johnny asked.

"No. No one but me," Jake replied.

"Who's Joan?" Dawn asked.

"You'll meet her later," Jake said. "Now, bring those tongs and come over here. See if you can get hold of that black thing down there to the left. I'd do it, but my arms and shoulders are too large." He pointed down at the wall at something wedged between the elevator car and the concrete. "It's right there, see?"

Dawn looked. With the tongs, she reached through the narrow crack and fitted the grippers around the object. Slowly, carefully, she drew her prize into the elevator car. A small black box.

"Good going," Jake said softly. "Now, set it down on the floor."

She did. Her arms were trembling from tension and effort.

"Thanks," Jake said, looking into her eyes.

And the magic was back. Dawn felt her knees turn to water. Not from fear. From other emotions.

"You look pale," he said. "Sit down for a minute."

"I'm all right." She took a deep breath, smelling the acrid stink of the smoke and the spicy scent of Jake. "It's just catching up with me, I think."

He frowned, not understanding.

"When I heard the explosion and saw the smoke, I thought..." *You might be hurt.* "I thought there might be injuries."

"So did I," he said. He reached out and touched her cheek in a tender and unexpected gesture. Quickly, he pushed the soft emotion aside. No time for that now. "But it was only used to scare us," he added. He stepped back and regarded the black box. "Now, let's see if we can..." He started to move it.

The box emitted a high-pitched beep.

Jake swore. "Johnny, get the hell away! Whatever it is, it's going to blow again!" He shoved Dawn through the partly open doors up to the hall floor and he followed close behind. His arm held her securely, by his side as they ran down the hall. Johnny was a few steps ahead. At the far end of the hallway, a crowd had been watching the drama. They all scattered as Jake yelled at them to get to safety.

The second detonation followed a moment later. Jake threw Dawn to the floor, positioning his body protectively on top of hers and covering her head with his hands.

The explosion was a small one, but if they had been near it, Dawn realized, they would have been hurt. Underneath Jake's hands, she shifted her head a little and peeked. Another smelly cloud of darkness billowed forth from the open shaft. The elevator car settled slowly downward, but didn't fall.

Against her back, she could feel the rapid, heavy beat of Jake's heart. "Someone," she said quietly, "doesn't like you."

"I know," he whispered, his mouth right at her ear, amazed at the sudden feeling of desire for her that rushed through him. Must be from the close call, he decided. And the close contact. "That's getting clearer with each passing day." He eased away from her body, reluctant to abandon the sensual feeling of her rounded form against his stomach, but well aware that if he stayed close, she would have little doubt about her physical effect on him.

Johnny Wilson struggled to his feet. "Jake, are you okay?" he asked, coming over to them. "What in hell was that?"

Jake rose and helped Dawn to her feet. "A self-destruct device, I think. Designed to disintegrate when moved. To keep me from discovering things about the perpetrator. Very clever." He kept her hand in his. "Are you all right?" he asked, his tone so low she almost didn't hear his words.

She avoided looking at him. "I'm fine. A little shaken, but otherwise undamaged."

Still holding her hand, Jake shouted, "Everyone out of this building. I want this place cleared in three minutes. I don't care what you're working on! It's not as important as you are!"

People scurried for the outdoors.

Todd, Farley and Laurie appeared, along with several other men and women who carried fire-fighting equipment. "Do we need to evacuate the entire building?" Todd asked.

"Jake, what was it?" Farley wanted to know.

"Dawn, are you hurt?" Laurie cried, running to Dawn and offering a hug.

A hug that removed her from Jake's touch. That brought Dawn's sanity back. The nameless telephone caller yesterday night had accused Jake of planning insurance fraud. Had he done this? Rigged a harmless explosion to frighten everyone? Possibly to set things up for sabotage of a more serious nature?

If she was any judge of character he was not the kind of man to do this. But when it came to Jake, her judgment was suspect. There was definitely sexual tension between them. She started to answer Laurie and discovered that she was trembling like a leaf.

At that moment Jake spoke.

"Laurie, would you take Dawn back to the main building," he said. "She's had a shock. Let Ginny take a look at her if Dawn seems to need it. I want to do some checking here, and I don't want anyone around who doesn't have to be. I don't want to be worried about safety."

Todd stepped closer. "Do we really need to get everyone out, Jake?" he asked once more. "Production will stop. It'll slow down work to—"

"Hang the production schedule! I don't care about that," Jake said. "Safety is more important right now. Clear them all out. And somebody get Joan over here. We've got some detective work to do."

They all went, leaving him with the team of fire-people.

Laurie kept her arm around Dawn's shoulders. "You sure you're okay? We have a doctor, Ginny, who you could see if you want. That was a close call! Whatever possessed you to run back to see what had happened? You might have been hurt."

"I don't need a doctor," she insisted. "I didn't think. When I heard the explosion, I just—" Dawn broke off when she saw what waited outside. Everything was covered with deep snow, and the white stuff was falling in heavy sheets. She gave a shaky laugh. "I guess the weather-service people ought to check with

Jake before they make predictions," she said. "You were right. I will have to bunk here."

"Let me take you to a room where you can stay while this mess goes on," Laurie said. "You might not want to see Ginny, but you sure look like you ought to lie down for a while."

"What about the rest of the tour?"

"Canceled for today. Anyway, if this weather persists, you'll have plenty of time to look around."

"True. And it seems there's more to look at than I thought," she said, almost speaking to herself.

"Oh, there is," Laurie replied, laughing. "You bet there is. But later, okay?"

"Okay. Show me my home away from home, please."

"Slog right this way." Laurie pointed toward a path covered with deep snow.

"Oh, boy. Where are my galoshes when I need them?"

"Forget galoshes. In a few more hours, we'll need snowshoes."

"Or sleds . . . With dogs."

Laurie laughed again. "Come on, I'm taking you to one of the main buildings. It's nice and warm there. I promise."

"I'll hold you to that." Dawn was shivering. And not entirely from the wet and cold. The impact of what had happened was beginning to hit her.

By the time they reached the main building, Dawn's feet were soaked. She squelched up the stone steps to the long wooden porch, griping about her own lack of preparation. "I really should have known better," she stated.

"Don't be so tough on yourself," Laurie coun-
seled. "Most of us were city folk who had to learn the
hard way how to dress for this climate. These mountains just seem to reach out and grab at snow. It's
amazing how helpless we become the minute we're
away from what we usually think of as civilization. No
county snowplows or city-sidewalk shovelers around
here."

"Even without knowing it was going to snow so
hard, I should have at least worn boots and an all-
weather coat," Dawn said, still fussing at herself as
they entered a small room that served as a place to
hang heavy coats and leave wet and muddy shoes and
boots. A long wooden rack already held several dripping pairs.

"If you'd known it was going to get like this, you
probably wouldn't have come out here," Laurie commented. "I mean the snow," she added quickly. "Not
the accident."

"Accident? I thought it was a bomb."

"I don't know what it was," Laurie said. "That's
up to Jake to determine."

"What about police?"

"They aren't needed."

Dawn didn't know what to say to that. She took off
a wet shoe. "What if someone had been hurt?" she
asked.

"Then of course Jake would have called in the au-
thorities," Laurie replied calmly, apparently content
to trust her boss's judgment.

Dawn took off her other shoe and turned it upside
down. Icy water ran out and spattered the floor.

The little room had a stone floor and served as a
means of keeping the worst weather from the main

living area. It was separated from the interior by a tightly shut door. Dawn shivered, remembering the tightly shut doors of the elevator and how she had stood before them, helpless, thinking Jake was inside and hurt.

Laurie gave her a friendly slap on the shoulder. "Don't look so gloomy. Come on in. We have a clothing bank for people who come here unprepared. All that's asked is that you return the stuff you borrow when you're ready to leave."

"I can do that."

"Then let's go get you some dry warm clothes. And some rest. You really look like you could use a good nap."

Dawn had absolutely no argument with that.

CHAPTER FIVE

THEY WENT through the door to the main room. A fire crackled cheerily in a large fireplace. The sweet smell of wood smoke was in the air. Warmth spread like sunshine over Dawn. The room was similar to Jake's cabin, but much larger and less personal. Made for a crowd rather than an individual. Sofas and chairs were informally grouped. Card tables were set up with chess and checker games in progress. But no one was playing.

"I expect everyone who knows about the trouble is over at Planning, trying to find out what happened," Laurie said. "Usually this place is jumping. The clothing bank is down here," she added, turning to the right.

Dawn followed. They left the main room and went down a long hall. Smaller rooms led off it. Finally they reached a large walk-in closet filled with shoes, boots, clothing and outerwear. Dawn helped herself, shedding her cold, wet garments right on the spot. When she was dressed again, she sighed in relief. "That's much, much better," she said. "Could you please show me where I can clean my stuff?"

"Laundry room is down the other way. Living quarters are to the right of the main room, utilities to the left, including the kitchen and mess hall. Some offices farther on that way, too."

"So who has an office here and whose are in Planning?"

"Jake's is here. And Joan's. Jake likes to keep Planning strictly for the science people. There are rooms reserved here for future expansion of administrative staff, too. Want to see?"

"Sure." Dawn gathered her wet clothes. "Lead the way."

An hour later, Dawn had her own clothes clean and dried and was trying to relax in her room. She'd been given a quick tour of the rest of the building and a chance to do her laundry. Then she'd had the pick of several empty guest bedrooms. Laurie had fetched fresh linen for her and located a key for her. Finally Laurie had left.

Alone, Dawn's muscles and nerves, tense as steel wire from all the action and excitement, began to ease.

This room seemed tailor-made for her. It was small, but well furnished with a bed, rocking chair, dresser, tiny desk and even a bookcase full of novels. Cozier than her own apartment.

She lay down on the double bed and patted the soft quilt that covered it, enjoying the feel of the heavy cotton. Beneath the quilt were thick blankets that would be warm during bitter winter nights. The air smelled clean and had a slight tang of pine and the sweetness of cinnamon.

Dawn shut her eyes. Warmth and comfort enfolded her, and she allowed her thoughts to drift.

Except for the bomb in the elevator, this seemed like a great place.

Was it?

The anonymous telephone caller's voice came back to her. *Jake Barr has perpetrated insurance fraud in the past, and he's set to do it again.*

But why? From what she'd seen already, Dawn was ready to swear the Well was making a good income. No immediate problems she could sense.

So why the bomb in the elevator?

Thanks to the unexpected snowfall, she was going to have a chance to do some serious snooping. Jake knew she was a reporter, but he hadn't told anyone else. She would have to ask him again about his reasons for that, but until she got his answer, she would assume everyone else thought she was a grad student.

Opportunity time!

Dawn slept.

She awoke to a gentle tapping on her door. She opened her eyes to see a woman she didn't recognize open the door a little and look in. "Hi," the stranger said. "I'm Joan Dawson. Laurie asked me to give you a ten-minute dinner warning."

Dawn sat up. "Hello, Joan. Dinnertime already?"

Joan nodded. Her hair was gray, but her face was that of a younger woman. Firm unlined skin. Her eyes were a faded brown, and the expression in them puzzled Dawn. Joan smiled, as if aware of the enigma she presented. "It's quarter to six," she said.

"I slept for two hours!"

"Maybe you were tired. I heard you were in the elevator when the fail-safe triggered that silly device."

"It didn't seen silly at the time. I was scared!"

"Of course it didn't. And you were right to be frightened. Do you want dinner?"

"Yes. I'll be along in a few minutes."

"See you then." The door shut.

Dawn got up and went into the bathroom. She washed her face with warm, then cold water. Looking into the mirror, she studied her features. How long would it be, she wondered, until her own blue eyes had the same faded look as Joan's?

Useless question, really. She had a life to live and goals to reach. If she faded somewhat as a result, so be it!

She managed to put those thoughts behind her as she left the bedroom and went down the hall toward the dining room. She was here to get the story about other people, not to analyze herself.

The dining room was filled with people, most of whom she did not know. Farley Wold met her at the door. "You look alert and rested," he said. "Manage to wind down enough to catch some z's?"

"I did. I can't believe it, but I slept for two hours. I guess I was more tired than I realized."

"You were strung-out, darlin'," he said, his tone friendly, not flirtatious. "No wonder, given what happened."

"What did happen? And where's Jake?"

Farley shrugged. "No idea. He and Joan were closeted for at least an hour over the remains of that smoke bomb, but neither of them is saying a word. Except that it looks like it was only meant as a practical joke."

"Some joke."

"Yeah. Well, most of the gang's already inside and seated. Care to join us?"

"Sure."

They went into the dining room and joined a round table with eight places set. Todd, Laurie and Joan were at the table.

"I understand you're doing research," Joan said. "On the Well or on Jake?"

"The Well. My work focuses on community-economy symbiosis."

"I see. But you tried to enter the area without permission."

Dawn tried a sheepish smile. "I was wrong. I got caught."

"But here you sit, an honored guest."

That got Dawn's attention. "If you have a problem with me, maybe you should take it up with Jake."

"I did. He says I shouldn't worry about you."

"Well then, why . . . ?"

"Don't mind Joanie," Farley advised, breaking into the conversation. He poured water for both of them. "She's still suffering from outsider paranoia."

"What's that?"

Laurie answered. "Outside means anyplace other than the Well, Dawn."

"It's my job to be suspicious," Joan said. "I'm what passes for the security expert here."

"Security?"

"I was a cop. I'm the closest thing Jake's got to a professional law enforcement officer."

"And you're a good one, too," Jake said, suddenly appearing and sitting down. Sophie was with him. She took a chair opposite her father. She had a withdrawn and sullen expression on her face.

"What happened with the bomb?" Dawn asked.

Jake just shook his head.

"Dad says I can't go into Deep Lab anymore," Sophie said, scowling at her father. "All on account of a dumb little smoke bomb."

"It was harmless, Soph," Jake said. "But next time..."

"Why should there be a next time?" Dawn asked.

"Deliberate sabotage." Jake fiddled with his eating utensils. "It's getting to be a problem, and I'm concerned about it."

"Then there've been other incidents?"

Just then, a person with a tray of food appeared and started serving.

"Let's not talk about it right now," Jake said. "I don't want to kill my appetite." He began to eat.

The others followed suit and the conversation turned from tense topics to jokes about the nasty early-winter weather. Dawn received some teasing about getting caught at the Well without proper gear. Even Sophie threw a gentle gibe at her, but Jake did not join in the friendly ribbing. He seemed to be consuming his meal without really tasting it, absorbed in thoughts that made his eyes glaze in that faraway stare Dawn was beginning to recognize as characteristic of the man.

The meal was a relatively pleasant experience, and the food was excellent. Everyone, including the silent Jake, ate well.

She didn't know what to expect after dinner. Given Jake's silent mood, she expected him to depart without much of a goodbye, leaving her on her own for the evening. So she was surprised when he stood and rapped on his glass for attention. When everyone was quiet, he began to speak.

"You've all heard about the smoke bomb in Deep Lab's elevator. I want to assure you that it was only a harmless device designed to frighten and annoy rather than actually damage anyone or anything."

Dawn glanced around the room. He had their undivided attention.

"You also know that this isn't the first time something like this has happened."

"Any idea who's responsible?" Farley asked, raising his hand as if he were in class. "I mean, have you and Joan any clues at all?"

"Joan has done her best," Jake said. "But we're no closer to exposing this prankster than we were a month ago when all the water turned purple." He smiled for the first time. "I guess Doc Ginny's still recovering from the relief she felt when she found out that was just from a harmless dye."

The crowd laughed.

"Anyway, I have something else to say," Jake went on. "We have a guest at the Well, as most of you know by now. This is Dawn Sutton," he said, indicating that she should stand.

"She's doing research for her doctoral thesis, and I encourage you to talk to her about why you're here and what the Well's meant to you, though, of course, whether you do or not is up to each of you."

From another table, Johnny Wilson spoke. "Jake, if you want talk, I think we need to talk more about what happened in Planning today."

Dawn sat down. Jake seemed to hesitate. Then he said, "You're right, Johnny. All of you came here to get away from fears and stress. Now you find yourselves confronted with a situation that engenders both. I agree we need to talk. How many of us are here right now?"

A count revealed seventy-four, including the serving persons and kitchen people.

"All right," Jake said. "Go round up your friends who aren't here and let's all meet at the auditorium in an hour. That okay with everyone?"

People talked, murmured, nodded assent.

"Jake?" Todd raised his arm. "Don't you think this is kind of overreacting? I mean, no one has been hurt."

"Not yet," Joan said, giving the scientist a hard look.

"We can debate that point in the meeting," Jake said. "Until then, save it. That's all I have to say for now. Thank you all for your attention. See you in an hour." He sat down and turned to Dawn. "I'd like to talk to you privately," he said, his whisper so low she could scarcely hear him.

"Okay. My room?" she replied in the same low tone.

"No. Get a coat and some boots and meet me at the front door."

"Outside?"

He nodded. "Dress warmly. Do me this favor, please."

She looked at him. Something in his eyes convinced her to do as he asked. "All right."

Ten minutes later, wearing a coat and a pair of boots she had found in the clothing bank, she walked with Jake into the storm. The snow was piled up nearly half a foot now, but the walkway leading from the main building was fairly clear. Obviously someone had shoveled it recently. Jake set a slow pace this time, adjusting his footsteps to her shorter legs.

"Why did you want to come outside?" she asked. "Why couldn't we talk in my room?"

Jake looked at her. The top of her dark, curly hair was covered with large snowflakes. They made a lacy covering like an old-fashioned prayer kerchief. "I wanted privacy," he said. "The only place I was sure we wouldn't be overheard is out here."

"Privacy? Be overheard?" She stopped. "What's going on, Jake?"

"I'll tell you what I know. Let's get out of the snow first." He steered her to the left and along another path toward the edge of the fort where a stand of pine trees rose into the night sky. "There's a log bench over here under the trees," he said. "The branches overhead will shelter us a bit."

Dawn hesitated. She was cold, but he was asking her to listen to him. This was an opportunity and an obligation, all in one. "Okay," she said. "But I still don't understand why you want to talk to me. It seems like you have an internal problem and I'm an outsider."

"It's because you're an outsider that I want to talk to you."

They reached the shelter of the trees. There was enough light from the main building's windows to provide illumination, and the snowfall shed its own white glow, as well. Jake scraped the small accumulation of snow off the bench and sat down. Dawn sat beside him, huddling close for warmth. "Talk," she said. "Before I freeze."

"What really brought you here today, Dawn?" he asked. "Straight answer, please. I deserve that much from you, I think."

"I told you, I—"

"No, you told me what you planned to do here. Not why you came today. What got you interested in Jacob's Well?"

"I can't."

"You mean you won't. Look, I understand about journalistic ethics. I'm not some judge asking you to reveal protected sources. I'm just a guy with some serious problems." Jake got up and started to pace. Then he stood still, his hands jammed deep into the pockets of his parka. "Dawn, since the last week of August, little things have been going wrong around here. Nothing vital, nothing fatal. Just...little things. I feel like I've been running from one brushfire to another, just getting one put out before another one pops up somewhere else."

"Sounds like a poltergeist. It will be Halloween in a few weeks," she said, trying to make a joke.

"Don't laugh. One of my great-aunts thinks we have a 'haint' living in the fort."

"A ghost? You don't seriously believe that?"

"No, of course not. I think my troubles are all too human in origin. I don't see a ghost delivering a sophisticated joke like the device we experienced today. That was put together by someone who had a good working knowledge of chemistry and physics."

"A scientist?"

"Exactly. Any one of two dozen people here, including me, have the capability of constructing the thing."

"So, where do I fit in?"

"Why did you come here?"

"I told you. I—"

"No, that's not enough. How did you hear about us? Why did you come today? There's just too much coincidence for my taste."

"Jake, everything I've told you is the truth."

He regarded her. "Maybe so. But it's not the whole truth, is it?"

She hesitated. Thought about it. "Okay. You're right. It's not." She drew in a deep breath and let it out. "Jake, if you hadn't acted the way you did this afternoon when you grabbed me and protected me, thinking the elevator was going to ignite, I wouldn't tell you this. I know from your actions that you fully expected a real explosion. So here it is. I came here because I got a phone call," she said.

"And?"

"And the caller said you might be setting things up for an insurance scam. That you'd done it before."

Jake stared at her.

Then, hands still jammed in his pockets, he sat down, hard, as if the strength had gone out of his legs. "Damn," he said, breathing the word onto the snowy air. "Hell and damnation!"

"I'd heard of the Well because of its success, and I did do a little quick reading before I drove here. But that call was what prompted me to make the trip."

"Any idea who it was?" He looked at her again.

There was cold, cold anger in his eyes.

"No. It was a woman, though."

"Old? Young? Anything special about her voice?"

"Just a woman's voice. Jake, do you want me to leave?"

His laugh was bitter. "You can't. And I don't want you to, even if you could. I'm going to have to trust you."

"Trust me?"

"I need your help."

Dawn paused momentarily. "Okay," she said finally. "What do you want me to do?"

"Just keep your eyes and ears open. You're a stranger, you don't know the drill. You can ask questions and get away with it. The storm's going to keep you here for a few more days, so if you learn anything that you think might help me, I would be most grateful if you let me know."

"You're looking for a rotten apple in your own barrel, aren't you?"

"Hard as it is to admit, that's true. It's not me, so it has to be someone else here."

"Is there any truth to what my caller said? Jake, I hate to ask, but I have to know."

He was quiet for a little while. Snow fell. "There's a story in my past," he said, not looking at her. "Some truth. Some lies. It's interesting, and no one else here knows it. At least, I didn't think so until now." He kicked at the snow at his feet. "I'll make a deal with you. Stay here and give me a hand, and I'll grant you an exclusive interview once the dust settles."

Dawn held out her hand. "Deal!" she said.

They shook.

Jake held on to her. The look in his eyes told her he would like to do more than just shake her hand.

"We have to get back," he said abruptly. "The meeting's going to start in a few minutes, and I'd better be there to keep things in line. People are pretty upset and with good reason."

"Okay. Let's go."

Neither of them moved.

"I'm really glad you came here," Jake said quietly, looking into her eyes.

"Me, too. Even if my reasons are less than agreeable to you." She tried to smile at him, but her lips seemed determined to remain softly poised.

For a kiss?

Jake seemed to lean a little closer.

And she could almost feel the touch of his mouth on hers.

A bell rang out.

He pulled back and released her hand. "That's the signal for the meeting," he said. He stood up and cleared his throat. "I'm glad we came to an understanding so quickly. I believe we can help each other."

"Me, too." She stood up. "Where's the auditorium? I want to stop by my room first."

He pointed through the falling snow to the structure on the opposite side of the fort from the main building she'd been in. "There. Just go in the front entrance, take a right and you'll find the auditorium at the end of the hall. You can't miss it."

"Okay." She put her hand on his shoulder. "I'll catch you in a few minutes."

"All right," He turned away, his features now set in a determined expression, his mind obviously no longer on her, but on his problems. He walked off toward the other side of the enclosure.

Dawn watched him go.

And thought about him and what she had agreed to do for him as she made her own way back to her room.

The main building seemed deserted. The fire in the big hearth in the living room was mere embers, and she could hear no sounds from the dining area. Everyone had left for the meeting, it appeared.

She hurried, not wanting to miss anything. First she retrieved her backpack with her tape recorder and camera and then headed down the long hallway to the front door.

But before she opened the interior door, she heard a sound. Down the other hallway, in the direction of Jake's office.

Dawn eased away from the door. With everyone at the meeting, what better time for an intruder to take advantage of the moment and . . .

And do what? She had to get her reporter's head back on straight! She had only Jake Barr's word for what had been happening and why. Though she found it easy to believe and trust him, so did many other people. That only meant that he had the gift of inspiring faith, not that he was actually to be believed in all things.

No one was.

But still, he had asked for her help, and the least she could do was to check something out when it bothered her. So she started down the hall.

She had gone about a third of the way when one of Jake's dogs came bounding out of a room. The big animal lumbered up to her and nosed her, sniffing and wagging his giant whip of a tail. Dawn laughed out loud, relieved she didn't have to confront an intruder. "Come on, dog," she said, patting the dark head. "Let's go see Jake."

She left the building with the dog trotting happily alongside her. She thought he might accompany her all the way to the other building, but instead, the animal veered off and ran across the snowy central field toward the section of the compound where Jake's cabin stood. Dawn let him go, figuring he was far more at home here than she was and knew what he was doing. She went on alone.

From the outside, the building that housed the auditorium looked like its sister building, but inside it was set up like a modern public school with classrooms, music rooms and even a gym. She found the meeting with no trouble. The auditorium was filled and the buzz of conversation would have guided her even if she'd had no directions. There were a few other latecomers, and Dawn joined them, shrugging out of her parka and taking a seat near the back of the room. Jake was on the stage fiddling with a microphone system.

The system squawked at him. That provoked some laughter from the audience. Jake stood and faced them.

"Since it doesn't look like I'm going to get cooperation from anything electrical tonight, I'll just try to speak loud enough for everyone to hear," he said, his voice raised to carry. "I guess it's no news to anyone that we're having problems," Jake went on, moving to the edge of the stage. "And I have to tell you all that the nature of the trouble seems to be escalating."

A hand went up. "What do you mean, escalating," a thin woman wearing a stained lab coat asked.

"I mean that in August you all know someone put salt in the sugar bowls in the dining room. In September, a harmless but startling purple dye was added to the water. It seemed funny, but the dye could have been poison, if the perpetrator chose to be lethal instead of humorous. Now, today's device was set next to the door of the elevator to Deep Lab. No one was hurt, but—"

"But they could have been," Fred Turner interrupted. "If I'd been in the elevator car when the thing blew up, I would have had a heart attack, I know it!"

"And just because the sugar-salt switch was funny, doesn't mean next time it won't be sugar and cyanide that's exchanged!" another woman in a lab coat exclaimed. She stood up. "I don't know about anyone else, but I'm getting scared."

"I don't think we need to be frightened," Laurie declared, also standing. "We just need to be alert."

"But that's not why we came here!" the first woman said. "We came here to be safe!"

"Who's doing it?" a man asked, his face drawn with worry. "Why are they doing it?"

Jake's shoulders sagged a little. "I wish I knew."

"Can't Joan catch the culprit?" a woman asked.

Jake looked into the audience. "Joan, could you speak to that? I . . ." He glanced around. "Where's Joan? She said she'd be here."

Just then, Dawn saw the security specialist enter by a door down near the stage.

And Sophie entered by the upstairs door. The girl slid into the seat next to Dawn.

"Joan," Jake said, "these people want to know what you've found out about the perpetrator of the so-called pranks. Any comments?"

Joan jumped onto the stage. She started to speak.

And all the lights went out.

Huddled down in her seat, Dawn braced herself for pandemonium. But no one cried out, no one screamed. A quiet exclamation. A short nervous laugh. A whispered question.

Then silence.

Jake spoke, his voice carrying power in the darkness. "Anybody got a match?" he asked.

CHAPTER SIX

HEARTY LAUGHTER followed Jake's question. A number of people held up lighters and flicked them on. Tiny flames flared, cheering the air. The room suddenly looked like an arena at the end of a rock concert. All that was needed now was for Jake to start singing.

And he did. In a pleasant baritone, he started the old gospel song, "This Little Light of Mine." Several other voices joined, some singing harmony.

Someone clapped in time. A moment later, another person joined in and the clapping becoming rhythmical. Soon everyone was clapping, and the entire group seemed to be singing along. Dawn listened, amazed at the changed mood. Only a few minutes ago, confusion and tension had been thick in the air.

Jake Barr was either lucky as hell or a genius when it came to handling a group of people. Could he have possibly been aware of what would happen and have arranged for the lights-out?

Was he capable of being that manipulative?

Dawn had to admit that she had no idea. He had responded to the crisis with suspicious smoothness, some might say.

Or, he had responded with such strength of heart and character that he had overcome the forces placed against him.

Whatever the case, she was more determined than ever to find out the truth.

Jake felt cold sweat running down his sides as he sang. He couldn't shake the sense of impending danger. The generator that powered electricity for the Well should not have failed. Until he checked, however, he couldn't know if the problem was in this building alone or all over. But he couldn't risk leaving the room and losing the cheerful mood he'd established by accident. Singing that song had occurred to him spontaneously. He was astonished himself when it seemed to do the trick and keep people from panicking.

When the singing finally ended, he stepped forward and asked two maintenance workers to investigate the electrical problem. The men left, using a flashlight to guide them. Jake got another flashlight from someone else.

Then he turned back to Joan. "You were saying?" he asked, shining the light in her direction.

Joan blinked in the glare. She shielded her eyes. "I kind of lost my train of thought," she replied. "What was the question?"

"Any progress on finding the person—or people—responsible?"

Dawn watched the security officer's face. The way the light hit it, she looked a thousand years old.

Old and scary.

Joan shook her head. "I don't have any idea who's doing these things," she admitted, her tone indicating how difficult it was for her to concede a failure. "All I'm sure of is that the person responsible is one of us. The enemy is within these walls, I'm positive."

Murmurs from the audience followed that statement.

Dawn frowned, sensing the mood change. Joan couldn't have picked a worse thing to say. She'd ripped away the feeling of community that Jake had established.

On the other hand, if what Joan had said was true, she was right to be so blunt. People needed to know the truth, even if it upset them.

Jake spoke. "Most of you came here to get away from trouble and find a quiet place where you could rediscover your own peace. When the road clears after this storm, I hope anyone who feels they need to leave the Well will do so. I can't guarantee that we won't have more of these kinds of incidents."

Silence fell.

And the lights came back on.

Dawn listened to the nervous, relieved laughter, but from the child sitting next to her, she heard a strange and unexpected sound.

Sophie whimpered.

The cry was so soft and clearly involuntary that Dawn wasn't sure she'd really heard it. But when she glanced at Sophie, she saw that the girl was scrunched down in her seat, her eyes wide open in a fearful stare and the skin around her mouth white as snow.

Had she been afraid of the dark? "Are you okay, Sophie?" Dawn asked, suddenly upset with herself for being so involved in other matters that she had failed to notice the frightened child.

But Sophie recovered instantly. So instantly Dawn wasn't sure she'd even seen the fear. "Sure," she said, sitting upright on her chair. "I'm fine."

"You looked like you'd seen a ghost," Dawn said.

"I don't like the dark."

"Oh, I see." *But you didn't whimper until the lights came back on.*

From the stage, Jake spoke again. "I guess the guys found the electrical problem," he said. "Must not have been anything serious."

Farley stood up. "I'd just like to say that I'm not about to let some prankster scare me away," he stated, his voice strong. "I'm going to stay and help Jake solve the mystery. I hope you'll all choose to do the same. Let's not allow Jacob's Well to be destroyed. Not after everything Jake's done for all of us!"

"Farley, that's kind of strong, don't you think," Jake began, clearly ready to reprimand the young scientist.

But Laurie stood and added her opinion. "I agree," she said. "Every one of us came here when no place else worked for us. To leave now that there's something or someone threatening the Well is just plain crazy! If something's wrong here, and it's one of us doing it, then it's up to all of us to fix it."

One of the other women stood again. "Where would we go?" she asked. "This is our sanctuary."

A spirited debate followed. Jake moderated, but Dawn noted that he allowed all voices to be heard. She leaned over and spoke to Sophie. "Your dad's a very capable leader," she said. "I'm impressed."

"You like him?" Sophie asked, her gaze fixed on the figure of her father on the stage.

"I guess I do," Dawn replied.

"Will you stay here and teach me, then?"

Dawn looked at her. Sophie was looking back, her small face drawn and tense. Waiting for an answer.

A positive answer.

"I'll think about it," Dawn said. "I really will."

Sophie didn't comment. She just looked away, back at the scene playing out below. Back at the adults who were talking and arguing, trying to decide what the future held for them. She sat there for a while, then without saying another word to Dawn, Sophie Barr got up and left the auditorium.

Although she was tempted to follow the child, Dawn stayed put. Sophie was not her concern. Unless Jake himself asked for her help, she would be unwise to get involved with his child. She settled back and turned on her recorder, determined to listen to the dialogue. But her thoughts kept moving back to the small face that had stared at her out of the trees that morning. Sophie might not be a real elf, but she was a real mystery. One that Dawn could not seem to let go.

An hour later, the debate ground to a halt. Jake looked exhausted and Dawn was not surprised. He was accepting responsibility for everything and everyone.

He needed help, she decided. He needed other people to relieve him of some of the burden. It was obvious that Joan was little help, and the only thing Farley, Todd and Laurie had managed to accomplish was heighten emotions by their comments. Todd especially had added to the negative aspects. He had a way of pointing out the dark side to everything. And it all landed back on Jake.

But that was the way things were at the Well. She was an outsider and an observer only, so all she could do was watch and record. When most of the audience got up and began to move to the exits, she followed, intending to go directly to her room and make some notes on what she had seen and felt.

"Dawn! Wait."

Laurie's voice stopped her. Dawn turned around and waited while the other woman climbed the stairs to join her. "I saw you come in," Laurie said. "But I was kind of caught up in things."

"So I noticed."

"What did you think?"

"About what?"

Laurie gestured. "The meeting. All this." Her expression was expectant and eager. Dawn realized that the woman was really asking for an honest opinion and not just a polite response.

"I think Jake Barr needs help," Dawn replied. "I'd be less than sincere if I didn't say I think you're all in over your heads right now."

Laurie frowned. "I guess I was afraid you might say something like that." She shuddered. "And I think you're right. I've always felt so secure here. Now it looks like no one is."

Dawn touched her arm. "No one's been hurt."

"Not yet." Laurie looked sideways nervously.

"Laurie, would you like to talk?"

"I sure would," she replied, nodding. "I've got a cabin of my own. Mind going there?"

"Not at all." Dawn glanced down to the stage. Jake was still surrounded by people and deep in conversation. She would catch him later. "Let's go."

LAURIE'S CABIN was smaller than Jake's, but just as homey. While Laurie went into her kitchen to prepare some tea, Dawn made herself useful by lighting the logs already set in the fireplace. The fire quickly warmed the small living room, and Dawn took off her parka. She sat down on the sofa and watched the flames. Her thoughts wandered over the events of the extraordinary day she had just spent. Time passed, and she almost dozed off.

Then Laurie returned, carrying a tray with a teapot and two mugs. "Here you go," she said, setting the tray on the narrow wooden coffee table. "It's herbal tea, so it won't keep you awake. Just warm you up."

"Herbal?" Dawn smiled. "Why am I not surprised? Another one of Jake's natural concoctions?"

"Yes." Laurie sat down and poured the fragrant hot liquid into the mugs. "I used to be a caffeine freak, but after living here a while, you lose your need to be wired all the time." She handed a mug to Dawn. "Enjoy," she said. "This is good stuff."

Dawn sniffed the aromatic steam rising from the mug. "Thanks," she said. "After all that's gone on today, the last thing I need is stimulation."

"I know what you mean." Laurie became somber. "It's usually quiet and very routine. Boring almost, by my old standards of life."

"You miss the excitement sometimes?"

"No!" She set down her mug. "I came here to escape... I mean..." Her words trailed off, and Laurie stared silently at the fire.

Dawn waited. She drank some tea. It had a sweet-soft taste. Like flowers. Or new-mown grass.

Laurie cleared her throat. "I had a great career in advertising," she said, speaking slowly as if remembering events from a long time in the past. "I'd been a successful model in my teens and early twenties, but I'd had enough sense to realize the age limitations of that profession."

"Smart," Dawn commented.

"Smart about that, maybe. But not about other things," Laurie said. She picked up her mug and took a long drink.

"I had some eating-disorder problems," she continued. "I couldn't shake them even after I left modeling, so I went to a physician for help and ending up marrying him."

"Were your problems cured?"

Laurie didn't answer right away.

Again Dawn waited. The only sounds were the soft ticking of a clock, the snap of a spark from the fire and the tapping of falling snow against the windowpanes.

"Jake said you wanted to interview us. To find out about the people who work here," Laurie said abruptly, looking at Dawn. "Why would you want personal interviews for a graduate thesis? Don't you just need statistics?"

"I'm hoping to get a book out of my research in addition to the thesis."

"Oh."

"Look, I'm not trying to be nosy. Just to understand why talented people would come and work for nothing just to be here."

"Could I tell you something and trust you not to write it?"

"Yes. I'm here right now as a friend. Not as a . . . student. If you want to talk off the record, I promise no one will ever hear what you say to me."

Laurie smiled. "You sound like a reporter."

"I wish!" Dawn lied quickly, thinking that if Jake hadn't requested she keep her profession a secret, she would tell Laurie immediately and reassure her that everything the woman told her in confidence would stay between the two of them. "I understand reporters make a little more money than grad students."

"How do you support yourself?" Laurie asked.

Dawn shrugged, unhappy to be drawn deeper into a lie. "I've been a teaching assistant in the past. This year, though, I'm concentrating only on getting my thesis finished. I don't want to still be ABD when I turn thirty!"

"ABD?"

"All But Done. It's a joke many Ph.D. candidates make while they're procrastinating on finalizing."

"Oh." Laurie smiled again. "I never got through college, myself. Modeling lured me away from any studies. I learned marketing on my own."

"You could still go back."

"No." Laurie shook her head emphatically. "I'll stay here. Maybe for the rest of my life. I'm safe here. I . . ." Tears filled her eyes.

Dawn set down her mug. "It's none of my business, and you certainly shouldn't tell me anything you don't want to, but, Laurie, this place isn't a desert island or a paradise. If I understand Jake's ideas properly, he expects people to come, stay for a while, then leave."

"That's right. He does." Her head was bent and her elbows rested on her knees. Laurie wasn't crying now, but her voice was tight and strained. "But I'm afraid to go."

"Why?"

"My ex-husband. The doctor. Turned out he was a control freak. He messed with my mind so badly I was sure I was insane. By the time I realized I wasn't the one with the mental problem, it was almost too late for what sanity I did have. I divorced him, of course, but then..."

Dawn could guess what was coming.

"He stalked me," Laurie said. "Telephone calls in the middle of the night. Dead rats left in my mailbox. All the terrible things you read about but never imagine anyone you know could actually do."

"Did the police help?"

"Some." Laurie straightened and spread out her hands. "But he was clever. Until he tried to kill me and some neighbors saw him do it, they couldn't touch him."

Dawn was shocked into silence.

"He's in prison," Laurie went on. "For a very long time. But I'm still afraid." She sighed, a deep shuddering breath. "At times I become paralyzed with fear. Can't move, can't think, almost can't breathe." She looked at Dawn. "I can't leave here."

"I think I understand." Dawn's heart broke for the other woman's pain. "But I confess I can't even imagine such a thing."

"Anyway, I wanted you to know, in case I start acting strange. With all this stuff going on, I just don't trust myself to..."

"But it has nothing to do with you."

"Maybe not." Laurie's hands twisted together, fingers twining nervously. She sat up straight and made a visible effort to relax. "But I really didn't ask you here to listen to my sad tale," she said. "I want to know if you'll stay."

"Here? At the Well? I don't think I have any choice for a few days."

"I mean after the roads are clear."

"I don't know. I..."

"You said it yourself. Jake needs help. I can't see him asking, so I'm doing it for him. Farley and I talked and we agreed I should do this."

"Laurie, I appreciate what you're saying, but I have commitments. I'll be here until the snow's gone, then . . ."

"Just think about it, please. Couldn't you work on your thesis here just as easily as anywhere else? You're an outsider, no connections with the Well at all, so you can't be involved in the trouble. If you would just stay for a while and give Jake some backup."

"I don't know what I could do that would be of any help to him."

Laurie sighed again. "I guess it wasn't such a hot idea."

"I didn't say I wouldn't think about it. It's just I don't believe I'd be able to do anything worthwhile."

Laurie sat back. "He likes you, you know. So does Sophie."

"Sophie? I don't think so. And Jake's still dealing with the fact that he caught me red-handed, sneaking onto his turf."

Laurie smiled. "Take my word for it. Both of them like you. Sophie came in and sat next to you this evening. She never sits by anyone of her own free choice. And I heard she asked if you'd tutor her."

"She asked twice," Dawn admitted. "But I can't teach a child. I don't have the skill."

"Sophie is no ordinary kid, Dawn. I guess no one's told you about her."

"What about her?"

"She's a genius. Actually, more like a prodigy, I guess. She's one of those children who have extraordinary minds and abilities with mathematics. She acts like a kid so much of the time, it's hard to remember that inside that little blond head is a brain that's as good as or better than most computers.''

"Then what's she doing here, going to a back-woods school where she can't possibly be getting the kind of training she needs?''

Laurie shrugged. "Her mother dumped her late this summer. Just drove up to the gate and set the child down with her suitcase. Told Jake it was his turn to baby-sit.''

"You're kidding! How could any mother do that?''

"Good question. From what I understand, the former Mrs. Barr is more than a bit weird. Jake took Sophie in without a fuss, of course. He's so happy to have her with him that I don't think he's really come to terms with the effect her mother's rejection must have had.''

"That's not good.''

"No, it's not. Anyway, I told you this so that you'd see it wouldn't be so far out to consider tutoring her. Anything you would care to throw at her, the kid can handle.''

Dawn considered. "I could start with some basics, I suppose. If math's her strong point, she'd have no trouble catching on to statistics.''

"Then you'll do it?''

"I'll think about it.'' Dawn thought and sipped tea. "I promise.''

"That's all I ask. That's all *we* ask,'' Laurie said. "Thanks.''

While they sat together in companionable silence, a cat wandered in from the bedroom. She was large, lazy and calico and she meandered over to sniff suspiciously at Dawn's feet before jumping up and settling on Laurie's lap. Dawn noted that one of the cat's legs was cut short. Laurie stroked the animal's back.

"This is Freda. Jake suggested I keep her when one of the local kids found her and brought her to Johnny for treatment," she said. "She got caught in a small animal trap and lost her leg."

"That's awful!"

"Yes, it is." The cat's purring increased in volume as Laurie scratched between the furry ears. "Poaching is a problem Jake's been trying to fight for years. That's one of the reason he patrols the forest around the Well so regularly, day and night. He hopes one day to catch the guy red-handed."

"Jake takes on a lot of causes, doesn't he?"

"Yes, he does. We're all worried about him, like I told you." Laurie paused, then went back to the subject of the cat. "Freda here is my best buddy," she said. "I can tell her things I'd never dream of telling a human. I hadn't owned a pet before and had no idea how good one could be to have around. Everyone is encouraged to adopt a pet when they settle in. Jake says it helps. I agree."

"I'd wondered about the veterinarian. So, there are lots of animals?"

"Yes. And the locals bring him their animals, too. Johnny's busy. Much busier than Ginny Reynolds, our 'people doctor.'"

"Folks tend to stay healthy?"

"Once they settle in. At first, most newcomers are in bad shape. But time spent here is so healing. I haven't even had a cold in the last two years."

Dawn made a mental note to have a talk with the doctor about the effects of living at the Well on general health. Another thesis chapter could come out of it. She could compare health statistics between this operation and a standard production enterprise. The project was taking on more depth and promise by the hour.

JAKE SQUATTED by the generator and did a careful inspection of his own. Not that he didn't trust his two maintenance men, but when Tom and Bob had returned to report that there had been no failure in the electrical system and no reason they could discover for the lights going off and then on again, Jake decided to investigate for himself. They had to be wrong.

But they were not. Sure enough, nothing out of order in, on or around the generator. He stood up, dusting off his jeans and thinking hard. There was only one logical solution to the mystery.

Someone had managed to bypass his personal lockout code and get into his computer. The intruder had accessed the files that controlled the physical plant and programmed the failure.

Jake spent the next twenty minutes rechecking the generator and the large room that contained it. It was possible in his weariness, he'd overlooked some clue. He studied every inch of machinery.

Nothing was wrong. The lights should not have gone out.

More to the point, once out, they should not have come back on until he'd gone into the master program and given the command to return the generator to normal operation. Running a hand over his head, willing the headache that gripped him to ease, he took a deep breath and exited the room.

He spoke briefly to the maintenance men, reassuring them that they hadn't missed anything. "I couldn't find a thing, not even with a fine-tooth comb," he joked. "Keep an eye on this room for a few days, though," he cautioned. "The weather's going to cut us off from outside help so we can't afford to let anything go wrong."

"We'll camp out here in the hall," Tom declared, his solid form and heavy features tense and grim.

"Yeah," Bob said. "Nobody'll get by us, boss."

Jake thanked them and headed out into the night, unwilling to tell them that their efforts and loyalty might come to nothing if the person who had sabotaged the system was as clever as he or she seemed to be. The two men were West Virginian to the core, hardworking and honest, but they were no match for a mind that could break a seemingly unbreakable computer code.

If that's what actually had happened.

He headed back to the main building and his office. A few minutes at the computer, and he would know for certain. Falling snow stung his face and the cold air cut through the woolen coat to make his bones ache, but Jake scarcely noticed the discomfort. His mind whirled, trying to locate and organize the possible explanations for the events of the day and evening.

He was too tired, he knew. But he had to try.

His office was dark and cold. Smelled musty, too. Like a wet dog. He hit the light switch and turned on the space heater for a few minutes. The room warmed quickly, and the air cleared. Jake settled down at his desk and turned his attention to the computer. He ran a diagnostic program through the security system and found no traceable evidence of a breach. No "footprint" of an unauthorized user.

Jake worked for another two hours, sifting the system, looking for some trace, some clue. Nothing showed up. Whoever had broken in was some kind of computer genius or a ghost who knew BASIC.

Jake covered his aching eyes. He had no choice but to reprogram everything. Without being able to track the intruder, he had no way to deal with him or her. So he had to protect his system and try to make it even more tamperproof. Somehow, he had to anticipate any avenue a brilliant mind might use to reenter the Well's electronic fortress. Had to anticipate it and put up a solid, immovable roadblock.

Everywhere!

He took a deep breath and started typing.

CHAPTER SEVEN

DAWN WOKE UP early the next morning, dressed quickly in her own clothes and went looking for a telephone to call her office at the *Wilmont Times*. Her editor needed to know she wouldn't be making her weekly column deadline. It didn't take her long to discover that the storm had taken down most phone and power lines in the mountain region.

Transistor radios provided information from outside. The weather was giving the country a real pounding. All up and down the East Coast, storm alerts were posted, and many other rural and mountain areas were cut off. The only reason the Well still had electricity was that its generator that had failed for nearly an hour last night was now working. Last night's outage should never have happened, since the system was designed to operate under extreme conditions of all sorts.

The weather was more than unusual, Dawn was told. It was a once-every-fifty-years sort of storm. A young local woman named Mabel, who was working as a cook, showed her the view from the kitchen window and explained, "Don't remember myself snow coming this early ever, but my gramma said when she was a young'un she 'membered gettin' stuck up in a cabin in the hills in September an' not gettin' out 'til near spring. Might happen like that this year."

"Oh, I hope not," Dawn declared, not sure if Mabel was kidding her. "Surely this will clear soon."

"Uh-huh," Mabel said, going back to work on a batch of pancake batter. "My gramma hoped same thing, I guess. But when spring came, she and my grandpa hadda get married and she never did leave that cabin for good. Stayed there raisin' kids for the rest of her natural life, she did." She stated the last cheerfully.

Dawn widened her eyes and thought of having to stay at Jacob's Well forever.

It was an interesting concept. Not entirely horrifying, but not exactly what she wanted for the rest of *her* natural life. She accepted a mug of fresh coffee and wandered into the dining room to wait for breakfast. Several other people were already seated, and they waved her over to join them.

They introduced themselves. Two of the women were scientists, one was a production worker. One man worked with the plant machinery, and the other was a theoretical mathematician who helped Jake with formula development. Dawn felt welcome immediately. She was chatting and enjoying her coffee when she saw Sophie enter the room. Something about the child's facial expression and body posture troubled her. But before she could get up and go to her, Sophie ran over.

Up close, Dawn could see that the girl's cheeks and nose were red from the cold. "Have you seen my dad?" she asked, her voice trembly. "He didn't come home last night at all!"

Dawn put her hand on Sophie's small shoulder. Her body was shaking. "No, I haven't seen him. Are you sure he didn't...?"

"His bed's still made up, and the dogs weren't fed! I looked at the front porch and at the back one, too, and there weren't any footprints." Tears formed in the girl's eyes. "He's gone!"

"Have you checked his office?"

"N-no." Sophie drew a shuddering breath. "I just came in and saw you and thought maybe you'd know."

"I don't." Dawn stood up, aware that the others were all regarding her speculatively. "Honey, your father has a lot on his mind right now," she said. "Let's go take a look in his office. I'll bet he's there, working."

"He didn't come home," Sophie declared again. She was beginning to pout. "He wouldn't work all night."

"Let's go see." Dawn started walking. To Dawn's surprise, Sophie took her hand. The gesture of trust seemed so natural, she was sure Sophie wasn't aware of it.

But the small hand fit into Dawn's as if they were made for each other. A sensation of gentleness settled over Dawn, and she felt a strange need to protect the girl who walked so innocently by her side.

They reached the door to Jake's office. It was closed. Dawn knocked softly. No answer.

"He's not there," Sophie said, moaning the words. "He's lost out in the snow or something. I just know it!"

"Calm down. If he did go out, you should know he'll be fine. He's part woods critter, isn't he?"

"I guess." Dawn knocked again, louder this time. Still no answer. "Let's go in," she suggested after a moment. Sophie stepped forward and opened the door. Dawn followed her into the room.

Sophie screamed.

Jake sat slumped over on his desk, facedown on the computer keyboard. Clearly, he'd been asleep, because at the sound of his daughter's scream, he sat bolt upright and crashed his chair into the wall behind him. He yelled, startled and shaken by his rude awakening. Sophie screamed again and burst into tears.

Dawn quickly shut the office door and took the girl in her arms. "He's okay," she said, soothing the sobbing child with her touch and voice. "Look. He's fine. We just woke him up."

Sophie buried her face in Dawn's chest and wrapped her arms around Dawn's neck.

Jake came fully awake and was out of his chair and by his daughter a moment later. "Sophie, honey! What's wrong?" He tried to gather her to him, but she clung to Dawn, refusing to go to her father.

He stepped away. Dawn gave him a look indicating her own puzzlement. But Sophie held on, now crying softly.

"She had a shock," Dawn said to him. "Give her a minute. Why were you sleeping here?"

"I came back here to check on something," Jake said, running his hand over his hair. "It took me half the night and I still didn't find what I was looking for. I guess I fell asleep near morning. I was..."

Sophie's crying stopped. She raised a tear-streaked face and said, "I didn't do it, Daddy. I swear!"

"Didn't do what, baby?" Jake moved close again, squatting to be nearer to the child. Dawn gently removed Sophie's arms from around her neck. "What's wrong?'' Jake asked, smoothing his daughter's gold hair. ''Sophie?''

''I didn't make the lights go out!'' Sophie's eyes were tightly shut. But she reached for her dad.

''I know that, honey,'' Jake said, pulling her close and hugging her. ''I don't know who did it, but—''

Suddenly the office door banged open. Joan Dawson stood there. ''I heard screaming,'' she said. ''What's wrong?''

''I was asleep at the switch,'' Jake said, standing up, his hand remaining on Sophie's head. ''I was face-down at the desk. Soph came in and thought I'd died on the job or something. Nothing to worry about.''

''Oh,'' Joan said. She gave the child a long look, and Dawn noted that Sophie seemed to shrink under the hard gaze. ''I thought someone had hurt you, Sophie,'' Joan added.

''I'm fine,'' Sophie replied, only a trace of the tears left in her voice. ''I just got scared when I saw Daddy. I'm sorry.''

''No harm done,'' Jake said, ruffling her hair. ''No need to be sorry, either. I should have come home.''

''As long as everyone's all right, I'll go to breakfast,'' Joan declared. She left, shutting the door behind her.

''I should have gone home last night,'' Jake said, directing his words to Dawn. Guilt haunted his eyes.

''You were tired,'' Dawn said quietly. ''Really tired.''

''Yeah, I was.'' He looked at her, his gaze searching for something she couldn't define. Then he said, ''Thanks.''

Dawn raised her eyebrows, questioning.

"For being there for Sophie," he explained. He returned his attention to the girl. "Okay, Soph. Why don't you take me to breakfast? I could use some coffee right about now."

Sophie grinned, her weepy mood vanishing entirely. "Okay. Coffee and cocoa flakes."

"Sounds great!" Jake took her hand. "Should we ask Dawn to join us?"

"Sure." Sophie turned her grin on Dawn. "Come on," she said, holding out her other hand.

Dawn took it.

The trio sat together at a separate table, eating breakfast like a small family. Dawn kept the conversation going when she noticed that Jake was having trouble staying awake, even with two mugfuls of strong coffee in him.

She talked to Sophie, giving Jake a chance to pull himself together. She wasn't comfortable with children as a rule, but as she dredged up stories from her own childhood, she found that Sophie became easier to talk to. For each of Dawn's stories, Sophie had one of her own to recount. By the end of the meal the two of them were yakking away like old friends.

Jake still felt groggy and bleary-minded from last night's marathon computer session. But he was awake enough to be aware of what was happening at the table. Since Sophie arrived on his doorstep two months ago, she hadn't exchanged more than a few casual sentences at a time with any adult on the premises. Even with him, her own father, she was not inclined to social conversation. They got along well, but they weren't really buddies.

Yet, here she was, talking away like a little magpie with a woman she had just met. Happy as Jake had seen her since she'd been at the Well.

Dawn Sutton had wrought a miracle.

And the snowstorm had wrought another. She wouldn't be able to leave for at least a week, if the cold held the snow on the back roads as he figured it would. A week.

And a lot could happen in seven days.

His heart missed a beat at the thought of having her here for a whole week. There'd be time to really explore his feelings for her and to see how her relationship with Sophie developed. He felt a surge of excitement at the possibilities that lay ahead.

But there were other—more pressing issues, he hated to admit—to attend to.

"I feel better, but I'm going to be tied up all morning and possibly the rest of the day trying to figure out what went wrong with the generator," he said when they were finished eating. "Dawn, would you mind giving Sophie a hand with her morning chores? The snow's going to make dealing with the dogs a little more trouble than usual. And she's got to shovel the porch and walkway in front of our cabin."

"Sure. I'd be happy to," she said, smiling at him, clearly pleased with the assignment.

Sophie looked equally happy at the prospect.

So Jake left them to each other, feeling surprisingly good about it.

DAWN SPENT a thoroughly enjoyable morning helping Sophie. Recently her life had been sadly lacking in physical exercise, but she found herself energized after throwing snow off the porch with a wide shovel and tossing snowballs for the three dogs to chase. Snow still fell steadily, but the air was fresh and pure and her body seemed to respond positively to the demands she made on it.

By lunchtime Jake still hadn't returned, so she and Sophie put together sandwiches and ate them in the cabin kitchen. They didn't talk much, but the silence was easy. The three dogs, damp from the snow, slumbered near the warm stove. The soft smells of wet dog, fresh coffee, wood smoke and food wafted through the room.

Dawn realized that she was feeling something she hadn't experienced for a long, long time. She felt relaxed and oddly at peace. Stifling a yawn, she said, "I don't know about you, Sophie, but I'm for a nap this afternoon."

"Okay." Sophie got up and carried her plate over to the sink. "I'm going to read. If you don't want to go back outside, you can use the other bed in my room."

"Thanks." Dawn stood and stretched. "I think I will." They cleaned the kitchen, then went into Sophie's room. Two narrow twin beds, a desk with a computer, a bookcase and a bureau comprised the furnishings. Sitting on the spare bed and pulling off her shoes, Dawn noticed that the computer monitor was on, a screen saver of fanciful color blobs roaming the surface. She commented on the pattern.

"I keep it on all the time when I'm not using the computer," Sophie said. "Daddy and I designed it."

"It's pretty."

"He's good with computers." Sophie took off her shoes and jumped up on her bed. "Not as good as my mom, but good."

"Your mother is a computer programmer?"

"No. She's a biochemist like Dad, but she doesn't do much anymore."

"Why not?"

"She's got a boyfriend." Sophie flopped back on her bed and placed a large book on her chest. A tome about theoretical mathematics, the title declared it. She opened it and began reading.

Dawn waited until she was sure no further confidences were forthcoming. Then she lay down and shut her eyes. Sophie's parents' lives were none of her business, no matter how curious she was.

No matter how intriguing she found the mysteries surrounding this place.

And no matter how fond she was quickly getting of this fey little kid.

Or her dad.

LATE THAT AFTERNOON, Jake held a meeting of the department heads. They crowded into his office and listened attentively as he outlined the situation.

"We could be effectively cut off right now," he said. "I can't even send messages with the computer since all the phone lines are out. But we do have an old-fashioned two-way radio that connects to my father's house. If any sort of emergency arises that we can't deal with or that we need outside help for, we can call out. Meanwhile, I'm counting on you people to observe emergency conditions. Keep a close eye on those working with you. I don't want anyone taking unnecessary risks physically. The last thing we need is the challenge of hauling someone with a broken leg out of here by snowmobile."

Everyone agreed and promised to spread the word.

"The other thing I want to suggest," Jake said, "is that we take this opportunity to declare a kind of miniholiday. The weather's going to keep us under for a few days anyway, so why not take time off and relax. It'll be good for us all."

"How about you, Jake?" Ginny Reynolds asked, her tone wry. "You planning to rest?"

Jake regarded the physician. "Yes, I am," he said.

"Good, because otherwise I was going to start chasing you with vitamin B shots," she declared. "Joan told me about you sleeping at your desk again last night."

Jake eyed the computer monitor. It danced with the screen-saver program he and Sophie had designed a few weeks before. "I was hunting," he said.

"Hunters need to sleep, too," the doctor commented.

"Point made," Jake said.

"Did you find anything?" Todd asked. "When you were hunting, that is? I assume you were trying to figure out why we had that electrical outage yesterday evening."

"Not a thing," Jake confessed. "There were no footprints in my system. I need to delve deeper, but I don't think I have the skill and know-how."

"If you don't, who here does?" Farley asked.

"Good question," Jake replied. "If I knew that, I'd know who was in without my authorization."

"Tell us about Dawn Sutton," Joan asked, changing the subject. "She arrives here unexpectedly, and odd things begin to happen. Just who is she and what does she want with us?"

"I told everyone at the meeting. She's a grad student. All she wants is information."

"Seems a little odd to me, too, her arriving just when all kinds of suspicious things start to happen," Todd stated. Several other people nodded agreement. "Did you check her story?"

"I did." Jake put both hands flat on his desk. "Dawn's not responsible for our troubles, and I think everyone here knows that. Once again, painful as it is, we have to face the fact that our problems are being caused by someone we know and trust. One of us."

"That doesn't mean she isn't involved," Joan said. "She could be working with—"

"I'll worry about Ms. Sutton," Jake interrupted. "Don't let her presence become a red herring, Joan. It's always easier to blame a newcomer, an outsider, than to look closely at one's friends and neighbors."

There was silence from the group.

"I don't believe one of us could be doing these things," Ginny declared, her arms crossed over her chest. "I'm the doctor here and I guess I know everybody about as well as it's possible to know anyone. There are no traitors here."

"I second that," Johnny Wilson said. "Hate to hear you even say such things, boss."

"I hope you two are right," Jake answered. "And if you are and I'm wrong, I'll make restitution somehow. But until we know it for an absolute certainty, we have got to stay alert and suspicious."

"That's not good for us," Farley intoned. "Not good at all."

"I know," Jake said sympathetically. "That's why I hope we can find the person responsible and clear this all up as quickly as possible." He paused and surveyed his team. "The Well might not survive otherwise,'' he added.

No one said anything after that.

DAWN WOKE UP from her nap to the soft sounds of keyboard clacking. She opened her eyes and saw Sophie sitting at her computer, tapping away. ''What time is it?'' Dawn asked. ''How long did I sleep?''

Sophie turned, a startled look on her face. Her fingers touched two keys and the data on the screen disappeared. ''Oh, not too long,'' she said. ''It's just five o'clock, I think.''

Dawn sat up and stretched. ''Better than I did yesterday. I must be catching up. What were you working on?''

''Nothing.'' Sophie hit another key and the screen saver appeared. ''Just messing around.''

Dawn got off the bed. ''I guess I need to get back to my room before dinnertime. Want to come over with me?''

''I'm not going to dinner.'' Sophie picked up the book she'd been reading. ''I'm not very hungry.''

''Okay. Will you be all right here by yourself?''

''Sure.'' Sophie flopped down on the bed and opened her book.

Dawn hesitated. ''Want me to bring you something from the dining room?''

''No. There's stuff here if I get hungry.''

Dawn smiled. ''You can cook for yourself on that wood-burning stove?''

''No. I'll just eat it cold.'' Sophie's nose buried deeper into the book.

''That doesn't sound very appetizing. I've never used a wood stove. Mind if I give it a try?''

The book came down. ''You can cook?''

''Some. I try not to burn water when I boil it.''

Sophie sat up, laughing. "Okay. Come on," she said. "I'll show you where stuff is."

"Stuff?"

"Pots and pans and things. I think I know where Dad puts them."

"You *think* you know!" Dawn rolled her eyes. "Oh, boy. We're going to be a great team!"

JAKE TOOK DINNER in his office and continued to work until his mind finally shut down and told him to get home to his own bed. Giving up on his hunt was hard, but he knew he had to get some real sleep on a real bed. Except for the continuing storm, nothing had gone wrong at the Well today, so maybe he could rest without undue worry.

He would probably worry anyway.

He trudged home through the deepening snow, his brain still burdened with the prospect of waking up to another day of fruitless stalking through the cyber-maze. He *knew* there was a clue, a trace somewhere in the system. He just didn't know if he had the intelligence and cunning to find it.

He clumped up the steps to his cabin, stomping the snow off his boots. He was so deep in his gloomy mood that it didn't occur to him until he started to open the front door that the dogs hadn't barked in greeting.

Sophie!

Fear hit him as he opened the door. "Sophie! Soph! Where are—"

"In here, Dad."

She was in the kitchen. That realization, the warmth of the fire burning in the hearth and the incredibly delicious aroma of chocolate hit him at the same time as the rush of relief. From the kitchen, he heard one of the dogs give a sleepy woof of welcome.

Then he heard a woman laughing, soft, sweet and low.

Dawn! He'd forgotten she had agreed to help Sophie with her chores.

"Dawn, are you here too?" he called out as he shucked off his boots and coat. "I didn't mean for you to baby-sit this long."

Sophie laughed, high and happy. "She's not baby-sitting me, Dad. We're making brownies."

Brownies?

He went into the kitchen. Dawn and Sophie were taking a large pan filled with dark chocolate goodies out of the oven. They were covered with soot from the wood stove, flour and a variety of brownie ingredients. The three dogs were sprawled on the floor, apparently stupefied by the warmth and liberal offerings of treats from the cooks. They wagged their tails for him, but remained motionless otherwise.

"You made brownies?" Jake asked. "I'm impressed."

"With whom?" Dawn asked, brushing her hair back from her sweaty face. Her hand left a streak of soot and flour on her cheek. "Me or Sophie?"

Jake laughed and sat down on the one kitchen chair that wasn't stacked with cooking gear or ingredients. "Both of you, I suppose." He regarded the pan of brownies. "Think they're edible?"

He was rewarded with theatrical glares. He laughed again, enjoying the release of tension that humor brought. "Well," he said, teasing, "I didn't know the two of you had hidden talents."

"Try them," Sophie said.

"We dare you," Dawn added.

Something wonderful and warm stirred in Jake. The sight of the two of them like this made him remember his childhood and the closeness of his family. It hit him that he had never seen Sophie in this kind of situation before. To avoid the pain *that* thought threatened to evoke, he reached for a brownie.

A minute later, he had to admit the brownies were delicious. The praise and the relish with which he ate restored him to their good graces. While he ate and watched, Sophie and Dawn worked together to clean up the mess they had made.

It was indeed a pleasing sight. One, he decided, he hoped would be repeated.

After that, they moved into the living room. Jake stretched out on the sofa, and Dawn and Sophie set up a chessboard on the rug in front of the fireplace. They told him they'd agreed to play while they had been cooking.

"Dawn says she's going to whip me at this game," Sophie said, her confidence clear. "She's been playing longer than I've been alive, but I'm going to win."

"In your dreams, kid!" Dawn stated. Her smile was wide and her eyes shone with glee. "Maybe you have the brains, but I have the experience! I've been kicking fanny at this game since I was old enough to read the rules."

"Ha!" Sophie laughed out her challenge.

And the game began.

And suddenly Jake realized the two had gone much further toward friendship and mutual understanding in just a few hours than he'd done with his own daughter in the years before his divorce from her mother and in the months she'd been with him now. The realization brought him mixed emotions.

From his position on the sofa, he watched the game. They played hard, giving each other no quarter. And they were surprisingly well matched. The play was noisy at first, the two exchanging good-natured insults and gibes.

Then as the strategies progressed, silence fell. The only sound was the crackling of the fire and the slide of chess pieces across the board. The dogs wandered in from the kitchen to settle near the fire, but neither player noticed. In spite of the tension from the game, Jake found himself relaxing.

Dawn won the first game.

Sophie wailed her disappointment and called for a rematch. Dawn agreed. Then she said something that brought Jake out of his drowsy state.

"You lost because you were thinking only of the physical setup, Sophie," she explained. "If you were playing against a computer, you'd have won. I don't doubt that."

"Then I should have beat you."

"No." Dawn smiled. "I'm human, and I faked you out." She picked up several pieces and set them up in fight position. "See, when you moved here, I moved here, and you thought..."

"I thought it was stupid, and that you were finished."

"That's what I wanted you to think. See, with a computer, it's all numbers. But with me, it's also emotional. You have to factor that into your calculations. If you can."

"I can!"

They started to play again.

Jake sat up a bit to watch. Something was going on that he knew he needed to understand. If only he wasn't so bone-tired, he'd figure it out.

But he could barely keep his eyes open. Could barely follow the play as it became more complex. Could barely...

Sophie won the second game.

"Good work!" Dawn declared, genuinely delighted. "You saw what I was doing this time. You're a good student!"

Sophie giggled with pleasure. "Then be my teacher." She glanced over to where her father lay snoring softly on the sofa. "We can ask Dad in the morning."

"Okay," Dawn replied, keeping her voice down, although she had a feeling she could yell out loud and not wake the sleeping man. "I think you can handle first-year economics. Now, I'd better get back to my room. It's late."

"You can sleep here."

"No, honey. I don't think that would be a good idea." Dawn helped Sophie put the chess pieces away. "Even though I'd be in your room, people would wonder. It wouldn't look good for your father. And right now, I think he needs his image as untarnished as possible."

"But you're my friend, not Dad's," Sophie protested.

"I'm a friend to both of you," Dawn said. "And I'm sleeping in my own room tonight. Okay?"

"Okay," Sophie said. "But in the morning...?"

"In the morning, we'll start class," Dawn promised. "Let's take care of your daddy before I leave."

"I'll let the dogs out the kitchen door," Sophie said. "That won't wake him up. He can just sleep out here. He's done it before."

Dawn bowed to Sophie's greater knowledge of her father's habits. While the girl took care of the animals, she went into Jake's bedroom and got a blanket. She covered the slumbering man and felt a surprising wave of tenderness toward him. He looked so peaceful.

Too bad it wasn't true.

CHAPTER EIGHT

THE SNOW CONTINUED to fall for thirty-eight hours, ending late Saturday night. The weather stayed winter-cold and overcast through Monday, keeping people inside and communication with the outside world impossible.

But on Tuesday morning, although it was bitterly cold and windy, the sun appeared shyly, as if ashamed for abandoning the countryside, and Jake informed Dawn that she could call out if she wanted.

She did. She closed the door to Jake's office and called her editor. She explained to David Pfaff the potential story she hoped to cover.

David was less than enthusiastic at first. "Sounds dangerous," he said. "You're too valuable to me to let you risk yourself like that. What if the bomb had been real?"

"It wasn't. David, this story will put the *Times* on the front pages. Come on. You can't turn down that kind of publicity."

"Yes, I can. If it involves the possibility of losing a friend as well as a good reporter."

"Listen to me," Dawn pleaded. "This is a once-in-a-lifetime chance."

A moment of silence on the line. Then, "You're going to do it, even if I say no, aren't you?"

"I hate to be stubborn, but yes."

"How long will you stay?"

"I'm not sure, David. Maybe two weeks or possibly even a month."

David sighed. "Okay. But don't say I was willing. Want me to ask someone to check on your apartment? Water your plants?"

Dawn laughed. "I don't have any plants, and you know it. And I'll be driving into town as soon as the roads clear to get my stuff. But thanks for the offer."

"Okay. Here's how we'll do it," David said, all business now. "I'd like a weekly telephoned report, if you can manage it," he told her. "I'll keep notes here on what you tell me."

Dawn agreed. It would be like keeping a diary, but one that was safe from prying eyes, since it would be in David's care, not hers. Although she had no reason to feel threatened, she nevertheless sensed that it would be wise to take precautions. If someone here really was trying to cause trouble, Dawn doubted they wanted an impartial observer on the scene, recording events. They certainly wouldn't want a reporter whose work was likely to get national attention once it was in print! So the low profile was the best idea all around.

When Jake came back into his office, she told him what she had said to David.

"Good idea," he said, his distracted tone and manner indicating he wasn't really thinking about her or her magazine. "You keep at it and let me know if there's any way I can help."

"I do have a question."

"What?"

"About my background. If you were able to check on me and find out about the magazine, can't anyone else? I'm thinking particularly of Joan. Won't she run a computer check on me now that the lines are open again?''

"She has no reason to." He sat down at his desk. "I told her I'd checked you out."

"But if she does . . ."

"If she does, she'll come to me and I'll take care of it. Don't worry." He tapped a few keys.

She saw that she'd lost his attention, so she started to leave the room.

"Dawn."

She turned.

"I want to tell you how much your taking time with Sophie means to me," he said, the abstracted look gone from his face. He was completely focused on her, and his expression was warm. "Thank you."

"It's no problem," she said. "I like her. She's extremely bright. She catches on more easily than many of my college-age students did. I'm having as much fun as she is. You don't need to thank me."

"Nevertheless, I'm grateful. I'm going to have someone open one of the empty cabins for you this afternoon. There are linens and basic housekeeping items available. When you're able to get out of here for a day, you're welcome to bring some of your own belongings from home to make your stay more comfortable. Not exactly a way of repaying you, but it will give you more space and privacy."

"Thanks. But I—"

"And in the morning, I think we'd better go out and mark your car."

"Excuse me? What?"

"Mark your car. When the snowplows finally get up this way, I don't want them running over it if it's buried too deeply to see."

"Oh. That hadn't occurred to me. Thanks."

He smiled, and the sunshine outside seemed to get brighter. "Just want to keep you here and happy," he said. "We'll talk more later." And he went back to the keyboard.

Dawn left the office, wondering what all that meant.

The rest of the day went according to the schedule she'd set. She kept busy and got a workout every time she left one building and trudged through the snow to another. Even though the walkways were kept shoveled, the wind was fierce and the snowy white carpet had a way of blowing back over the cleared areas and presenting a challenge to foot travelers.

After the general state of alarm on Thursday night, however, everyone seemed to have returned to a normal relaxed attitude and were taking the inconvenience of the cold and snow with good humor. Jokes were even made about the smoke bomb and the mysterious electric failure. As Dawn observed this change in temperament, she wondered if matters actually had been taken too seriously, blown out of proportion, as it were.

But she could draw no concrete conclusions, since she hadn't been at the Well long enough to be sure. One thing she did know: the residents were resilient, able to deal with problems and uncertainty much better than she would have imagined, given the reasons most of them had come to the Well.

Her relationship with Sophie had progressed nicely. The girl had taken to Dawn's teaching like a duck to water, showing a fine aptitude for theory. Sophie was an endearing combination of kid and genius, a mix that Dawn found amazingly easy to deal with.

And to like.

Tuesday evening she had dinner in the dining room with Jake and Sophie, but they'd shared the table with others and there had been no opportunity for any personal talk. By late evening she was worn-out and ready for sleep.

As she prepared to get into bed, a soft knock sounded at her door. Throwing on a robe, she asked who was there before opening.

"It's Jake," he said. "Mind if I talk to you for a minute?"

Dawn opened the door. "Sure. Anything wrong?"

He stepped inside and shut the door. "It's about Sophie," he said.

Dawn sat on the bed. "What about her?"

Jake sat down beside her. "I know that for the last few days I've seemed in a kind of a fog. I've been concentrating on tracking whoever got into my computer program."

"You have been busy."

"But not so busy that I haven't been aware of things."

"What things?"

"Quite a few things, actually." He looked at her and smiled. "First, like I said this morning, how well you and Soph have hit it off. And let me repeat how grateful I am for that." The smile faded. "Dawn, I'm worried about her. She's afraid of something."

Dawn laughed. "Sophie? I don't think so."

"She's been acting withdrawn around other people. Not you, but people she's known much longer. She's waking up several times a night with bad dreams, and last night I found her working on her computer at two in the morning. I had to threaten to unplug it before she'd go back to bed. I stayed up in the living room until I was sure she was asleep. It was nearly four before she settled down.''

"Maybe she's just overstimulated by everything that's happened. I mean, it was exciting with the smoke bomb and the lights going off and the snowstorm. And she's absorbing all the material I'm throwing at her as fast as I can..."

"She's afraid, Dawn. And I'm worried that there's a connection between her state of mind and the events that have been plaguing us.''

Suddenly Dawn felt cold. "You're not thinking she had anything to do with...?"

"No! That is, I don't know. I can't imagine it. But in my five days of investigation, I've about torn my computer apart and I've found that the only person besides myself who has accessed the files controlling the electrical system is Sophie."

"That doesn't mean she did—"

"All it means is that she was able to get past my security and into my program. She could have done that and then left it for someone else to do the dirty work." He looked down at the floor. "Hell, I don't know what to think. She plays with computers like other kids play electronic games. She might have wandered in and out without even knowing what she had accessed. But if she's the only one I can find, then I have to assume that she was somehow involved in the generator failure."

"Maybe it was done as a prank. Have you asked her about it?"

"Yes. She categorically denies responsibility, and I can't bring myself to call her a liar. She's very defiant about it."

"She's tough."

"She's afraid. I..." He paused. "I just want to ask you another favor, I guess."

"You want me to try to find out what's bothering her?"

"You're the only person I can turn to." Another pause. "Ironic, isn't it?"

"You mean because I don't belong here?"

Jake waited a moment. Then he said what had been on his mind for some time. "I think you do belong here, Dawn. I wish I knew who placed that call to you last week because I want to thank her."

She laughed. "Whoever it was hardly had your best interests at heart."

"Sometimes even enemies do you favors."

"And sometimes even friends do you harm?"

His expression turned bleak. "I don't know. I've spent most of the last decade trying to build a place where people would be able to trust one another. I'm afraid I've been too much of a dreamer."

She felt a prickling of sympathetic emotion. "Dreams do have a way of turning into nightmares sometimes."

"And when that happens, all you want to do is wake up."

"Jake, tell me about what happened in your past. Why the insurance-scam thing is such a threat."

He shut his eyes. "It wasn't anything, really. When I was a very young man, I tried to start a small business. Selling herbal-based products. Like the Well, but on a much smaller scale. To make a long story short, I went broke. The insurance I'd taken out covered my losses."

"That's hardly a secret scandal."

"Well . . . there was some resistance from the insurance people to paying up."

"And?"

"It went to court. I won. But there were a lot of aspects about the case I didn't care for. The insurance company did a good job of tarnishing my reputation, and I was too young to realize I should pursue that issue as well as the financial one."

"How young were you?"

"Nineteen."

"You were just nineteen, and you started a business?"

"It was a poorly thought-out idea. My folks and friends tried to help, but we were all naive. My lawyer was one of my second cousins. He did the best he could, but looking back, I wasn't well represented. Cousin Paul wasn't wily, just eager. The tarnish lingered for years." He stood up. "Until you told me about the phone call, though, I thought I'd put it all behind me."

"But anyone who cared to look up the court records and match them with newspaper articles published at the time could resurrect the incident."

He ran his hand over his hair and looked at his watch. "It's late, I'll be going. Tomorrow we'll go out to the gate and make sure that your car is safe, all right?"

"All right. And I'll see if Sophie is willing to open up to me about what's on her mind. But you have to realize that if something is bothering her, it might not have anything to do with your problems at the Well."

"It might have to do with me as a father, you mean?"

"Or with her situation. As I understand it, her mom dumped her on you. That's got to hurt."

He considered that. "It might. Sophie hasn't said a word about her feelings. She's been with her mom since we divorced seven years ago, but I was granted unlimited access to her. No contest in the divorce settlement. Our marriage was a battle zone, but oddly enough after we split, we got along pretty well. No hard feelings on either side, I believe. Joyce has been very generous about it all."

"She's never left Sophie with you like this?"

"Not during the school year. Sophie went to a school for gifted kids."

"I can understand why. Seems to me her mom would be concerned about keeping Sophie's education at that level.... Have you talked to Joyce recently?"

"No."

"Have you tried?"

"Yes. She's not home. I know she's been seeing another biochemist. A guy named Tony Edwards, someone we both knew in graduate school. I've tried to get hold of him, but I can't find him, either. They may have gone off somewhere."

"Does that seem like her?"

"No, it doesn't." He looked at the floor. "But then, I don't think I ever really knew Joyce. I thought because we were both in the same field, we'd be able to work and live together in harmony. It didn't turn out that way. Joyce never loved the work for its own sake the way I did. She only wanted what it could bring her."

"Money?"

"That. And prestige. When I decided to move here from Philadelphia, she couldn't accept it. We'd lost our love before that and were just hanging on."

"So, she has reason to hate this place?"

Jake smiled wryly. "She couldn't be behind the sabotage."

"Just a thought."

"Even if it was off base, please keep having them. I need all the input I can get." He stood and walked over to open the door. Dawn followed.

At the doorway, he paused. "Now that I'm just about out of your bedroom, Dawn, there's something I want to say."

"Go ahead."

"If I weren't so knotted up about what's going on at the Well, I want you to know that I'd be paying you a great deal more attention than I have."

"Oh, don't apologize. I've been fine. Laurie's a good tour guide, and everyone's been happy to talk to me."

"That's not what I mean." His expression turned softer, serious yet beguiling. His green eyes seemed to deepen to the shade of the dark forest.

Dawn stood still, her heart beginning to beat faster.

"I mean that while I appreciate your kindness to my daughter and the help you've agreed to give me, those are not the only reasons I'd like you to stay here. I'm attracted to you, Dawn. I'm just real sorry I don't have a chance to explore that fact." He put his hand on her chin and touched her lips with his. Kissing her. Gently.

"Good night, Dawn," he said. "There *will* be time for us, I promise," he said.

And with that, Jake left, shutting the door behind him. Dawn stared at the closed door for a few minutes, her lips still tingling from his kiss. He'd referred to the two of them as "us." Was there an "us"? she wondered. The thought both scared and excited her. With difficulty, she managed to put aside her emotions and concentrate on what she had just learned about him. She got a pad and pen and made some notes to herself.

Things to check out when she had the chance.

THE NEXT MORNING Jake and Sophie appeared at breakfast in the main dining room. They both seemed cheerful and behaved in an outgoing manner toward one and all, making Dawn wonder if the conversation and kiss she'd shared with Jake the night before had all been a dream.

Or a reflection of a man who was hiding something. A man who might be doing exactly what her mystery caller had implied. While she found such ideas distasteful to consider, she reminded herself firmly that it was her professional duty to entertain them until she had proof that Jake Barr was as good and innocent a man as he seemed.

Her emotional response to his confession last night had to be left out of the equation. And her response to the touch of his lips was something she needed to put out of her mind entirely! A good reporter should not be distracted by personal passions, no matter how compelling.

Sure.

She went over and took a seat beside Sophie. "You're looking bright and chipper this morning," she said. "Is it because the storm's over and you're going to be able to go back to your regular school?"

"No." Sophie gave her a blank look. "Dad says I can stay here while you're here."

"Oh. That's good. I called my... I can stay for a full month. That way, we can cover just about all of Economics 101."

Sophie grinned. "Stay longer. I want you to tutor me all through to graduation from college."

Dawn realized she was being teased. It felt good. "I'll give it the consideration it deserves," she retorted, tousling Sophie's blond hair." She looked at Jake. "Sleep well?"

"First night in a while," he replied with a smile. "I actually feel human this morning."

"Dad's going to take you skiing," Sophie announced.

"Skiing? I thought we were going out to my car."

"We are." He drank coffee. "We could take one of the snowmobiles, but I want to scout the trees by the fence. The local poacher's been laying his trap lines inside my territory, and with this snow, I want to make a careful search. Don't want any of our animals hurt."

Dawn looked around the table. The others seated there included Faye Reynolds, the nurse, her sister Ginny, the doctor, as well as Laurie and Farley. Everyone nodded agreement with Jake's comment. "I met Laurie's cat," Dawn said. "It's terrible that an innocent animal would get caught and hurt like that."

"I hate trapping," Jake said angrily. "But I have to grant that some folks have the right to do it out on open land. Trapping's an old way of making a living here in the hills, and I don't have any business interfering with a man's legal livelihood, no matter how distasteful I find it personally. But on my land, it's different. It's my animals, both wild and domestic, that I aim to protect.''

Dawn saw a cold light in his eyes and was very glad not to be the reason for his anger. "I appreciate what you're doing,'' she said. "But if you're skiing out to the gate, forget about taking me along. I don't know how to ski. I'll just be in your way.''

"This is cross-country. If you can walk, you can do it. I'll show you.''

"Jake, I'm not very athletic.''

He chuckled. "The way you got hung up on the gate, I suppose you have a point. But really, it's not hard. Ask anyone here.''

Dawn looked around the table once more. Everyone was grinning. "Why do I think that's a bad idea?''

"Come on.'' Jake put his hand across the table to cover hers. "Besides being fun, I thought it might be a chance for me to enjoy your company.''

Dawn felt herself blush and was amazed. Were her feelings *that* close to the surface? "Okay,'' she said as breezily as she could manage. "Since you put it that way, how can I refuse? I'll give it a try.''

The teasing laughter from the others made her blush even harder.

Why?

She had little time to consider that question. An hour later, Dawn was moving across the new snow, the soft stuff making strange squeaking-squishing sounds beneath the unfamiliar skis. Jake had outfitted her in cross-country gear as soon as they'd finished breakfast. Wasting no time, he'd shown her the rudimentary moves and they had headed out of the fort, down the slope and into the trees. She fell twice on the way, but then began to get the hang of it. It was not as difficult as she'd thought. In fact, after a few minutes, she found she was moving in a natural rhythm, gliding and skating along.

She was even able to notice and appreciate the scenery.

As it had been on the morning she had climbed the gate, the air was thick and white. No snow fell, but cold humidity caused a misty fog and the overcast sky made it seem as if the storm still held sway. The sunlight was almost too pale to matter. Dim enough to be less help than moonlight.

That caused another problem. Depth perception was nil, and Dawn learned quickly that if she tried to concentrate too hard on keeping her balance, she would fall. A furrow in the snow that seemed only inches deep would prove to be deeper and she'd trip. And an area that looked dangerous turned out to be smooth as a skating rink. Her eyes tricked her. Only by ignoring what she saw, not thinking about it and letting her body take control was she able to remain upright.

That all served to make the journey rather dreamlike in spite of the physical exertion.

In addition to his green backpack with a rifle strapped to it, Jake wore a red jacket, so she had no trouble seeing him, but the woods around her remained shrouded in the ghostly light and mist. The temperature was hovering around twenty-five, he had told her, but she didn't believe him. It was colder out here in Jake's forest than anything she had ever felt.

Soon, however, the exercise warmed her enough to raise a good sweat. That, together with the concerted effort not to think about keeping her balance, provided a new kind of challenge. And, after a while, she realized she was enjoying it.

Ahead of her, Jake skied slowly, expertly, breaking the trail, as he'd explained he would. He was giving her a slightly tramped-down path to follow. Around him, the three dogs romped and chased one another through the drifts, barking and yapping and generally having a fine time. They were as at ease in the deep snow as they would be running in a sunny meadow on a soft grassy carpet.

In his own way, Jake was the same. He seemed to have no problem with the strange light. He never tripped, never fell. Instead, he acted as if he'd been born on the narrow boards. Every so often, he would stamp his skis on the snow, take off from the path and chase one of the dogs, laughing and calling out. The dogs loved it, and Dawn was able to appreciate that the man was getting to let off some of the terrible pressure that had built up in him. Seeing him at play made her smile. She plugged along on the track, watching the action. No side trips for her!

Finally they reached the gate. Her poor little Saab was just a white bump on the road outside. Jake waited until she caught up and stood beside him.

"You're terrific," he said. "For someone who's never had skis on, you maintained the pace and kept on your feet very well. I'm impressed."

"Don't be," she said, although his praise warmed her. "I've left a few marks of my fanny in the snow along the way. But it is getting easier. And it actually seems like it could be fun, once you really get used to it."

"Wait. A little more practice and you'll just fly along. It's the only way to see the woods in the winter."

"You've been doing this for a while, I think," she said, bending over and breathing deeply, trying to catch her breath in the cold air.

"I've been skiing since I was a kid, if that's what you mean. Before we could afford real ones, I made my own out of old boards and leather straps."

"A pioneer from beginning to end."

"You might say." He balanced easily on one ski and knocked snow off the other with a pole. "You don't have to have modern manufactured stuff to manage. When it's available, of course, I use it."

"And when it's not, you improvise."

"I do what people have done all through history. I use my brains to figure out—" He stopped talking and just looked at her.

"What's the matter?" she asked, alarmed. "Is something wrong?"

"Yes." He set his ski poles against the fence. "Here we are, all alone, and I'm talking about myself, when all I really want to do is kiss you." He shrugged out of his backpack, took off his gloves and hat and moved to stand next to her.

Dawn held her breath, feeling frozen in place. But not cold. Not cold at all.

Jake touched her face, his fingertips caressing her skin. She felt the very air start to tingle with the same excitement she was feeling. She shivered with anticipation.

He leaned closer, watching her eyes.

Dawn sighed and opened her lips a little.

They kissed.

And embraced ...

And the skis they wore skittered against one another and Dawn fell back, pulling him with her. They landed in soft snow, Jake on top of her, their legs tangled awkwardly with the long skis. She sputtered as the cold snow rolled onto her face. Brushing it away and laughing, she saw him looking down at her.

Desire shone in his eyes. Even when he began to laugh with her, the gleam remained, not fading as he picked up a handful of snow and gently rubbed it on her cheeks.

"Do you have any notion how pretty you are?" he asked. "All rosy and white and warm with your hair lacy with snowflakes?"

"I know I'm not all that warm," she replied. "And if these skis lock together, we're likely to freeze here."

"No, we wouldn't," he said. "There's too much heat between us for that to happen." But he rolled to one side and took off his skis.

Dawn sat up and struggled with hers.

"Here," he said. "Let me help. It's just a matter of tripping this lock on the binding." He did, and the skis fell clear of her boots. "Now," he said. "Where were we?"

CHAPTER NINE

DAWN REACHED OVER and put her arms around his neck. "We were kissing, remember?"

"Oh, yes." Tentatively, Jake brushed her full, moist lips with his, and her heat flooded over him. Dizzied by the sensation, he felt his body's response, and sensual power filled him. He wrapped her in his arms, marveling at the feel of her. She had seemed so small and fragile, but now, holding her, he knew she was a strong, solid woman.

One he desired. As he allowed himself to slide into a state of barely controlled passion, it occurred to him that he was falling for a woman he hardly knew. At a time in his life when romance was not an option.

But that didn't seem to matter. *This* was what he wanted. Easing sideways, he pulled her back down onto the snow.

Dawn relaxed in his embrace, scarcely aware of the cold bed on which they were lying. The warmth of his kiss and the security of his arms made her feel as if they were in a quiet room, safe from the elements.

But they weren't. At least not from some elements. A moment later, the barking of the dogs broke the spell. The three animals arrived in a great rush from whatever adventure they had been pursuing, spraying snow all over the two humans. A wet furry face pushed close to his, and Jake sat up, laughing and swearing good-naturedly.

"Next time I won't bring my pets along on a date," he said. The dogs danced near them, then barked again in chorus. Pearl eased close for attention. Jasper sniffed Dawn. Onyx took off into the woods again after more interesting sport.

"I think they're trying to tell us this isn't exactly the best place for us to get to know each other better," Dawn said. She touched his face. "Although, I must tell you that it was very nice."

"Just nice?" He raised his eyebrows.

"More than that, and you know it!" Dawn stood up, dusting snow off her rear. Without Jake's arms around her, the cold clamped down once more, and she shivered. "I have to say, I find you very different out here, away from the Well."

"I'm not carrying my troubles with me right now," he said, standing. "But don't be surprised when I pick them back up on my way home."

"I won't. That's who you are. I'm just pleased to see another side of you, that's all."

Jake kissed her again. "I hope you'll stay around until this side is the one you see most of the time."

"I . . . I can't make you any promises."

"I understand. But I wanted you to know what I was thinking."

She smiled at him and took a step through the deep snow toward the gate. The older dog, Pearl, growled.

Dawn stopped.

"Wait," Jake said. "She's not growling at you. Something else is bothering her."

Dawn felt a chill that had nothing to do with the freezing temperature. "What?"

Jake moved forward. "I don't know, but I'm going to find out," he said. His expression had turned from gentle to grim. He unlocked the gate. "Wait there," he cautioned her. "Stay," he said to the two dogs. They whined, but stayed within the boundaries of the fence.

Dawn wasn't about to move. "Be careful," she said.

Jake looked back and smiled. "Thanks. I like the sound of that," he said as he turned away.

Dawn watched, her heart pounding in fear, as he circled the lump that was her car. She wasn't sure what frightened her more: the idea of some unknown danger out there that could be lying in wait for Jake or the emotions that were now growing in her. Emotions that seemed to cast long, long shadows over her future and her plans.

She *really* liked Jake Barr. Was drawn to him more than she could remember being attracted to a man in a long time.

Maybe ever!

The big female dog quit pacing the fence and came over to sit on the snow by her feet. Dawn reached down to pet the animal's head. Pearl looked up, her dark eyes reflecting the worry that Dawn felt.

She heard Jake's voice—a more serious swearing this time.

"What?" Dawn asked.

"Not sure," came the answer. He was hidden behind the car. "Someone's been here since the storm started, though."

"How can you tell?"

Jake stood. "Tracks," he said. "Snow's filled them, but I can tell that a person has walked here not too long ago. Whoever it was circled your car several times. Tried to open the doors, I think.''

"There's nothing of any value inside.''

"Wouldn't matter. A casual thief wouldn't know that.''

Dawn started to move through the gate. "Come on, girl,'' she said to the dog by her side. Pearl woofed, then followed. The other dog, Jasper, whined. He looked off into the woods and whined again.

"Jasper!'' Jake called. "Find Onyx.'' Jasper yipped with obvious relief and bounded off into the woods after the younger dog. "Come on,'' he said to Dawn. "No danger here.'' He started to clean snow off the car.

Dawn helped. Soon they had it clear enough for her to set her key in the driver's-side door. Unlocking it and looking inside, she said, "Nothing's disturbed. No one got in.''

"But they thought about it.'' Jake tromped back through the gate and picked up his backpack. He took out a telescoping rod with a red flag at the tip. He planted the rod deep in the snow near the rear of the Saab. The flag fluttered in the cold air as if trying to keep itself warm by the movement. "That should keep any overly enthusiastic snowplower from running over your car,'' he said.

"I appreciate it.''

A series of barks sounded from some distance away. Pearl growled again. Jake looked in the direction of the noise. "I'm going to check that out,'' he said. "Stay here with Pearl. Don't try to start the car. The exhaust is buried in the snow.''

"I'll uncover it before I try.''

He hoisted the backpack to his shoulders. "I'll only be gone a few minutes," he said. "From the sound of them, they've treed a raccoon or something like that. But I want to check."

"Okay. Be—"

He kissed her.

"Careful," she finished.

Jake smiled.

Then he was gone.

Dawn waited until his red-jacketed figure all but disappeared up the road into the mist. Then she set to work digging out the rest of her car, exhaust pipe and all. Pearl waited patiently, sitting on the snow and watching her. When she was satisfied with the job she'd done, Dawn opened the door and got in. The Saab started after only one stutter.

Pearl sat on the snow watching. Her head tilted to one side.

"Come on," Dawn said, opening the back door and patting the rear seat. "It's going to be a lot warmer in here in a minute."

Pearl whined.

"Come on." Dawn slapped the seat. "He'll be back in a few minutes. No reason to be uncomfortable, is there?"

Pearl got in. She sniffed around on the back seat, then settled with a satisfied grunt.

"See?" Dawn said. "Told you you'd like it." She got back in front and cranked the heater. A few minutes later, the Saab began to throw out warmth. "Ahhhh," she said. "That's more like it."

Pearl grunted in agreement. Dawn looked back. The dog had relaxed, put her head on her paws and shut her eyes.

"I understand," Dawn said. "All that snow tired me out, too." She reached over and petted Pearl. "What do you say to a little nap while we wait?"

Pearl sighed. Her tail thumped the seat.

Dawn leaned back and closed her eyes. The warmth enveloped her, bringing a physical kind of peace. The skiing had been fun. Kissing Jake had been even more fun. *I could live like this,* she thought. Out in the middle of nowhere, close to nature, with a man...

But not yet. Too much to do. She had plans and ambitions, and it just wasn't time, no matter how strongly Jake appealed to her.

"Tell me about Jake," she said, talking to Pearl and glad no one else was around to hear her doing it. "Is he a reasonable kind of guy? Will a short-term romance with him work, if that's what I decide I want? Will he...?"

Pearl growled.

"Hey. I was just talking. Nothing that really meant anything, understand... Hey!" She looked around.

Pearl's head was up, her hackles raised and she was uttering a continuous deep-throated, threatening growl. Her attention was not on Dawn.

She was looking out at the road.

Dawn sat up. "What is it, Pearl?" She squinted, trying to see through the mist. "Do you hear something I can't?"

Pearl now stood on the back seat, still growling, her tail down between her legs and the hair along her backbone stiff and upright.

Dawn opened the doors. The air was as still as smooth glass, and just as silent. Except for the growling dog, the beating of her heart and the rush of blood in her ears.

She was suddenly unaccountably terrified.

The sound of a shot shattered the stillness.

Dawn and Pearl jumped out onto the snow together. Moving as one, they ran up the road, Pearl quickly outdistancing Dawn. But the dog looked back as if to make sure Dawn was following.

"Jake?" Dawn called. "Jake, where are you?"

She heard him calling her name.

Pearl disappeared into the whiteness.

Dawn ran on.

She found them a minute later. About twenty feet off the road and to the left, away from the fence, under a large oak tree. Jake lay on the snow. Onyx sprawled beside him, whimpering in pain. Pearl and Jasper paced around them, whining and growling.

Blood speckled the white snow.

"Jake!" Dawn ran to him. He was on his back, the rifle in his right hand. But his left hand and arm . . .

His left arm was caught in the jaws of an animal trap. Onyx's left front leg was caught there, too.

"Oh, Jake!" She knelt in the snow beside him.

He opened his eyes, pain flashing over his face. "You heard the rifle shot," he said. "Good." He groaned, and his eyes shut again, and she could only see white. No pupil. He had apparently fainted.

"Jake, what can I do? How can I help?" She reached for him, almost touching his face, then drawing back, not sure what was the right thing to do. Her first-aid skills were almost nonexistent. "What happened to you?"

He didn't answer. She moved toward the trapped dog. He growled at her, baring his teeth, but Pearl barked once, reproaching her offspring. Onyx whined, cowered and let Dawn come near.

What she saw told her the story. Both man and dog were caught in the same trap. The animal's foreleg was thinner than Jake's arm, but although the man had taken most of the punishing force of the closing jaws, the dog was still unable to get loose. Obviously Jake had seen his dog about to be trapped and had intervened with his own arm.

Both were hurt and bleeding, and Jake had passed out.

She had to do something! If she left to go for help, they might die in the cold. She reached over and took the rifle from his hand. Maybe if she fired it again, someone else would hear and come investigate. She pointed the weapon skyward and pulled the trigger.

Nothing happened.

"The safety," Jake said weakly. "You have . . . to take the safety off."

He was conscious again! She put down the rifle and kneeled beside him. "If I do manage to shoot, will anyone hear?" she asked breathlessly.

"Probably not . . . They'll just figure . . . hunter out . . . ahead of the season . . . trying to make most of early snow. The effort his words took visible on his contorted features, Jake paused for a moment. "I just fired in hopes you'd come."

"Okay. What can I do?"

"Ahhh." He eased himself up on his right elbow. Sweat beaded his face. "Look . . . in my pack. There's a knife."

She felt nauseated. "I can't cut you!"

"No. No cutting. Use it to pry the jaws open enough . . . so Onyx can get loose."

"What about you?"

"I'll survive. Get him loose . . . then go for help."

She rummaged in the pack. "I won't leave you here alone." She located the knife. It was long-bladed with a thick, black handle. "I'll get you free, too."

"No. Just Onyx. Then go for help."

"No way." She looked at him.

He'd passed out again.

Okay. It was all up to her, and she was not going to leave him. She worked the blade down to the place where the trap jaws came together and exerted pressure.

Nothing happened. Onyx whined and licked her hand.

"Be patient, boy," she whispered. "One way or another, I'll get this." She leaned on the knife handle, using her body weight to add pressure.

The dog yelped.

She looked at Jake. He hadn't stirred. She looked back at the trap. Even if she did manage to widen the jaws far enough for Onyx to pull out his paw, it would likely cause the poor animal a great deal of pain and scrape him up more than he already was. And if the trap snapped shut again, once the dog was free, Jake's forearm might be crushed.

There had to be a better way.

She went back to the pack and hunted around inside. Extra clothing, gloves, some food, matches. Nothing that would pry apart steel teeth and keep them apart.

But...

If she got the jaws to open a little and jammed the gloves and sweater inside, would that protect Jake's arm and keep Onyx from tearing his leg?

It was sure worth a try!

She carried the items over to the trap, stumbling in the deep snow as she went. Kneeling down once more, she set the knife in place. Using all her strength, she pressed, prying the trap apart. With her knee, she pushed the sweater into the gap. Rocking back on her heels, she grabbed a glove and added it to the padding. Repeating this process, she finally got the jaws open far enough for Onyx to pull himself free, which he did with a yelp and a howl.

That brought Jake back to consciousness again. "Wha... what're you doing?" he asked. He tried to sit up, then fell back. His face was as white as the snow he lay on.

"I'm trying to get you loose," she replied, levering the knife blade again and jamming the other glove into the gap. "So hold still."

"Don't try." His voice was weak. "Go for help."

She continued to work.

Minutes later, he was free. As gently as she could, Dawn eased his arm out and immediately wrapped it with her scarf. Jake turned from white to gray and breathed hard while she worked. When she was done, he said wanly, "I think you saved my life. Thanks."

"We aren't home-free yet." She released his skis from his boots and stood up, brushing off snow. "Stay still," she told him. "I want to check Onyx before we move."

Jake shut his eyes, but he remained conscious. He said nothing else, just cradled his hurt arm to his body.

She went over to the dog. He was quiet, probably on the edge of shock. He started to growl at her again, but shut up when Pearl nudged him. Jasper also came close, adding canine support to his brother. Warily, Dawn lifted the injured animal's foreleg. The wound was bleeding, but it seemed no bones were broken, since Onyx could put some weight on it. He might limp along, but he could walk.

"I'm going to get the two of you to my car," she said, standing up and returning to Jake. "You'll be out of the cold there while I go for help."

"There's a quicker way." He managed to get to a sitting position, and his color looked better. "A road to the fort. Take it instead of going back through the woods. It'll be easier and faster. You can ski it by yourself with no problem."

"A road? Where?"

"About a quarter of a mile farther on. The snow'll be deep, but the trees won't get in your way." He grimaced with pain, but made it to a kneeling position. She steadied him as he got to his feet. "You go on," he said. "Use my equipment. Ski to the fort. I'll get Onyx to the car. We'll shelter there until you send someone for us."

"I'm not leaving you out here." She hoisted the pack onto her back, settled the rifle under her arm and moved close to him. "Put your weight on me. We're going to my car together."

Jake considered arguing, but he knew he didn't have the strength. The situation was far out of his control now. His arm felt broken, and he was weak and close to passing out again from shock. He needed her help.

So they walked. Slowly, painfully through the snow along the path she had made to find him, back to her car. The dogs followed, the older ones flanking and protecting the younger one. Dawn helped Jake into the front passenger seat and somehow got all the dogs into the back.

Then she walked around the vehicle, sweeping the rest of the snow away with her arms.

Jake sat inside, watching her, wondering what she was up to. He was too weak to yell at her to get going. The sooner she left, the sooner he'd get help.

But she didn't leave. Once she had finished completely uncovering the car, she got in and turned the key in the ignition. "Okay," she said, gunning the engine. "Just exactly where is this road?"

"You can't drive. Snow's way too deep."

"This is a Saab," she said. "With all of us on board, we have plenty of ballast. That'll keep us from high-centering. We'll make it." She slammed the gears, and the car chugged forward, gaining speed slowly. They broke loose from the snow and ice and moved up the road.

Jake wasn't aware of much during the trip. He knew when they reached the back gate because she muttered something about fences, gates and false senses of security. She got out to open it with his keys, then returned to drive through. She didn't close and lock the gate behind them, but kept going through the snow.

That was all right with him. He knew he needed medical attention and needed it fast. Even with the powerful heater blasting away inside the car, he was shivering uncontrollably. Shock had him in its grip. He closed his eyes and fought to stay conscious.

Dawn felt sweat tickling her skin as she forced the Saab through the heavy snow. Several times she was sure they would be stuck in a deep drift, but somehow she got past the worst of it, and after what seemed like hours of struggle, the palisades of the fort appeared out of the mist in front of them. She pressed the horn, hoping to attract attention as quickly as possible.

It worked. The front gate swung open and people came running out. She turned to Jake.

He was watching her. "You did well," he said, his voice so weak she could hardly hear him. "Very well!"

His praise filled her with an unexpected sense of accomplishment. Her eyes teared. Then the others were there, and she got out to tell them what had happened.

AN HOUR LATER she sat in front of the big hearth in the main living room, sipping coffee that was liberally laced with whiskey. A fire blazed, but she still shivered occasionally. Sophie sat next to her, drinking hot chocolate. Seeing her father injured and so weak he couldn't walk by himself had terrified the child, and it was clear she was going to cling to Dawn for support until Jake was back to normal.

Whenever that would be. Dawn swallowed the booze and coffee. Sophie imitated her, chugging the chocolate, spilling a little on her turtleneck shirt.

"He's going to be fine," Dawn reassured the girl. "We'll even get to talk to him in a little while."

"Sure."

"And Onyx is okay, too."

No response.

Dawn decided to keep quiet for a while. Sophie needed her near, but she didn't seem to want to talk. Dawn didn't blame her. The girl was bright enough to imagine what might have happened. Thank goodness the Well had a doctor and a veterinarian on staff. She didn't want to think what they would have done if Ginny Reynolds and Johnny Wilson hadn't been right there to start treating Jake and Onyx. As succinctly as she could, Dawn had explained the situation to the two physicians, and they had gone right to work. Johnny reported that Onyx had sustained only a deep cut and some tissue injury. But Ginny told them that Jake's arm was badly broken, and he was suffering from shock.

If he'd gone out alone, he might still be in that trap.

He might have died before anyone found him.

She almost gagged at the thought.

Joan Dawson came into the room and took a seat on the stone hearth, facing Dawn. She held a glass half-full of a brownish liquid that looked like unadulterated whiskey. "Jake was lucky you went along," she said, almost echoing Dawn's own thoughts. "He was in bad shape." She glanced at Sophie. "I've seen severe shock like that in gunshot victims."

Dawn willed the woman to shut up. "He'll be fine," she said pointedly.

Joan didn't get it. She took a drink. "Dog'll be fine," she said. "Jake may not be."

"You're not a doctor," Dawn replied, angry now.

Joan shrugged. "I overheard Ginny talking about nerve damage. I have to figure from what she said that Jake's got some problems ahead."

"My dad's going to be okay!" Sophie yelled. She stood up, spilling the chocolate, and ran from the room, heading down the hall toward Jake's office. Alarmed, Dawn rose too. A minute later, they heard the door slam.

"Good work," Dawn said, glaring at Joan. "You didn't have to say all that in front of her."

Joan glared back. "Maybe not. But maybe the kid deserves the truth." She took another long drink. "Somebody 'round here needs to be speaking it."

"What do you mean by that?"

"Nothing. Anyway, you can take her over to see him if you want. I talked to him myself just a bit ago."

"You did? Why didn't you say so right away? Joan, what's the matter with you? You're drinking when Jake needs you to be alert. If he can't function, he's going to need all his staff to take on extra work."

"Uh-uh. He's got himself a new CEO. Guess that's whatsa matter with me. See, he told me I hafta take orders from this newcomer."

"What? Who?"

"You, Missy Sutton. He wants you to run the place until he's back on his feet. Can you believe that?"

"He what? Me?"

"Yeah. Don't that beat all?" Joan downed the rest of her drink. "Hey, boss. What're your orders?"

Dawn shook her head. "No orders. He's got to be out of his head. He'll change his mind when he's recovered a little."

"I don't think so."

"Why not?"

"'Cause he's nuts about you, case you haven't figured that out."

She really was drunk, Dawn decided, sitting back down on the sofa. "That doesn't matter. The way Jake may feel about me has nothing to do with my skills in business. Joan, I know nothing about this place. I'm not any kind of administrator. I won't take the job."

Joan didn't reply.

"Hey, Dawn!" Laurie entered from the dining room area. "I understand you're taking over temporarily." She smiled and sat by Joan. "Jake's going to be all right, but Doc says he needs to rest and he's put you in charge until he's better."

"I just don't believe this . . . He can't mean it."

"He does." Laurie looked at Joan. "And you ought to go over and see him," she said to Dawn. "Joan, what's up?" she asked.

"Nothin'."

"You're hitting the sauce again. You know you shouldn't. It'll kill you if you keep it up. You've said that yourself, and I've heard you. So something's bothering you."

"I think it's me," Dawn said. "Joan doesn't seem exactly thrilled with the prospect of having me in charge."

"Well, I think it's a great idea," Laurie declared. "I think you're just the person we need right now."

"I don't." Dawn stood again. "Jake's made a mistake, and I'm going to tell him so. Joan, don't slug down any more booze. We need our security person sharp and ready to deal with any problem. Laurie, get some coffee into her, please. And Sophie ran off to her father's office. If you'd check on her after you deal with Joan, I'd appreciate it. I want to talk to Jake alone. Excuse me."

Both women stared after her as she left.

CHAPTER TEN

THE INFIRMARY was down toward the laboratory/
production section of the enclave. Dawn huddled inside her coat and looked at the path as she walked.
Although it was getting late in the afternoon, the weak
sunlight still struggled to shine through the overcast
sky. The atmosphere was heavy and everything felt
surreal.

The infirmary was like all hospitals. When she
walked inside and shut the door behind her, the moist
warmth and antiseptic smell made her eyes water and
her throat sting. Shuddering, she took off her coat.
Faye Reynolds came out of the reception office to
greet her.

"Hi, Faye," Dawn said to the young nurse, tossing
her coat on a chair. "Is he able to have visitors?"

"Sure." Faye smiled. "He was badly hurt, but he's
tough. He'll be out of here tomorrow."

"Really?" Was Joan being overly concerned? Was
her pessimism a reflection of her own problems, not
Jake's? "That's good news."

Faye's expression clouded. "Of course, once the
weather makes it possible, he's going to need to see a
specialist."

"Oh? So there was more damage than just a broken arm?"

"You'll have to ask Ginny about that."

Dawn hesitated. "You know, none of this is really any of my business. I'm not a relative, and I don't work here."

"That's not what I hear."

"Faye, Jake can't mean it. I'm not equipped to run this place!"

The nurse shrugged. "All I know is that when Jake Barr makes a decision, it usually turns out to be the right one. I trust his judgment. Why else would I stay out here in the middle of the woods when I could be running a nursing unit of my own back in the city?"

"I'm clueless," Dawn replied.

Faye smiled. "You've been recruited, honey. Happened to me and Ginny the same way. This place, that man and his dreams, they get to you."

"I think I'd better talk to Ginny. Where is she?"

"In her office. Come on, I'll show you the way." She started walking down the hall.

Feeling very much out of depth, Dawn followed. Faye left her at the door. When she entered the office, Ginny told her to take a seat. "I'm glad you came over," the doctor said. "I was going to send for you."

"As I told Faye, not being a relative or close friend, I feel strange about this," Dawn confessed. "I've only known Jake a week. But I do want to ask how he is and what his prognosis is."

"You haven't seen him yet?"

"No."

The doctor removed her glasses. "He's already mending," she said. "He's relatively young and very strong. In good health, generally. But I want to get him over to the medical center in Francisville as soon as possible. I'm concerned about nerve damage. And he's been pushing himself pretty hard lately. Too much tension and responsibility. Not enough sleep or proper food. He may be his own worst enemy when it comes to full recovery.''

''I see.''

''I'm also aware Jake has put you in charge of the Well until he's able to return to his regular work schedule. I'd like to talk to you about that, if you don't mind.''

''Actually I plan to talk to Jake as soon as we're through,'' Dawn replied. ''I can't take on that kind of responsibility. He knows that. He must have been out of it when he—''

''He's in full possession of his mental faculties, if that's what you're implying,'' Ginny said, clearly amused by Dawn's discomfort. ''Sorry, but you can't wiggle out so easily. If anyone challenges your authority, I'm more than willing to back you up. I was there when he made the decision. Jake wants you to run things. He trusts you.''

''I can't do it. I just can't.''

''Or won't? Seems to me, if you don't mind my saying, that you've gotten a whole lot more than you bargained for when you came here.''

''You can say that again!'' Dawn stood up. ''I guess I'd better go face Jake. Get this mess straightened out, one way or another.''

''Good luck. I've been here long enough to know how he works, and I'll warn you that once he's made up his mind, it usually stays made.''

''Thanks for the warning. But I'm sure he'll listen to reason.''

''Famous last words! Good luck, as I said. You're going to need it!''

Jake was awake when she entered his room. Awake and watching the door as if he'd been waiting for her. When he saw her, he smiled, and the light in his eyes brightened to high voltage. "There you are," he said, struggling to a sitting position. "I was about to send out a search party."

"They wouldn't have had any trouble finding me," she said. "Once I was sure it was okay to visit, I headed here to see you."

"Here I am, and here I'll be," he answered. "At least until Doc Ginny lets me go home. Are you okay? That was an ordeal for you, too."

"Oh, I'm fine, Jake. The question is how are you?"

He didn't look sick at all. He looked good. In fact, if she ignored the cast and sling that bound up his left arm, the sight of his naked upper body was having quite an effect on her. He was muscular without being overbuilt and had zero body fat that she could see. His skin was smooth with a sprinkling of coppery hair across his chest.

But he stopped smiling at her question. "I've been better," he admitted. "It was really dumb of me to stick my arm down that trap, but when I saw Onyx step into it, I didn't think. I just acted."

"It was very brave of you to save Onyx." She paused momentarily, gazing at him. "Now, we have to talk, Jake," she said at last.

"Talk?"

"About the crazy rumor I'm hearing that you've appointed me CEO until you get better."

"It's no rumor. I've done it, and I'm counting on you."

"Jake, I cannot take over the Well. I don't know a thing about running a place like this."

"Maybe not exactly this kind of operation. But you're smart, you've successfully handled a small business and you're an outsider. We've already discussed that aspect. You know why I need you. Besides, if I appoint one of the regular residents, there's bound to be some jealousy, and I can't have what little harmony is left destroyed. I know I should have asked you first, but you weren't here when Joan demanded to know who would be running things. I had to make a decision on the spot."

"I'm afraid you'll regret it."

"I don't think so."

She was speechless for a moment. Then, "Jake, I've honestly never met anyone like you before. Do you always get what you want from people?"

"No," he replied.

And in his eyes, she saw pain. To her utter amazement, she felt something inside herself twist and change. A flash of heat enveloped her as she realized what was happening.

She was falling in love with this man.

"But will you do this for me?" he asked. "And keep Sophie under your wing, as well. I can't trust anyone else with her right now, and she is so precious to me."

Dawn stared, unable to answer, so powerful was the strength of the emotions she was feeling. She *yearned* to help him.

"Dawn, I need you. I'll be indebted to you for the rest of my life if you'll do this for me."

She *had* to. Not because of his promise, but because of her feelings. "All right, Jake. Of course I'll look after Sophie while you're here. The Well is another matter. As long as I'm stuck here, I'll give it my best shot,'' she said brusquely, with no intention of letting on how she really felt. ''But don't blame me if it all falls apart.''

''I'm not worried,'' he said, closing his eyes.

''You should be,'' she replied, not as harshly as she had intended.

He said nothing. It took her a minute to realize he'd fallen asleep. He'd used up his energy, extracting her promise. Dawn sighed, leaned over, kissed his lips and left the room.

SHE FOUND SOPHIE back at the Barr cabin. The child was sitting on her bed in her room, nose in a book. She didn't look up when Dawn knocked on the door frame and came in. ''Your dad's doing all right,'' Dawn said. ''After supper you can visit him.''

''Okay.'' Flat, unemotional.

''I'm sure he'd like to see you.''

''Sure. Okay.''

Dawn went over and sat on the bed. ''Sophie, would you like me to move here? I mean just while your father's in the infirmary. So you'll have company?''

Sophie put down the book. Tears filled her eyes. ''Is Daddy going to die?''

''No, of course not! Why did you . . . ?''

Sophie started to cry. Dawn put her arms around the girl and held her while she sobbed. Dawn's anger at Joan's tactlessness resurrected and grew.

After a little while, Sophie settled down and seemed embarrassed about her outburst. Dawn explained what Dr. Reynolds had said, and the child seemed satisfied that her father was not in any immediate danger. She said she wanted to go see him, but not until morning.

"I don't want him to see me with my eyes all red like this," she said.

"He wouldn't mind," Dawn assured her. "I know he'd be touched that you cared enough to cry over him. But he is sleeping, so it might be better to wait."

"Don't tell him I cried, okay?"

Dawn agreed, but she wondered why Sophie was unwilling to let her father know how she felt. "Would you like me to move here?" she asked, repeating the question. "It would be for a day or so at the most."

Sophie rubbed her eyes and smiled. "I wanted you to move here before, remember?"

Dawn hugged her. "Sure I do. But I wanted your permission, so I asked."

Sophie hugged her back. Dawn could feel tight tension in the little body, tension that gradually eased as the child relaxed in Dawn's embrace.

"I feel lots better," Sophie announced, finally letting go of Dawn.

"I'm glad to hear that," Dawn said. "Why don't you take a little nap while I go get my stuff. Your dad asked me to do some work for him, too, so I need to stop in at his office. I'll be back around dark, and I'll bring us some dinner."

"Okay." Sophie lay back, clearly almost asleep already.

Dawn bent over and kissed her forehead.

"Dawn?"

"What?"

"You're going to stay here, aren't you?"

"For a while, honey."

"Good. Then maybe the bad things won't happen." Sophie shut her eyes.

"What bad...?" Dawn didn't finish. Sophie was asleep.

Like father, like daughter.

She shut the bedroom door. The two uninjured dogs were lying on the floor in the living room. They watched her walk toward the front door. Tails did not wag. "I'm coming back," she promised them. "I'll put a fire in the hearth then, and I'll fix your dinner, too. I promise."

Nothing.

"Onyx is going to be fine! I swear it!"

Pearl's tail hit the floor once at the word, "Onyx." Jasper just watched her as if he didn't believe a word she said. Thinking that she had been blessed with not only a new job, but also a fascinating and lovable child and several unhappy pets, Dawn put on her heavy coat and headed back to the main building that housed Jake's office.

An hour later, seated at his desk, she sighed in despair. She knew how a business should be run, but she'd never tried to handle one like this where the people mattered more than the profit.

She got up and went over to the window to watch the day end. Sunset tried to blaze a path through the clouds, but succeeded only in tinting the whiteness an opaline pink. The view was beautiful. Snow covered everything, everywhere.

She turned and studied the room. It was a work station, plain and utilitarian. The furniture consisted of a large desk, scarred and stained from years of hard use, a truly ugly but incredibly comfortable desk chair and two wooden client chairs for visitors. The floor was plain wood. A map of the area covered one wall.

No other art or photographs. Two walls were covered floor to ceiling with filled bookcases.

And on the desk was the most advanced computer she had ever had the pleasure to use. Looking at it, she realized just how much she'd changed in the week she'd been at the Well.

The old Dawn Sutton would have had little compunction about breaking into Jake's computer, taking whatever information she needed for her article and leaving—as soon as the snow allowed—with the business story of the decade.

But the Dawn who'd seen what Jake Barr had achieved, who'd kissed the man and probably saved his life could never betray him. Not if her life depended on it. And her career probably did. She moved back to the desk and turned off the computer.

A knock on the door punctuated her action. Laurie looked in. "Sorry to bother you, but you have a meeting in five minutes," she said.

"I do? What kind of meeting and with whom?"

"Come and see."

Dawn picked up a pen and notebook from the desk. She wanted to keep a careful personal record of everything she did. "Did you take care of Joan?" she asked.

"Yes. I filled her up with strong coffee, then made her go outside and shovel a few hundred feet of walkway. She's stone-cold sober now. A little hung over, but repentant."

"Will she stay that way?"

Laurie shrugged. "She came here because of the drinking problem. She's been dry for months, but who knows. Jake almost had to ask her to leave in May when she tied one on and got unpleasant with an-

other member of the staff, but since then, she's behaved herself.''

"Until now."

"She'll be fine. Give her some slack."

"I will. But I need to be able to depend on her, and
I don't think I can do that if she's going to indulge.
Any idea what sent her over the edge?''

"None. You'll have to ask her."

"I will. Now lead me to my meeting."

Laurie smiled. "Right this way."

The meeting was in the dining room at a long table
set up for that purpose. Although she had met almost
everyone at the Well already, Dawn was reintroduced
to the people in charge of the various departments and
activities. Then she was asked to make some deci-
sions. Before the meeting was over, she'd assigned
more work teams to clear snow on the fort grounds,
authorized disbursement of some emergency supplies
and agreed to spend some of Jake's money on e-mail
communication through the company computers so
that residents could contact relatives and friends
whose phones still weren't working and let them know
things were all right at the Well.

All in all, it was an interesting experience and she
got to know her crew in a hurry. Jake had been right
to worry about chaos ensuing without leadership.
Pressure from the semi-emergency weather situation,
along with fears about further sabotage and concerns
about Jake's condition had contributed to the collective tension, and the infighting was surprisingly fierce.
At one point, the two men heading competitive sec-
tions in research verbally sparred with each other for
a few minutes before she broke in.

"Excuse me," she said loudly, interrupting what was quickly becoming an unpleasant exchange of insults. "Dr. Boyd and Dr. Corman, will you please sit down."

After a startled pause to stare at her, they did.

"Thank you." Finding their project folders, Dawn picked them up from among the many that Laurie had given her before the meeting began and looked at the figures on the reports. "I can see value in both of your arguments," she said finally. "But for the short term, neither one of you needs more funding. So unless you can present me with facts that will change my mind, I'm afraid I'm going to have to hold back any more monies for your projects."

"You can't do that!" Boyd sprang to his feet, his face red with anger.

"It's outrageous," Corman agreed hotly. "We need more money. That's all there is to it!"

"Well, no it isn't." Dawn paused. Joan Dawson entered the dining room and took a seat at the table. The security officer looked pale and sheepish. Dawn acknowledged her with a nod and a friendly look, hoping to indicate that the woman's lapse was forgiven if not forgotten. Joan nodded back, her brown eyes opaque and unreadable.

Dawn went on. "Look, I understand how unsettling all this is for you," she said gently. "I'm only here to try to help. If you'd like to prepare a fresh report, we can discuss funding again."

Silence.

Then, "What kind of facts?" Boyd asked. The color had faded from his face. He looked less angry and more thoughtful.

"Productivity and profit," Dawn said. "As long as I'm in charge," she added, speaking to everyone, "I'd appreciate your all thinking in those terms. Remember, I'm with you. I want us to work together to get through this crisis, for the Well's sake . . . for Jake's sake."

More silence. Then some nods. A smile. Dawn relaxed.

The meeting was soon adjourned to make way for dinner preparations. Dawn went into the living room to wait for the meal the cook was readying for her to carry back to Jake's cabin. Others joined her. Some availed themselves of drinks. Most did not.

Joan was among the abstainers.

"I guess I owe you a big apology," the security officer said, taking a place next to Dawn on the long couch in front of the fireplace. "I was way out of line. It's no secret I had a drinking problem before I came here, and the pressure of the last few days just got the best of me, I guess."

"It's history now. Almost forgotten," Dawn reassured her.

"No," Joan declared. "It's not. Been a long time since I've fallen off the wagon like that. Thank God for Laurie. She kept me from turning it into a real drunk."

Dawn shifted position on the couch. "That's what friends are for," she said softly. "To help when you need it the most."

"That's what the Well is for," Joan said. "I came here hoping to sort out my problems under nonstressful conditions. But life follows, doesn't it?"

"Sure does."

"Anyway... What I want to say is, you've got my support and skills, such as they are, at your disposal. I had no business acting like I did and saying what I said. You can count on me." She held out her hand.

Dawn smiled and shook it. "That's good to hear. Hopefully, nothing more will happen that needs your attention, but I'm really glad you said all this to me."

Joan smiled back. "My behavior was wrong. I figure I owe you," she said. "Speaking of that, we need to talk."

"Go ahead."

"It isn't about me. This is Well business, but it involves another member." Joan looked around the room. A dozen or more people were standing and sitting in groups, talking. "Later, when it's private. You going to be in the office tonight?"

"I might. I'm going to take dinner to Sophie. She's pretty upset about her dad."

Joan scowled. "I really blew that! I'm really sorry. I need to apologize to the kid."

"She'd like that, I think. But wait until tomorrow, why don't you. We're sort of pretending everything's okay right now."

"But it's not."

"No," Dawn agreed. "It's not. I'll try to be back here by nine. Ten at the latest. I want to make sure she's settled and calm before I leave her tonight. Can you wait until then to see me?"

"Yes." Joan grinned wryly. "I'm hungover, but I can deal with that." She got up and left the room.

Dawn was puzzled about the woman's behavior and worried about what she wanted to discuss. But she felt much better for having the talk. She was going to need Joan's cooperation, if not her help. She was almost ready to check on supper when Johnny came through the front doors and over to her. He stamped his feet and rubbed his hands together, then eased close to the fireplace to warm himself.

"Sorry I didn't make the board meeting," he said. "I've been busy getting Onyx patched up, and one of the local farmers brought in another dog who needed some medical attention."

"No problem," Dawn said. "I'd rather you be doing your good work with animals than sitting around listening to other people argue."

"Like that, was it?" Johnny winked good-naturedly. "Better get used to it. Actually, I did hear you rattled some cages."

"I spoke my mind. A few people listened. That's all I expect right now."

"Good for you."

"So how's Onyx doing?"

"That's what I need to talk to you about." Johnny sat down beside her, his manner now serious. "Onyx is a young dog, full of life and energy. Like his owner, he's already on the road to recovery. But he's going to need special attention and supervision. He needs to be with someone he trusts."

"But Jake's still in the infirmary. He might get out tomorrow, but Ginny's not sure about that."

"I know. That's why it's up to you."

"All right. But I don't know much about dogs."

"I made up a sheet of instructions." Johnny reached into a pocket and took out some folded paper. "Here you go."

Dawn took the paper. "You're sure he won't be better off in the animal hospital?"

"He needs to be home. He's scared and hurt and pining for his mama and brother. He'll do better in his own environment, and I'm just a loud holler away if you need help."

"Well, I'm staying at the cabin with Sophie until Jake's back, so I suppose the two of us can manage. I have a meeting with Joan later this evening, but I'll come by and pick him up after that."

"Good." Johnny stood up. "I'll have him ready. Read the instructions. I'll see you later." He smiled at her and wandered off to talk to some other people.

Beverly Clarke, the head cook, came out carrying two take-away meals. Dawn took them, put on her coat on and trudged back to Jake's cabin, thinking about the load of responsibility suddenly thrust on her. She'd come to the Well on a simple quest for a story. Now, she was head of a complex and confusing business empire.

Jake, please get better quickly!

CHAPTER ELEVEN

DAWN SPENT the next hour with Sophie, eating dinner and talking. Sophie seemed calm, although she would lapse into silence now and then, requiring Dawn to chatter to fill the spaces. Nevertheless, it was a comfortable time, and Dawn garnered more information about the girl's relationship with her mother than she had in past conversations.

It began when Dawn asked if Sophie wanted to come along and wait while she talked to Joan, then pick up Onyx, rather than stay in the cabin alone.

"I don't mind staying here," Sophie said. "I'm alone a lot. Besides, my mom's gonna e-mail me tonight, so I have to wait at my computer."

"E-mail you? Why doesn't she call? The phones are working again."

"Don't know. I guess it's easier. Anyway, she says it's safer than a telephone. Nobody but me can read it."

"I've heard there are ways to get into private e-mail," Dawn said. "But I don't imagine anyone would bother trying to read your mother's letters to you."

"Maybe not." Sophie dug a fork into the stew on her plate. "Dad might."

"Your father wouldn't violate your privacy," Dawn declared. "If he wanted to know something, he'd ask you."

"He wants to know where Mom is," Sophie said.

"Why don't you tell him?"

"She told me not to. And besides, if he did know, he'd just try to dump me back on her and I don't want to go."

Dawn sat back, considering what she had just heard. "You mean, you think your father wants to get rid of you? But you don't want to leave here?"

"He's too busy to mess with me. So's Mom. She dumped me on him. But I'd rather stay here than go back to..." Her voice trailed off.

Dawn touched Sophie's shoulder. "If you don't want to talk to me, don't. But if you want to tell me anything secret, I promise you I won't blab. Not unless you give me permission."

Sophie regarded her thoughtfully. "Do you have secrets?" she asked.

"Everyone does."

Sophie returned her attention to her food. "I don't know where Mom is right now. She and Tony were going to Hong Kong so he could try to sell some stuff, but..."

"Tony?" Dawn knew who Tony was. Jake had told her. But she hoped Sophie would elaborate.

"Mom's boyfriend."

"Oh."

"Dad doesn't know about him. Please don't tell."

"I won't. It's not my business, anyway. What kind of stuff does Tony sell?"

"Stuff like Dad makes. He and Mom are trying to go into business. Like Dad."

Faint alarm bells went off in Dawn's mind. This was something that needed investigating.

But not in a way that exploited Sophie.

"Why do you want to stay here?" Dawn asked. "With your mother, at least you wouldn't have to live in the wilderness."

"I like it here. I like being able to stay by myself. Dad trusts me. He lets me do things by myself. Mom doesn't."

"What about school?"

"You're my teacher now."

"Sophie, listen to me. Even though I like teaching you, once the snow melts, it's back up the mountain again for you. I'm not qualified."

Sophie didn't rebel as Dawn had feared. "I don't really mind. The kids at Fairway are regular kids. The place my mom sends me is full of jerks and dweebs."

"The teachers or the kids?"

"Both." Sophie ate more stew and chomped off a bite of bread. When she finished chewing, she said, "It's a special school for weird kids."

And you prefer being with regular ones. This was, Dawn decided, something she'd discuss with Jake in the near future.

"I have to go," she said, looking at the time. "If you'll clean up, I'd appreciate it. I have to meet Joan in your dad's office in a little while."

"Joan's a creep," Sophie declared.

"How so?"

Sophie pushed her plate away. "I just don't like her. Don't tell her what I said, okay?"

"I made you a promise. I won't talk about our conversation with anyone else. Finish eating, honey. I'll be back with Onyx soon."

"I'm not hungry anymore. Can I give the leftovers to Pearl?"

"Sure." Dawn ruffled Sophie's hair gently. "Make sure Jasper gets some, too, or he'll be jealous."

"Tony's jealous of Dad."

Dawn paused, not moving, thinking rapidly. "Why?" she asked.

"He says my dad's the best chemist, but he won't do what he could."

"Such as?"

"I don't know. I just heard them talking once."

"What about your mother?"

"Tony says she's not as good as Dad. Nobody is."

Dawn smiled. "I expect you're right about that. What does Tony do?"

"Boss me around. He thinks he's a big shot. He's not. I hate him."

Dawn decided to leave the topic alone for a while. Sophie was probably reacting to the man she felt was trying to take her father's place. It was a problem many stepparents had to face.

"I'll be back soon," she said. Then, "Have you talked to your mother since I got here?"

"Once."

"So she knows about me?"

"Yeah. She said she knew you were coming."

Bingo! The only person who knew Dawn was coming to the Well was the mystery caller!

"Well, tell her hello for me, will you? And if she wouldn't mind, I'd like to talk to her sometime."

"You mean write her on the computer?"

"No. I'd like to talk to her on the phone."

And compare her voice to the one that called me!

JOAN WAS WAITING when Dawn got to Jake's office. She was sitting on one of the client chairs, but got up when Dawn entered the room. "Hope you don't mind," she said. "I came on in rather than wait down in my office." She smiled ruefully. "My head's hurting, and I didn't feel like trying to work."

"You need some sleep," Dawn said. "You'll feel better in the morning." She took a seat behind Jake's desk. On the computer monitor, a screen-saver program danced silently.

"I know." Joan scooted her chair close to the desk. "I wouldn't have asked to meet with you tonight, except that I think it's important you know about Laurie."

"What about her?"

"She's been getting notes and presents from someone who calls himself her secret admirer."

"So? That's not a problem. It sounds romantic."

"Maybe. But not if you're Laurie. Did she talk to you at all about her past?"

"The ex-husband? Yes."

"In her case, any attention is scary. The ex is in prison and has no idea where she is, but she's so sensitive that even though she knows the stuff can't be coming from him, she's reacting as if it is."

"She doesn't seem upset."

"That's a cover. She's a mess. And the guy who's responsible has no idea."

"You know who it is?"

"Farley Wold."

Dawn swallowed her surprise. "They seemed like friends to me. Why wouldn't he just tell her directly if he feels more than that?"

"My opinion is that he's too shy to deal with her openly."

"Well, he needs to—"

"Don't say anything to either of them, please," Joan cautioned. "I'm only telling you because you're in charge now. I think you need to be aware of what's going on."

"Thanks. I appreciate it. But..."

"There's another possibility that I hesitate to bring up," the security officer said, sitting back and tapping her blunt fingers on the arm of the chair.

"What's that?"

"This may sound crazy and maybe it is, but take it for what it's worth. Suppose Farley and Laurie are behind the things that have been going wrong here?"

"Not possible! They were with me when the bomb exploded. Besides, if they were working together, what sense would that secret-admirer stuff make? They'd have no secrets from each other."

"Not necessarily. I told you this was far out. Just supposing that they are conspirators and Laurie told me that story about the notes and gifts to throw me off track."

Dawn sat up straighter. "What motive could they have to sabotage the Well?"

"I don't know."

"Anything else?"

"No. I hate to dump this on you, but I thought you ought to be briefed."

"Jake knows?"

"Not yet. I was going to tell him, but..."

"I will. I'll see what he says when—"

"I wouldn't burden him with this right now," Joan interrupted, her brown eyes showing inner pain. "I realize I was overstating things this afternoon, but Doc did say he was stressed-out. From what I understand, he needs to be as tranquil as possible."

"But he'd want to know about people as important to him as Laurie and Farley. He'd certainly want to know if it's possible they are behind the trouble."

"Think so?"

"Well, I . . ." Dawn hesitated.

"See. You shouldn't tell him. Let him rest. You and I can work together on this. He put you in charge. Act like it."

The challenging tone angered Dawn, but she accepted the logic of what Joan was saying. "All right. This is between you and me," she said. She stood up. "Now you get some sleep and get yourself back in fighting trim."

Joan stood and made a little salute. "Aye, aye, boss," she said, smiling.

They shook hands, and Joan left.

Dawn sat at the desk for a while, thinking. Then she remembered her promise to pick up Onyx. It was almost ten. She got up, turned off the computer and headed out into the frigid night.

Before she went to the animal hospital, she stopped by the infirmary and checked on Jake. She had no intention of telling him what Joan had said; she simply needed to be near him for a few minutes. But Faye, who was still on duty, told her he was asleep and that Ginny had warned her not to let anyone disturb him.

"Until you showed up this afternoon, he wouldn't close his eyes," Faye said. "It was like he was waiting to talk to you before he'd allow himself to rest."

So much for being with Jake.

Disappointed, she trudged back outside to the small building located near the upper left part of the fort. Inside the animal hospital, Johnny waited with Onyx.

Seeing her, the dog whined and wagged his heavy tail furiously.

"He's been anxious," the vet said. "Jittery and restless. I told him you were coming to take him home." He petted the big animal's head.

"How'll I do that?" Dawn asked, eyeing the large bandage on the dog's foreleg. "Won't his dressings get wet?"

"He's going to travel by dogmobile." Johnny said, pointing out a large kennel set on a red wagon. "I figured you wouldn't want to carry him."

"You're right about that," Dawn answered with a smile, realizing she was being teased. She patted Onyx. "Okay, fella," she said. "Let's get you home."

Onyx barked delightedly. He continued to bark as she hauled him down the path to Jake's cabin. When they got there, Sophie was already fast asleep. She didn't wake up even when the other dogs made a welcoming racket in honor of Onyx's return. Dawn noticed that the computer was on, and clicked it off, leaving Sophie to slumber on in the soft darkness.

That night, Dawn slept in Jake's bed.

AT SUNRISE the phone rang. She automatically fumbled for it and found it on the bedside table in approximately the same place as her own phone. Dazed and still half-asleep, she answered it, using her name just as she would have at home.

"What the hell are you doing in his bed?" the female voice asked angrily.

Dawn sat up. The line wasn't all that clear. "I'm sorry. What did you say?"

"Get out of his bed or the same thing that's going to happen to him will happen to you!"

"Who is this?"

The caller hung up.

Dawn swore softly and replaced the receiver. The phone rang again immediately, but when she lifted the receiver, it buzzed at her. The caller had hung up.

The three dogs, who had slept on their dog mats on the floor at the foot of the bed, stood and woofed, disturbed by the rings and by her swearing. Onyx limped over to the side of the bed and licked Dawn's hand. He whined.

"Let me guess. You all have to go out."

They barked. She got out of bed.

The phone started ringing again as she stumbled across the icy living room floor to let the animals out. By the time she got back and picked it up, it had gone dead. She held the receiver and asked herself who would be doing this.

It wasn't until she was sitting in the kitchen with a hot cup of fresh-brewed coffee giving her brain a good solid kick that she realized that of course she knew the voice. It was the same woman who had called her anonymously to suggest she investigate Jacob's Well. The same woman who had told her Jake was involved in insurance fraud.

Very likely, unfortunately, it was Sophie's mother. Jake's ex-wife. Joyce Barr.

JAKE WOKE UP feeling completely disoriented. His entire body hurt. As if he'd been run over by a truck. His mind was on red alert, however. He had the strong sensation that someone was watching him. He'd had that sense several times during the night. Once he'd awakened completely to find Faye changing his IV bottle. Later she'd come and unhooked it entirely, taking it away. Another time he was sure he'd seen another woman, but he'd fallen back asleep before he could identify her.

He opened one eyelid. He was still in the infirmary. He opened the other eyelid.

And focused on the female figure sitting on the chair near his bed. Another woman.

Dawn Sutton.

Suddenly he felt much better.

"Good morning, Sleeping Beauty," she said. "You slept in late."

Jake blinked, clearing his vision. In the pale sunlight she looked gorgeous. Her skin appeared creamy-soft with an appealing pink color on her cheeks. The short dark hair, the big blue eyes ... Why, she looked like a real-life version of Snow White.

The idea made him smile. "If I'm Sleeping Beauty," he said, "you must be the princess come to give me my life back by kissing me. How about it?"

She didn't smile in return, although he could have sworn he saw an answering light in her eyes. "Jake, how are you feeling?" she asked. "I hate to do this while you're still in here, but we need to talk. Business. I'll go tell Faye to bring you breakfast and after you wake up completely, I'll be back. I need your full attention."

"Not more sabotage!" He sat up, regretting it immediately as a wave of dizziness hit him.

"No. But I have some ideas on that score. Take it easy," she added, smiling. "The good guys are going to win. I'll be back."

And with that, she left the room.

Jake lay back down. The ceiling turned overhead, whirling at least three times before it settled and steadied. He felt sick as a dog.

"Faye!" he yelled.

Faye came in, carrying a breakfast tray. "You sound grouchy this morning," she said. "Thought seeing Dawn first thing when you woke up might make you a little more cheerful."

"I'm damn dizzy," he said. "And I don't have time for this. Get Ginny in here to give me something to fix it!"

"You're dizzy because you've had a bad shock to your system and you haven't eaten anything since yesterday morning," Faye replied, unruffled. She set down the tray. "Now, you eat, then you can fuss." She moved over to raise the head of the bed. "Never met a man yet who was able to be a decent patient," she muttered.

"Sorry." Jake managed to sit again and didn't suffer the dizziness. "I guess I'm in a bad mood because I can't do anything myself. I'm dependent on all of you."

Faye smiled. "Eat your breakfast. It'll make a world of difference."

He needed no more encouragement.

After a shave and a careful shower, he felt nearly normal, and when Ginny came in to check on him, he demanded to be let loose. "I'll go home and rest," he promised as the doctor silently went over his vital signs and listened to his words. "I asked Dawn to take over my work, and I'll let her do it without any interference. I promise. Just let me out of here."

"You can promise yourself blue in the face, Jake Barr," the doctor said finally. "But until I'm sure you're safe, you're staying right here where I can keep a close watch on you.''

"Safe? What's the matter?''

Ginny smiled reassuringly. "Nothing. Your blood pressure's a little elevated. You've complained several times of dizziness. Understandable under the circumstances, but I'd rather watch it for another few hours before—''

"Dawn wanted to talk to me,'' Jake interrupted. "If she's around, my blood pressure's going to rise, and you know it, and I don't see how it's going to hurt me.'' He tried a winning smile.

Ginny didn't bite. "She's not here right now, Jake. And your pressure's up.''

"I got extremely dizzy when I first sat up this morning,'' he admitted.

Ginny nodded. "Thanks. Faye already told me, but I appreciate your honesty. Together we can work on this and get you back in form as soon as possible.''

"Thanks, Doc,'' he said, giving her another grin. "I'll behave.'' He lay back down. "You've convinced me.''

"Don't go getting all cooperative all at once,'' she warned, "or I'll figure you have something planned.'' She put her stethoscope around her neck. "But I will call Dawn and tell her you can receive visitors now.''

"Tell her I'd like to see Sophie.''

"Sophie's waiting out in the front room.''

"Well tell her to come in!''

When Sophie entered the room, Jake could tell something was wrong. Carrying a little paper sack, she walked slowly over to the bed and looked at him. "Hi, Daddy,'' she said. "Does it hurt?''

"What?" Jake held up the cast. "My arm? No. Not a bit."

"When I saw you yesterday, when Dawn brought you in, you were acting funny."

"Honey, I was hurt. But Dr. Reynolds has made me all better now."

"Are you coming home?"

"As soon as she lets me. Do you miss me?"

"Dawn's staying in your room."

"She is?" Jake had figured Dawn would sleep in the other twin bed in Sophie's room. The idea of her being in his bed warmed his heart.

"Yeah. She says the dogs wanted her there, and she didn't want to wake me up when she got home with Onyx. Onyx is home."

"Ah." That explained it. "How's he doing?"

"Okay. He . . . misses you. A lot, I think."

Jake felt a surge of fatherly emotion. "Sophie, will you tell Onyx for me that I'll be back as soon as I can. And that he's to do what you tell him while I'm here?"

"Okay." She reached into the sack and handed him a folded piece of paper. "Here's a get-well card I made," she said.

Jake unfolded it. The little cartoon of him was hardly flattering, but he had to admit it was sort of accurate. "Do I look that much like a raccoon?" he asked.

"With your glasses on, sometimes." Sophie grinned.

"Well, thank you very much, honey." Jake reached out and pulled his daughter in for a hug. "I love you," he said.

"I love you, too, Daddy."

Jake blinked back tears. This was the first time she'd said that since she had arrived at the Well. He swallowed hard against the sweet emotion. "Got anything else for me in that sack?" he asked.

Sophie took out a muffin. "Dawn and I made these this morning. It's a little burned on the bottom, but it tastes all right."

Jake took the muffin. "I'll eat it right away," he promised. "So Dawn's learning to cook on a wood stove?"

"Yes. She swears she's going to burn the place down, but I'm not worried." Sophie giggled. "All we have to do is open the door and shovel snow over any fire."

"It's still cold out there?"

"Yes."

"Do you miss California?"

Sophie shrugged. "Not really."

"Have you heard from your mom?"

Another shrug.

Dawn knocked on the door frame. "Hi there. Am I interrupting?" she asked softly.

Jake felt his heart beat a little faster. "No, no," he said, sitting up straighter. "Come on in. Look at the great card Sophie made for me." He held out the paper. "And thanks for the muffin. It looks delicious."

Dawn made a wry smile. "Wait until you taste it." She took the folded paper and admired the drawing.

Jake picked up the muffin and took a big bite. "Mmm," he said. "Yum, yum."

Sophie giggled. "You're teasing us, Dad," she said.

"No, I'm not. It's good." He swallowed. "I could use a little water or something to wash it down, though. Would you run out and ask Faye for some juice for me, please."

"Sure." Sophie scampered from the room.

"I can't thank you enough for what you're doing with her," Jake said quietly. "She's opening up, showing her feelings more now than she has since she's been here."

"Jake, there's something I have to tell you." She paused for his approval. When he nodded, she continued, "I can't be sure about this...but I think Sophie's mother was the one who called me at the *Times.*"

Jake put down the muffin.

"I think she called your cabin this morning. When I picked up the phone, a woman spoke to me. It was the same voice, I'm sure of it."

"Damn!"

"Please, Jake, try not to get upset." Dawn paused once again, clearly concerned about Jake's agitation. "After she spoke to me in a less than pleasant manner, she called back twice. Just rang the phone until I answered, and then hung up."

"No idea where she called from?"

"None. And really I can't be absolutely positive it was the same voice as my anonymous caller's or even that it's your ex. I'm only going on a hunch."

"It sounds like a pretty solid one to me." Jake swung his legs over the edge of the bed.

"What do you think you're doing?"

"Getting up. I have to find out where Joyce is. Just to eliminate her as a suspect if nothing else."

"Get back in that bed. Suspect in what? All she did was make a nuisance call."

He put his hand on her arm. "Dawn, what if the person who called you and the one causing the problems around here are in league?"

"I've thought about that myself." She put her hand on his forehead. "Are you all right? You look funny all of a sudden."

"Just a little woozy. I'll be fine in a minute."

"Don't move so quickly. Your system's had a shock, remember."

He sat back. "The broken arm's the least of it."

"What can I do, Jake? I feel partly responsible."

"Why?"

"If I hadn't taken that call in the first place, if I hadn't listened to innuendo, if I hadn't been so ambitious for my own career..."

"If you hadn't responded, the caller would have found another reporter," he said. He touched her face. "And we'd never have met."

"That would have been awful." She leaned forward and kissed him gently.

Jake hooked his good arm around her neck and pulled her close. His kiss was not so gentle.

Dawn settled in toward him. His body felt solid, strong and warm. Through the thin material of the hospital gown, she felt his heartbeat against hers, felt his heat, felt his need for her. She pulled back a little. "This is—" She broke off. "Jake, you're really looking flushed. Are you sure you're okay?"

He smiled. "I'm excited. Is that okay?"

"Yes, but..." She put her hands on his chest. His heart was beating far faster than she thought was right, even for a man who was more than a bit excited. And he was starting to sweat freely, even though the room was cool.

"Actually," he said as his face started to turn a gray color, "it might be a good idea to get Ginny in here. I'm not feeling very good at all suddenly."

Dawn ran for the door.

CHAPTER TWELVE

THE WHOPPING SOUND of the Medi-Vac helicopter cut through the chilled, misty air above the fort. Snow swirled wildly as the chopper set down in the central area. From all the surrounding buildings, people came out to see what was going on. In the waiting room of the infirmary, Dawn sat with her arm around Sophie, attempting to console the crying child and trying not to give way to tears herself.

Jake was in serious trouble. From the moment Faye had returned to the room at Dawn's frantic summons, it had been clear that a medical crisis was occurring. Chasing Dawn and Sophie out, Faye had yelled for Ginny and the two had gone to work on Jake. Under their shouted orders, Dawn had called the state emergency team.

And now they were here to take Jake away.

"He's going to die," Sophie cried. "They're going to take him and he's never coming back!"

Fighting her own grief and not sure Sophie wasn't right, Dawn didn't correct her. She said simply, "I'm staying with you, honey. We'll be together until we find out." No false promises, no lies. Just the simple truth.

Sophie seemed a little calmer after that. She still cried softly, but her body wasn't shaking so violently and she wasn't gasping for breath between sobs.

The helicopter medical team rushed by and went into Jake's room. Moments later they emerged, an unconscious Jake on a gurney and Ginny running beside it as they rushed outdoors to the waiting chopper. An oxygen mask covered Jake's face and he looked whiter than the sheet pulled up to his chin. A heavy blue blanket was wrapped around his body. The gray in his brown hair stood out starkly, like snow. Faye followed the medical team, slowing when she passed Dawn and Sophie.

"What's happening?" Dawn shouted, grabbing the nurse's arm. "Just tell us. Is he going to be okay?"

"Let's hope so," Faye replied. "Looked like a heart attack at first, but Ginny's not sure now. I'll talk to you both in a minute," she added. Then she followed the crew out the front door and across the snow-covered ground to the helicopter. Many members of the Well stood near and watched, silent and solemn. No one wore a coat or boots, but no one seemed to notice the cold.

Dawn and Sophie also stood waiting and watching from just outside the infirmary. A short while later the big machine took off skyward. Only Faye remained on the ground. Dawn shielded her face from the flying snow and felt the hot tears run down her cheeks.

He was dying! Just when she'd realized she might be falling in love with the man, he was leaving forever! She held Sophie more securely, vowing that at the very least she would make sure Jake's child was well cared for. She had no rights, no rights at all, but she was going to do it!

After the snow churned up by the chopper settled, Faye came back. "Let's go inside," she said, her voice hoarse as if with unshed tears. "I'll tell you what I can."

"You'll tell us everything," Dawn said, rubbing the signs of grief from her eyes. "Sophie has a right to know what's going on. And we'll need to get in touch with her mother."

"No!" Sophie cried. "I want to stay here!"

"Come on," Faye said. "We'll talk about all that inside."

She led them to Ginny's office and made them sit. Sophie was now shivering, but the crying had stopped. Dawn felt cold as ice.

Faye sat down at Ginny's desk. "Jake's in bad condition," she said. "But he's not in immediate danger of dying."

Sophie let out a little gasp of relief and leaned against Dawn's shoulder. Dawn put her arm around the child's shoulders again.

"As I said, his symptoms made us think he'd suffered a massive heart attack, but Ginny has some questions about that diagnosis. He showed an elevated blood pressure this morning, but nothing that would indicate an attack was pending. She wants to get him stabilized and out of any danger, then run a battery of tests to see what went sour and why he exhibited symptoms so suddenly."

Dawn's attention perked up. "You mean it might not be his heart?"

"I mean we don't know. It sure looks like his heart went haywire, if you'll pardon an unscientific description. Exactly what did you observe, Dawn? Before you called for help?"

Dawn described his symptoms. "We were, um, getting kind of close," she said, phrasing the subject delicately because of Sophie. "You don't think that...?"

"Kissing you wouldn't have given Jake Barr heart failure," Faye said, a smile finally appearing on her face. "If anything, it ought to have settled him down if he was experiencing anxiety. It's just a good thing you were right there and noticed the changes. I'll write down your observations." She made some notes on a piece of paper. "Thanks. This might help."

"Anything else you can tell us now?" Dawn asked.

Faye shook her head. She looked at Sophie. "Listen to me, Sophie," she said, "your daddy's a strong man. You go home and pray for him. You have to stay strong and healthy so you can help him when he gets back."

"Can I go see him?" Sophie asked.

"As soon as it's okay, you can," Faye promised. She looked at Dawn. "Guess you've got more on your hands here than you bargained for, don't you?" she said.

"That's a fact," Dawn replied. She would've liked to speak to Faye alone to try to get more substantial information than the nurse was willing to dispense in front of Jake's daughter, but it was obvious Faye didn't intend to let that happen right now. Nor was Dawn really willing to be parted from Sophie. The child needed all the support and security she could get.

"Let's go back home," she said to Sophie. "I need to check on Onyx and then we'll go to the office. You can bring something to read, and when I get a chance, we'll do another economics lesson."

Sophie nodded, but didn't speak.

"You should get hold of her mother," Faye said. "If Jake's going to be unable to care for her..."

"Dawn will take care of me," Sophie declared. "I don't want my mother!"

The vehemence in the child's voice shocked both women. Faye started to speak, but Dawn held up a hand, warning her off. "You know how we talked about laws the last time we had a lesson?" she asked the girl. "How sometimes laws make businesses behave a certain way? How sometimes it's not the best economic thing, but it is the law?"

Sophie nodded wordlessly again.

"Well, this situation is like that. We have to let your mother know that your father is sick. That I'm taking care of you. It's the law."

Sophie looked up. "Will you get in trouble if I don't tell her?"

"I might."

Sophie considered this. "All right. I'll tell her. But she won't be surprised."

"Why won't your mom be surprised?" Faye asked. "Your father seemed to be a perfectly healthy man."

"She said he wasn't going to be around much longer," Sophie said, her eyes brimming. "That something was going to happen to him." She started crying again. "She told me to be ready for her to come and get me and take me with her and Tony. And I don't want to go with them!"

Dawn felt a slow horror creep over her. This threat echoed the words the unknown caller had shouted at her this morning.

She needed to talk to the police!

She cleared her throat and spoke to Faye. "I'll deal with the mother issue," she said, putting her hand on

Sophie's shoulder. "Perhaps the police should be notified."

"There's Joan." Faye looked worried. "But she's not really a policeperson anymore."

"I wasn't thinking of Joan," Dawn said pointedly. "She's too close to the situation, if you get my drift."

"Right. I'll do some checking."

"Let me know," Dawn said.

"I will, Dawn. You can depend on me."

"I'm counting on it," Dawn replied. "You'll find me in my. . . Jake's office."

And with those words, Dawn knew she had accepted a new level of responsibility. Now she was really in charge of Jacob's Well. And probably the target of any new trouble at the fort.

The trouble started quickly.

The moment Dawn and Sophie emerged from Ginny's office after talking to Faye, they were met by a group of people who all wanted to know what had happened. Laurie, Todd, Boyd, Corman and Fred among others clamored for information. Dawn held up her hand.

"We don't know much yet," she said. "Jake's been taken to the trauma center at Francisville, and as soon as Ginny calls to let us know how he is, I'll let everyone else know. For now we have to be patient. From what Faye tells me, he's going to be all right." She tried to smile, hoping to convey confidence.

"If he's going to be all right, why was he evacuated by helicopter?" Dr. Corman demanded. "That's for near-death emergencies in this kind of weather!"

"I'll tell you when I get more information," was all Dawn would say. "The best thing we can do is go back to work and do our jobs. Jake would be asking each of you to cooperate if he were here now,'' she added. Then she pleaded for some privacy with Sophie. The others left, but she could tell they were far from satisfied. She was going to have to tell them something soon.

"Let's go home,'' she said to Sophie.

They spent a long, nearly sleepless night together.

THE NEXT MORNING Faye told them that Jake's condition had been upgraded. He was doing better. Greatly cheered, after seeing to the dogs' needs, they went over to Jake's office and settled in. Scrounging in one of the storerooms, they acquired a small desk and chair, which they set up for Sophie. Dawn worked out a lesson for her and left her working figures and graphs with as much pleasure as other kids experience doing a jigsaw puzzle. She decided to wait before getting in touch with Joyce Barr. Sophie needed a break, and for her, working with numbers was relaxing.

Dawn switched on Jake's computer, wishing it was all as easy for her.

Then she suddenly had a memory flash. Day before yesterday she had deliberately turned off his computer. When she had returned to the office later and found Joan waiting, the computer had been on.

She was chewing on that when the computer made a strange sound. The screen went blank.

Sophie looked up. "What's that?'' she asked.

Dawn hit keys. The screen stayed empty and the hard drive made a growling, grinding noise. "I don't know,'' she said. "Sounds like the thing's trying to throw up.'' The mechanical yowling suddenly stopped.

"Oh no!'' Sophie ran over. She touched keys. "The hard drive's crashed,'' she said.

"What?"

"The computer. The hard drive crashed. It's dead."
Sophie started to cry. "Daddy's hurt and now somebody ruined his computer, too."

"Hush now," Dawn patted her back. "It's not so
bad. Surely there's a backup somewhere." Surely!

"I don't know. Maybe Dad kept one in his desk.
But you'll have to get the drive replaced, anyway."

"No one here can fix it?"

Sophie looked at her. "Someone here broke it," she
said.

"Sophie, drives crash. Why should it be anyone's
fault?"

"Because." The child stared at her. "Everything
else has been somebody's fault."

Dawn was about to challenge that statement when
a knocking on the door interrupted her. Joan stood
there.

"May I come in?" she asked.

"Sure," Dawn said. "I've got another problem
here. Maybe you can help."

"What is it?" Joan entered. "What else could possibly go wrong? Hi, kid. Sorry about your dad. Hear
he's doing better today."

Without answering, Sophie shrank from Dawn and
scurried back to her little desk.

"Jake's computer crashed," Dawn said. "Any ideas
about backup?"

"He keeps disks in his desk, I think. Did you look
there?"

Dawn did. She pulled open every drawer.

No disks.

"This is very strange," she said. "If I were paranoid, I'd be thinking this was more sabotage."

Joan sighed and took a chair. "It might be," she said, her tone so deadly weary that Dawn was afraid the woman might be getting ill herself.

Or thinking about drinking again.

"Maybe Jake moved the files," Dawn suggested. "I'll look around the cabin. Meanwhile, is there someone here who can fix the machine?"

"I'll ask Todd," Joan said. "He'll send someone over." She took a deep breath. "What I came here to talk to you about, though, might make that a useless effort."

"Why?"

"I'm hearing people talk about closing the place. Some are ready to walk away the moment the roads are clear enough."

"No! Jake will be back. We have to keep things going for him."

Joan glanced over at Sophie. The child's back was to the women, but the attitude of her body indicated that she was paying close attention to the conversation. "Sure you want to go into all this now?" Joan asked.

Dawn appreciated her tact. "No," she conceded. "But closing down is not an option. Pass that on, if you hear rumors or grumbling."

Joan stood. "Okay. Just thought you ought to know."

Dawn smiled. "Thanks, Joan. Good work, even if it was bad news. Now see if Todd can find me a computer wizard, please."

"Will do. By the way, there's also more trouble on that matter I talked to you about yesterday. Remember? The letters and presents?"

Laurie and Farley. "What sort of trouble?"

"She's waiting to talk to you. She's real upset."

"Send her in."

"My professional advice is to listen, but don't attempt to solve the problem. This isn't your job, you know," Joan said, her tone and expression indicating sympathy for Dawn.

"I know. But I agreed to try. I'll take your suggestion. Thanks. Now, go on. Get me someone to fix this thing and let me talk to Laurie. I'll see what I can do. I'll do my best."

"That's all anyone can ask of you," Joan said. She left and Laurie came in, her eyes red and her color blotchy.

Laurie sat down. "I'm sorry, but I have to leave the Well," she said. She sniffed and dug in her pocket for a tissue. "I can't stay. I'm too upset."

"We're all nervous and upset," Dawn replied. This sudden show of emotion bothered her. If Laurie was involved in all the sabotage, would she be trying to leave the Well at this point? Everything seemed to be going according to the saboteur's plans?

But Dawn had to take Joan's advice. At least she had to think about it. If she did or said something that caused anyone further harm, she'd be responsible and would carry the guilt for the rest of her life.

How did Jake handle this responsibility day after day? Month after month? Year after year?

If he hadn't had a heart attack, it wasn't because he wasn't due!

"Can you tell me why you feel you have to go?" she asked.

And Laurie started crying hard. "It's Farley," she said. "He's gone! And it's my fault!"

WHEN JAKE WOKE UP again, he felt far worse than he had before. He was nauseated as hell. The aches in his body had quadrupled, and tiny pins of pain danced all over his skin. He opened his eyes, saw a white, bright light and groaned, then swore.

"If this is hell or even if it's heaven," he declared, his voice croaking in his sore throat, "I'm mad! I've got too much to do! Let me go back, damn it all!"

A man laughed. "He's coming out of it," he said. "Going to be all right."

A woman spoke. "Hello, Jake. This isn't heaven, it's Francisville."

Another woman, one he recognized. "It's not hell, either, boss. But for a while there, we weren't sure about your final destination."

Jake turned his head and saw Ginny. "Francisville? How'd I get here?"

"Medevac chopper," the man said. He leaned into Jake's field of vision. "Hi. I'm Dr. Bolton, cardiologist. We thought you'd had a heart attack."

"Me? Why? I was about ready to..." Jake frowned. All he remembered was kissing Dawn and wishing they were somewhere private where no interruptions were likely to happen so that he could...

Another man's voice spoke. "Vital signs are all normal. Whatever it was, he threw it off in one heck of a hurry."

"We'll have a better idea when the lab results come back," the first man said. "I think I know what it was, but I need confirmation."

"Have you called the police?" Ginny asked.

"Not until the lab work—"

"Police?" Jake attempted to rise from the bed. At least three people put their hands on him and kept him still. "What about police?"

"Jake, just relax," Ginny said. "Your system's had a bad shock. Two bad shocks, and you—"

"Damn it, Ginny," Jake roared. "Tell me what the hell is going on!"

"Calm down, man," the cardiologist said. "What we think is that you've been poisoned."

Ginny put her hand on his shoulder. "Jake," she said. "Someone tried to kill you."

LAURIE CONTINUED to cry as she talked. "Farley's been sending me letters and presents. At first it freaked me out, because I didn't know who was doing it. But when I discovered it was just him, I relaxed. We're friends, so I figured he would come to me directly after a while and tell me how he really felt. But he didn't. I got worried then that he might be weird like my ex. But Farley, well, you've met him. He doesn't seem like he'd ever hurt anyone deliberately."

"I agree. But people can hide things about themselves."

Laurie rolled her eyes. "Don't I know it! Anyway, yesterday, I got another love letter. I went to Farley's desk, found a sample of his handwriting and compared them. They were a match. I confronted him with the evidence this morning, not long before the helicopter came for Jake. He got white as a ghost, then he turned and walked away. He wouldn't talk to me. And now..."

"He's gone. He can't have gone far with the snow like it is. Are you sure he's not just hiding and avoiding you?"

"He's gone. I looked everywhere in the fort. None of his personal stuff seems to be missing from his cabin. Just his heavy coat. I think he's left. I think he's so ashamed, he can't stay anywhere he might see me."

"I bet he went to the cave," Sophie said. "That's what I'd do."

"What cave?" both women asked at the same time.

"It's just a little ways from here," Sophie said. "Up in the hills on the way to Fairway. I can show you."

"I didn't know there was a cave nearby," Laurie said. "How could Farley know about it?"

"He knows because I showed him," Sophie said. "One time when Dad couldn't take me to school, he sent me with Farley. We stopped at the cave because it was raining." Her face seemed to cloud when she spoke of her father, and Dawn felt her own heart tighten in pain.

"Farley's nice," Sophie continued. "He wouldn't do anything to hurt you, Laurie."

"I know." Laurie started crying a little again. "But he's not here to tell me that. And what he did scared me. We have to talk about it."

"Yeah, he's at the cave for sure," Sophie said, talking thoughtfully as if to herself. Listening to an inner logic. Then she looked up at Dawn and spoke more directly to her. "It's got all kinds of stuff in it. Dad set up the cave so if we got caught in snow or rain we could stay there until we could get home."

"All kinds of stuff?" Dawn asked.

Sophie nodded, but didn't elaborate.

"No one can walk far in this deep snow. If Farley went out, he must have skied or used snow shoes." Dawn tapped her fingertips on the desk.

"We can take the snowmobiles," Laurie said, sounding considerably cheered.

Dawn debated inwardly. She didn't want to leave in case more news came in about Jake. And she was reluctant to abandon the office until someone had taken a look at the computer.

On the other hand, what she should do was what she figured Jake would do if he were in her place.

She should delegate as much responsibility as she could, then go find the missing member of the Well. She should bring Farley home. Whatever else was going on here, she knew that people were far more important to Jake Barr than things, and at the moment one of his people could be in trouble. Even if the cave contained camping gear, she doubted Farley was much good as a survivalist.

And the sooner he faced Laurie and admitted sending her the letters and gifts, the better for both of them.

People first, things next. Dawn started delegating.

AN HOUR LATER she and Sophie on one snowmobile and Laurie on another roared out of the fort across the snow, following the trail left by Farley's snowshoes. Pearl bounded alongside them. Dawn had figured taking the oldest, most experienced dog would be best.

Also, if something happened and they needed help, she could send Pearl back to the Well. Enough people knew they were going out so that if the dog returned alone, it would signal another emergency.

Just what everyone needed!

It was warmer than it had been in the morning, and the mist was even thicker, reflecting the rapid and extreme changes in temperature and humidity. Land and sky were still held in a white blanket, muffling the noises of their machines and making depth perception and direction difficult to fathom.

Just as it had been when Jake had stepped into the trap.

Dawn's snowmobile hit a lump of soft snow, and she struggled with the steering for a moment before regaining control. Sophie tensed, but didn't yell. She pointed a little bit to the right of the path Farley had made. Dawn turned, trusting the child to know the best way to go.

Laurie's snowmobile pulled alongside hers, and Dawn indicated that Sophie had called for the change. Laurie nodded and fell slightly behind. They drove close to some low hills, along the bank of a small stream that flowed darkly and sluggishly under icy snow and then upward along a path into the mountains.

The only variation in the gray surroundings came in the darker gray rocks that jutted upward as they rode up on the side of the mountain. Even the evergreen trees looked black instead of green. After a while, Sophie signaled for Dawn to slow.

They were near the cave.

"Over there," she shouted, pointing to an area of the mountain that looked unapproachable. "Stop!"

Dawn stopped, and Laurie followed suit. Pearl hesitated, and when Dawn told her to stay, she circled the snowmobiles and sat down nearby. In the silence, Dawn could almost hear the blood rushing through her own veins.

"The cave's right up there," Sophie said, taking off her helmet. "I'll go see . . ."

"Hold it," Dawn said. "Let me . . ."

"No." Laurie set her helmet on her snowmobile. "It's my responsibility. I want to talk to him alone first. I've run away from so many things in my life. I want to face this and help Farley do the same. Please."

"Take Pearl with you. Call out if there's trouble."

"Okay." Laurie snapped her fingers at the dog. "Come on, Pearl."

Pearl looked at Dawn.

"She wants your permission," Sophie said, her tone indicating surprise. "She usually acts that way with Dad. I've never seen her do it with anyone else."

"She must remember I helped Onyx. Go on, Pearl," Dawn said. "Stay with Laurie."

The dog stood and jogged off at Laurie's side.

Dawn and Sophie settled down to wait.

JAKE FINISHED SPEAKING, outlining what he wanted to do, and the police detective sat silently, considering what had been said. Jake waited. The man's name was Sam Groner, and he was a person Jake was comfortable with, a native West Virginian from a family that had lived in the hills for generations. He was relatively young for a detective, in his late twenties, solidly built and solemn. Red hair, blue eyes and a slow but steady manner. Sam looked at his notes and scratched the back of his neck.

"It's not exactly by-the-book procedure, what you're proposing, Dr. Barr," he said, speaking slowly. "Don't know how I'll explain it to my superiors."

"Don't explain until you've made the collar," Jake said. "Look, Detective. You have evidence a crime was committed. An attempt to kill me. But you have nothing else. Doing it my way will catch the perpetrator. And any accomplices."

"It's dangerous for you."

"It's been dangerous for me all along."

"I don't know, Dr. Barr. This really goes against my professional grain."

"Tell you what. You know the law, I know the situation at the Well," Jake said, his West Virginia accent strong. "Why don't you call me Jake, I'll call you Sam, and then together we can fix ourselves up a plan that'll make both of us happy."

Sam looked at Jake. Then at his notes. Then out the hospital window at the melting snow. He stood and walked around the small room. Then he sat back down.

"I have to be crazy, listening to you, Jake. But go on and talk. I'll be here when you're done."

So, Jake talked.

CHAPTER THIRTEEN

DAWN, Sophie, come on up here!'' Laurie's voice summoned them.

Dawn looked up. Laurie was standing on a ledge right outside the mouth of the cave, signaling for them to come in.

"Is Farley there?" she called. "Is he all right?"

"Come and see for yourself," Laurie replied. She sounded happy, but a little puzzled.

"Let's go," Dawn said to Sophie. They started up the rise. When they reached the inside of the cave, Dawn saw why Laurie had sounded strange.

Farley was there, looking extremely embarrassed, but otherwise seemingly unharmed.

The cave was a cozy haven, protected from the weather by a large, heavy, canvas drop cloth hung a few feet inside the natural-rock entrance. The floor was mostly bare rock, swept clear of any debris, but over in an alcove lay a carpet of woven material. Also in the alcove were a cot and rolled-up sleeping bags. A small stove stood to the other side of the open space.

But most astonishing of all was the office. Covered completely in protective plastic were a computer, telephone, fax machine and television. A large piece of equipment on the floor seemed to be some kind of generator.

"Hello, Farley," Dawn said, staring at the setup. "I see you found a pleasant place to stay."

"I wasn't thinking straight," the chemist said, shamefaced. "I just had to get away from the Well." He glanced at Laurie. "I couldn't face you after what you found out about me," he confessed.

"Farley, I forgive you," Laurie said. "Now come on home. We need to talk."

"Wait a minute," Dawn said. "Sophie, what's all this stuff for?"

"Dad set it up here just in case we were stranded." Sophie went over to the cot and sat down. "There's lot of food. Freeze-dried stuff."

"But the computer? Is it a mirror of the one in his office?"

Sophie frowned, looking confused by Dawn's reference. Then she got it. "I think so," she said. "He never said, but I remember him working here and sending information back to his office. And nobody else except Farley knows about it."

Except Farley. Dawn looked at him. He seemed mystified by the conversation. Could he be that good an actor? she wondered. Was it possible that he'd not only downed the computer in Jake's office but trekked all the way out here in the cold to do the same to this one?

She didn't think so. "Show me how to turn on the juice," she said to Sophie. "I'm going to make a backup of all the data files to take with us."

"What's going on?" Farley asked as Sophie helped Dawn unzip and remove the plastic covers that protected the equipment. "Laurie told me Jake is better. What's this about a backup?"

"I don't understand either," Laurie said. "Has something else gone wrong?"

"Jake's office computer crashed," Dawn told them. "I left to come find Farley before Todd could send someone over to fix it. But something tells me the data is gone for good. The backup disks are also missing so I'm pretty sure someone has done it deliberately. I'm hoping that person didn't know about this computer."

Laurie sat down on the cot. "You suspect everyone, don't you," she said. It was not a question, but a statement of fact. "Including me."

Dawn stopped working. "Laurie, if I were Jake, I'd suspect *me*, and I know I'm innocent." She paused. "Farley, when did you leave the Well?"

Farley blushed. "This morning. Right after Laurie showed me the handwriting comparison. I was so ashamed of causing her grief that I just—"

"It's all right, Farl," Laurie said. "You made a mistake. But that's in the past."

Farley took a deep breath and continued, "I got my coat and snowshoes and ran," he said. "I knew about this place, but I wasn't even thinking of coming here until I got away from the fort and started to worry about what to do."

"Okay." She went back to the computer, and Laurie and Farley moved to another part of the cave and began to speak in low tones.

Dawn turned to Sophie.

"Sophie, why don't you sit at the keyboard and let's see if we can access and copy everything." It took the girl a few minutes to get into Jake's files but to Dawn's relief, it seemed as if all information pertinent to the Well was in fact stored on the small but powerful system. It was as if he'd anticipated the need for a full backup away from the fort.

"That's everything," Sophie said, handing the disks to Dawn who wrapped them carefully before stowing them in her pocket.

"Let's all go home," she said.

Laurie and Farley looked at each other.

Sophie gathered up her coat and mittens. "Will we find out about Daddy now?" Sophie asked morosely.

"We will," Dawn promised. "If Ginny hasn't called with information, I'll track her down myself. I promise."

Sophie looked more cheerful at that.

Laurie cleared her throat. "I know you need us, but we'd like to stay out here for a little while longer. We're talking things over, and we just won't get this kind of privacy back at the Well."

"Okay. But please don't stay out past dark. I don't want to have to send out another search party."

"We won't."

So Dawn and Sophie returned alone. Neither spoke much; each keeping her worry about Jake to herself. When they entered Jake's office, Todd and another man were tinkering with the computer.

"It doesn't look good," Todd said to Dawn. "Larry has been working on it for several hours with no results."

"It looks like someone's inserted a virus into the hard drive and all the data's been corrupted," Larry announced, a frown on his youthful face. "I've done everything but an exorcism, but I'm afraid there's no way to recover any of it."

"You didn't find any backup disks?" Todd asked Dawn. "If we had those, Larry could put the data on another system."

"No." Dawn glanced at Sophie, willing the child to silence. The fewer people who knew she had outwitted the saboteur, the better.

Sophie said nothing. She just wandered over to her little desk and sat down.

"I haven't really searched everywhere," Dawn replied. "But a quick check of the office didn't turn up anything."

"From the looks of this," Larry said gloomily, "I'd bet you won't find 'em. Whoever planted the virus wasn't likely to leave restoration data around." He pushed back from the desk.

"So you think it was deliberate and not just an incremental failure that was due to happen anyway?" Dawn asked.

"Be my guess."

"But isn't the data on the Well network? I thought all the computers here were interconnected."

"They are," Larry said. "But Jake's system was set up so he could separate his own stuff from the rest." He shook his head. "I doubt if you'll find anything of his on any other system here."

"Then it's all lost." Dawn turned back to Todd. "Have you heard any more about Jake's condition?" Out of the corner of her eye, she saw Sophie move jerkily.

"No," Todd replied. "Not a word."

"Okay," Dawn said. "Thanks, Larry. Can you bring me in another computer while this one is in the shop?"

"Consider it done." Larry started to unplug Jake's system.

Todd moved to the desk. "Dawn," he said, "you know what this means, don't you? The Well can't function without Jake. And as good a job at substituting as you might do, you certainly can't function properly with all his data destroyed."

"I don't know everything he had in here," Dawn said, waving a hand at the computer, "but I do know how businesses operate, and yes, we can probably function for a while, even with Jake gone. Unless he walks in and tells me to quit or unless the entire staff of the Well vanishes, we'll have life go on as usual, starting now." She crossed her arms over her chest. "Don't you have work waiting to be done?"

Todd reddened. He left without another comment.

Larry vanished with the computer a few moments later.

Dawn shut the door and looked at Sophie. "Let's call," she said. "I can't stand not knowing."

Sophie nodded. "I bet Todd knows and won't tell," she said.

"Honey, he's as worried as we are." Dawn crossed over to the desk and picked up the receiver. "Well, maybe not *as* worried, but he is concerned. After all, he does live and work here. He owes Jake a lot."

Sophie didn't comment.

Dawn checked the internal numbers and dialed the infirmary. When Faye answered, Dawn asked the nurse for a report.

"I haven't heard from Ginny since this morning," Faye replied, her tone thin with anxiety. "I'm going to call her in a few minutes."

Dawn felt cold. "We're in Jake's office," she said. "Please let us know as soon as you find out something." Faye agreed. Dawn hung up. "I think it's time we call your mother," she said to Sophie. "She needs to be told."

"She won't care," Sophie said.

"She will want to know about the situation, I'm sure. By the way, thanks for not saying anything about the disks to Todd. Right now I'd just as soon not have anyone know I've managed to restore the information that went missing. Is it all right if I use your computer? That way no one will know if I don't want them to."

Sophie shrugged. She stared at the papers on her lap.

Dawn pulled a client chair over to the child's desk and sat down, facing Sophie. "Look, honey," she said, "I think I know how you feel about my getting in touch with your mom, but I'm not sure. I do know that you ought to be with a responsible relative if Jake's not able to take care of you. So if you won't help me contact your mother, how about your grandparents?"

Sophie raised her face. Her eyes were wet with tears. "My grandparents are okay, but I want to stay here with you," she said. "Don't send me away. Please."

Dawn's answer was immediate, from her heart and totally wrong from a logical and legal point of view. "I won't send you away!" she declared. She reached out and hugged Sophie. "I promise!" she added.

The phone rang, and Dawn felt Sophie shudder. When she picked up the receiver, her own hand was shaking badly. She shut her eyes when she said hello, terrified of what she was going to hear.

The news was almost the worst it could possibly be.

THE STATE POLICE came to fetch them. Because it was a life-and-death situation, an official escort was provided.

They were taken to the main road by snowcoach and from there to the hospital at Francisville by police car. Once out of the forest, they made excellent time because the roads were relatively clear. Since no one would tell them exactly how near death Jake actually was, Dawn was in a state of horrified tension but had little time to dwell on her own feelings. Sophie needed everything she had.

Sophie was obviously in shock, never letting go of Dawn's hand nor saying a word. The little girl had turned gray when Dawn had repeated the awful news that Faye had passed on to her: Jake wanted to see Sophie, before...

Before he died. Dawn's eyes filled with tears. The ache that had begun in her heart swelled until she could scarcely breathe. This was a man she could have loved. *Did love!* It was so *wrong* for him to be taken like this!

It was early evening when they reached Francisville. Rosy sunset light gleamed golden off the red brick of the hospital. Dawn helped Sophie out of the police car, noting with dismay that the girl's small hand was ice-cold. Colder than her own, if that was possible.

And Sophie was shivering in spite of the heavy coat and clothes she wore.

"Ms. Sutton?"

"Yes?"

A red-haired man came out of an alcove by the hospital entrance and walked toward her. "I'm Detective Groner," he said, not extending his hand in greeting. His features were set in a grim expression. "Come with me, please."

"Is Jake ... ?" Dawn couldn't bring herself to finish the question. Sophie's hand seemed to spasm, then grip tighter. "We need to know," Dawn stated.

"Just come with me," the cop said, his expression void of emotion. He turned his back on them and walked into the hospital.

Dawn and Sophie followed.

They went along a hallway, but instead of heading for the bank of elevators, Groner continued past the shiny doors. When he turned and headed down a deserted corridor that looked as if it led nowhere, she halted, all her senses alert to trouble.

The cop kept walking.

"Wait," Dawn whispered to Sophie. "I don't like this."

"I don't either. I want to see my daddy," Sophie whispered back, finding her voice for the first time in hours. "Where is he?"

"Right behind you," a familiar voice said, speaking low.

Dawn and Sophie both whirled. Dawn felt an explosion of emotions in her heart. Jake stood there, looking very much alive. With simultaneous cries of joy and surprise, they flung themselves into his arms, one of which was wrapped in a blue castlike bandage.

Jake hugged them both, then guided them quickly down the hall to where the policeman waited by the door. He would not answer their barrage of questions, however. "Just be patient," he told them. "I'll explain it all as soon as we're safe."

Safe? Dawn felt the word lodge like a knife in her midsection. So this was all an elaborate setup to avoid danger. To her, to Sophie? Or to Jake?

Why had they been told he was dying? From the looks of him, except for a little paleness, he seemed healthy. Why the lie? Why put Sophie through that? Why put *her* through it? She felt anger now as well as relief.

Jake bundled them into the rear seat of a four-wheel-drive car parked right outside the exit door. Detective Groner got in the driver's side and Jake got in the front passenger seat. The windows, Dawn noted, were darkened so that no one could see inside.

Groner pulled away from the parking place slowly and drove carefully through the snow and ice that still covered the back streets. Night hadn't fallen yet, but the sun was gone and the light was gray and dirty. Neither Jake nor Groner said anything. They studied the pedestrians, the streets and the passing traffic as if looking for an enemy, so Dawn kept her questions to herself for the moment. Sophie sat still as a mouse, but she watched her father intently and her green eyes shone with joy.

They drove into an older section of town and the streets quickly deteriorated in quality. On either side of them, snow-covered lots rose sharply away from the road and dark, slightly shabby houses perched precariously on hillsides. The trees were thick around the dwellings, and the bare branches looked like skeletal hands protecting the homes.

Groner slowed and pulled up into the vertical driveway of one of the most run-down. Snow-covered

junk littered the front yard. Several windowpanes were
patched with material that looked like cardboard. The
front door appeared to be solid enough, but the over-
all effect of the place was one of decay. "Safe house,"
Groner said. "You'll stay here for now."

"Why?" Dawn asked, unable to keep quiet any
longer. "Why does Jake need to be in a police safe
house? I thought those places were only for protected
witnesses and people like that."

Jake didn't answer.

"Inside," Groner said. "Then we'll talk."

"Daddy," Sophie said. "I don't like this. I'm
scared."

"It's going to be okay, honey," Jake said, reaching
for Sophie's hand. "You have to trust me."

"How about trusting us?" Dawn countered, her
anger very near the surface. "Listen, Jake. We were
told you were near death. You can't imagine what Sophie's been through." *You certainly can't imagine
what I've felt!*

"Ms. Sutton," the policeman said. "Please cooperate. What I'm doing is unorthodox enough. I don't
need more complications."

Dawn started to retort. Jake's hand on her shoulder stopped her. "Dawn, listen. I really was near
death," he said. "Someone tried to kill me. I didn't
have a heart attack. I was poisoned."

"It was a clear attempt at murder," Groner said.
"Jake's one of the luckiest guys I've ever met. He
ought to be dead right now. Fortunately, it seems like
the killer wasn't sure of the dosage. Gave him a less-
than-lethal amount."

Dawn was speechless with horror.

Suddenly Sophie cried out, "Was it Mom?" Then she started to cry.

"We don't know, honey," Jake answered, his voice full of emotion. "I hope not, but we just don't know."

Dawn's heart broke for the child.

They went inside the house. Dawn kept Sophie close, not concerned about what the interior would be like, if the grim exterior was any indication. But once the front door shut behind them, she discovered the place was relatively pleasant. Clean, warm, fresh-smelling and spacious. Groner turned on lights and led them into the dining room.

"We can talk here," he said, shedding his winter coat and inviting them to do the same. "No chance of being overheard. This place is as bug-proof as they come."

Sophie was no longer crying, but she sniffed back tears as she sat on a chair beside her father. Taking her from Dawn, Jake held her hand and spoke soothingly and seriously. "Tell me how to get in touch with your mother," he said. "Sophie, if Detective Groner can just talk to her, maybe he can clear her of any suspicion."

Sophie looked at the policeman. "You'd put her in prison, wouldn't you," she said. "I wouldn't be able to see her again."

Groner looked extremely uncomfortable. He didn't answer.

Dawn did. "If she did try to kill your dad, she'd be in a lot of trouble, Sophie, but maybe she'd get some kind of help so she wouldn't want to try again."

Sophie stared off into a distance. Jake started to speak, but Dawn shook her head, silencing him.

"I don't know for sure," Sophie said after a few interminable minutes. "But I do have her e-mail address, and I write her almost every day. I could ask. Sometimes from the way she answers things, I can figure out where she's writing from and what she's doing."

"Is there a computer here?" Jake addressed Sam Groner.

"Yes, but—"

"Let Sophie send her a letter," Jake went on. "Maybe she can get Joyce to talk to us."

"I can," Sophie said. "If I ask her to, Mom will be here to get me." Her demeanor was now determined.

Groner looked skeptical, but he stood up. "Come with me, young lady. I'll show you where you can work."

Sophie gave her father a hug. She looked at Dawn. Then she followed Groner out of the room.

Dawn turned to Jake. "Now," she said. "Before I hear every single detail of what happened to you and why you're looking so fine and fit when we thought you were on the way out, I have to say something."

"What?"

"This. I'm mad as hell at you, but there's lots more to my feelings than anger." She put her hands on either side of his face. "Since I first set eyes on you, you've had a strong and strange effect on me, Jake Barr. I've been mad, annoyed, enchanted, bewildered and downright flustered! It's only gotten weirder as time has gone by. But today when I thought you were going to die, I knew what it all meant."

"And that is?"

She smiled at him and her voice took on a softer tone. "I'm in love with you," she said. "No other explanation makes sense." Then she kissed him.

Jake felt a thrill go through him. But he forced himself to relax and accept her kiss without responding as he would have liked to do. He wanted to wrap Dawn with his good arm and pull her to him. He wanted to make love to her there and then. But Sophie was in the next room, and also he didn't want Sam Groner walking in at an inopportune moment.

But his heart soared. No doubting his own feelings in the matter. No doubting at all! How he wished he could celebrate these feelings with the two people who meant the most to him. The ironic thing was that both Sophie and Dawn were here with him...but for a very different reason. This was no time to rejoice.

Not while the threat of his own death and the destruction of his life's work hung over the future like a dark cloud. Those matters needed to be dealt with first. Then...

Gently, he pushed her away. "Dawn," he said. "Before anything else is said or done, you have to know that staying with or near me or even at the Well now is extremely risky. Please listen to reason on this. I'm not letting Sophie return, nor should you."

"I'll listen." She had seen something in his eyes that satisfied her need for reassurance about his feelings for her. She sat back. "Tell me what happened."

Jake ran his hand over his head. "Someone slipped a dose of heart medicine into me. From what the doctors here can tell, it was done in incremental dosages during the twelve hours I was in the infirmary at the Well and it wasn't quite enough to kill me. Obviously the poisoner didn't know enough about the drug. My system was strong enough to fight the insult, but the strain combined with the shock from breaking my arm was almost enough to be fatal.''

"Who did it?''

"Don't know. I'm leaving out only a few people, including Faye and Ginny. While they were in the right place at the right time, it makes no sense that they would fail. Proper dosage is something they'd know. Last night I'd swear I saw another person in my room, but I can't remember anything about him or her, save for size. Could have been a woman or a small man. Groner's got forensics people working on other possibilities. All we know for certain is that the person had to be at the Well last night. That's when I got the last dose.''

"You seem all right now.''

"I am. They pumped me full of antidote and then gave me a cocktail of vitamins and minerals that upgraded me from nearly dead to almost well.'' He smiled, but it was not a warm expression. "I'm ready to do battle again.''

"In that case, you need me with you.''

Jake shook his head. "Sam Groner's my sidekick for this. We had a long talk, and he's agreed to go undercover and announce to everyone at the Well that he's an agent for my insurance company and—''

"Jake, he'll be spotted as a cop the moment he steps foot in the grounds.''

"I hope not. In any case, he's going to do it.''

"What's your plan? Do you intend for all your friends to think you're dead or dying?''

His expression grew bleak. "I don't know who my friends are. It seems one of them tried to kill me.''

"What do you intend to do then? How are you going to find out who it is?"

Jake sighed. "You're not going to stay out of it, are you?"

"No."

He sat back down. "I'm going to play as if I'm really nearly dead," he said. "The idea is to flush out the culprit—or culprits—by pretending that the Well is going to have to close because of my condition. As an insurance officer, Sam will go out to the fort and start arranging the details. We think whoever's behind all this wants to take over the Well. To close it would be to ruin their plans. Our hope is that the bait will be too tempting."

"How will you flush out the culprit? What's the bait?"

His green eyes took on a cold light. "Me. They'll have to try to kill me again."

Dawn stared at him. "You can't be serious!"

"As serious as I've ever been. If I'm dead, the Well can't close until all the legal formalities are formalized. That would give someone plenty of time to take over. I've taken Sophie out of danger. Now I can let out all the stops. As far as anyone else knows, I'm laid up in the hospital with a police guard. To keep the story believable, Sam will let it out that you took her back with you to your place, but really she'll be staying at her grandpa's in Fairway..."

"Are you sure she'll be safe at his—" She broke off. Jake had turned much paler and beads of sweat had formed on his forehead. "What's that matter?" she cried.

Jake leaned back, shutting his eyes. "Just weak for a moment there. Sorry."

"Sam!" Dawn called.

The policeman came in a hurry. Sophie was right behind him. "The doctor said he needed to take it easy," Sam said, addressing Dawn, his tone angry but his manner concerned. "He's not supposed to get too stressed or push himself physically too much for a few days."

"Daddy?" Sophie went to her father and put her hands on his chest.

Jake opened his eyes and managed a smile. "Guess I was getting a little bit ahead of myself," he said. He looked at Dawn. "You seem to have a way of making me get faint," he said, smiling. "I seem to be like putty in your hands."

"I didn't mean to upset you but you're just not being smart!" As she fussed at him, Dawn felt tears in her eyes. "You don't know I wasn't the one who poisoned you," she said. She was shaking as if she had a chill. "There's no reason to rule me out."

Sam and Jake both uttered negatives at the same time.

"You were the prime suspect at first," Sam said. "I figured you'd been sent as an assassin. Someone Jake would take in and then lower his guard because . . ." The cop turned a little pink.

"Because you were able to get under my skin," Jake finished, his tone surprisingly strong. He sat up. "Dawn, you need to know something. The muffin that Sophie gave me on Thursday in the infirmary had some trace of the drug in it."

"What?" Dawn looked at Sophie. "We both baked and ate them ourselves."

Sophie nodded. The child was unaware of the awful implication. She just looked puzzled. "I don't get it," she said. "The muffins were burned, that's all."

"Sophie." Sam squatted so that his face was level with hers. "Did anyone at any time besides Dawn have a chance to look at or touch the muffin you gave your father?"

"No."

"You're sure?"

Dawn intervened. "Sophie, did you leave the muffins in the kitchen when you let the dogs out that morning?"

"Sure. But I..."

"Then someone could have entered through the back kitchen door and doctored the muffins."

"But there was only one left and..." Realization hit. "Did I poison you, Dad?" Sophie's face turned chalk white.

"No, honey!" Jake pulled her to him. "But somebody tried to make it look like Dawn did. Did you tell anybody about the muffins?"

Sophie nodded, choking back tears. "I...I let the dogs out and went over to the main kitchen to get a bag." She looked at her father. "You're out of small disposable bags, you know."

"I'll take care of it, honey."

"Okay. Anyway, I told Mabel I needed something to carry a muffin to you. She gave me a paper sack."

"Who heard you say that?" Dawn asked.

Sophie looked at her. "Mabel. And Joan," she answered. "She left right after Mabel said she'd give me the sack." Tears streamed down her cheeks.

"Honey, what is it?" Jake asked, gathering Sophie to him with his good arm.

"Daddy, I lied to you," Sophie said in a rush. "Joan made me turn off the lights. I set up the computer to do it. Mom told me to do whatever Joan told me." She started to tremble. "Joan said she'd hurt me if I told on her. I was really scared, Daddy. I still am."

CHAPTER FOURTEEN

"NO ONE'S GOING to hurt you, honey." Jake seemed calm enough as he drew his daughter closer in a comforting hug. But Dawn saw the green glint of barely concealed fury in his eyes. "Did you get hold of your mother?" he asked.

Sam answered for Sophie. "She sent the message. No reply yet."

"Okay," Jake said. "Here's what we're going to do." He wiped away Sophie's tears and set her on the sofa beside him, his good arm still protectively around her. "Honey, we'll all sleep here tonight, but tomorrow I want you to go to Grandpa's house. Sam will arrange for you to get there."

"But I want to stay with you," Sophie began to protest.

"No argument, Sophie," Jake stated firmly. "You'll be safe there. And I need to know you're safe before I can do anything else."

"You're sure that's a good idea?" Sam asked, echoing Dawn's earlier question. "I mean, wouldn't that be the first place her mother would look for her?"

Dawn agreed. "I could take her somewhere no one would know about."

"No. She needs people she knows and trusts around her, I've changed my mind and decided I'd like you to be with me, Dawn," Jake said. "Sophie, tell these two about your cousins, please."

Sophie made a face. "All of them or just some of them?"

"I was thinking of the big ones," Jake explained. "Uncle Ed's boys. Tell Dawn and Sam what would happen to someone who tried to get you while you were at Grandpa's."

Sophie grinned through her tears. "They'd get pounded. My cousins are real big. And tough. They work in the coal mines."

"She'll be safe enough in Fairway," Jake said. "Sam, will you arrange it?"

"If you're determined, I'll do it," the cop said, clearly reluctant. "I'd rather she stay here under police protection, though."

"She doesn't know the police," Jake replied. "She does know her grandparents and relatives. They're a strong family, and a protective bunch. They won't let Joyce...or anyone else near... This is a...this is hard for her, you understand?"

"Yes, I do," Sam said. "Okay." He got up. "I'll go make some phone calls." He left the room.

Jake spoke to Sophie. "Is there anyone else at the Well who scares you?"

"No. Just Joan. She gets mean."

He turned to Dawn. "Joan and Joyce can't be the only collaborators. They simply don't have the skills to mastermind all the things that have happened. There's got to be someone else."

"I know there is." Dawn explained about the computer in his office. "Someone who knows the system has to have been the one who destroyed your data files. You said Joan wasn't much good with computers."

Jake sighed. "But there are a number of people who are."

"Maybe Joan's been set up," Dawn suggested.

Jake's expression changed. "You mean maybe Joyce set her up by using Sophie? If Joyce told Joan to get Sophie to help her, knowing that Sophie would probably get angry or upset and..."

"Of course. Sophie would let you know how she felt about Joan but not implicate her mother in the process and then you'd naturally suspect Joan while overlooking the real..." Dawn stopped talking. Jake was looking down at the top of Sophie's head and shaking his own. He wanted to get the child out of earshot, she realized. They could discuss the fine points of the situation later.

"I did have the presence of mind to ask Johnny to take care of the dogs when we left," she said, changing the subject. "So they'll be in good hands until—"

"It's all set." Sam reentered the room, rubbing his hands together. "First thing in the morning, a team will take Sophie to Fairway and settle her with your folks, Jake."

"Thanks. Hear that, Soph?" Jake asked.

Sophie, who seemed to have fallen into a light doze, stirred against her father's side. Clearly the events of the day had taken their toll on her. "Yeah. Say, I'm kinda hungry," she said drowsily.

Dawn stood up. "Me, too. Where's the kitchen, Sam? I'll find something for us to eat."

"Down the hall," the policeman said. "Around the turn to your right."

Dawn took Sophie's hand. "Come on, Soph," she said. "Let's go see what it's like to cook on a newfangled stove."

As they walked down the hall, Dawn heard the two men start to talk again. The pitch of the conversation gradually grew louder until they were almost shouting at each other. Dawn felt Sophie squeeze her hand.

"Don't worry, Sophie," Dawn whispered. "They're only talking loud, not fighting. That's just the way guys have sometimes of working things out. Kind of silly to us women, but it makes them happy." She looked down and to her relief, Sophie gave her a wan little smile.

The kitchen was clean and well appointed. It came with all the usual appliances, plus a cop. The large man sitting at the table looked up and nodded to Dawn and Sophie when they entered. He didn't introduce himself, but went back to reading his newspaper. Dawn didn't object. They were in a safe house. Police officers were there to keep them safe, not make friends.

There was plenty of food and in a short while, Dawn had a simple spaghetti dinner ready. As she set things out on the table, she thought wryly that for a woman who had avoided domestic duties as long as she had, she was getting to make up for it with a vengeance lately. Sophie fetched her father. Sam joined them. The unnamed cop excused himself and went out into the living room to keep watch while the four of them ate.

Not much in the way of light conversation went on.

When the meal was over and the dishes cleared and washed, Jake took Sophie upstairs to the small bedroom reserved for her. Dawn waited with Sam while father and daughter talked in private.

She sat down at the table and curled her hands around her mug of coffee. "I'm going to ask you some questions," she said to Groner. "You don't have to answer, but I need to ask."

He smiled. "Fair enough. Ask away."

"It doesn't strike me as normal procedure for a police investigation to let the potential victim of a homicide run the operation."

"It's not." Groner shifted on his chair. "Jake told me what you do for a living, and I can guarantee I'll get in a lot of trouble if you write an article about what's going on here."

"I don't intend to do that."

"Maybe not, but just so you know, if I saw any other way of apprehending whoever's behind the murder attempt, I'd ignore Jake's plan."

"So it is dangerous?"

"Sure. He's setting himself up as a sitting duck."

"You can't substitute a cop?"

"I could. But the culprit might discover the switch. No, much as I hate to say it, Jake's way is the only sure way."

"That sounds familiar." Dawn sipped her coffee. "What happens if his wife is behind it?" she asked, thinking of Sophie. "What happens to their child?"

"No matter how the investigation turns out, Jake's going to sue for custody, I believe," Sam replied. "He was on the phone to his lawyer earlier today."

"Good." Dawn pushed the coffee away. She was wired enough as it was. "Now I have some information for you."

Sam looked attentive.

"You know about the things that have been going on at the Well?"

"Jake told me."

"He told you about the phone call I got and why I showed up on his doorstep?"

"Yes."

"Did he mention the call I received the other morning when I was staying in his cabin, baby-sitting Sophie and the dogs? The call that sounded like it was from the same women who gave me the tip? The call that threatened I would come to the same harm as Jake?"

"No, he didn't."

"Sam, much as I hate to say this, I'm sure it was Joyce. Find her, and I think you'll find the person responsible for trying to murder Jake."

Sam was quiet for a moment, then he said, "Maybe."

"Sophie told me her mother knew I was coming to the Well before I arrived. The call I got that threatened me was the same voice that I heard in Wilmont. What do you need? A blueprint?"

"I need proof I can give to the D.A. to take into court, Ms. Sutton. You should know that."

The reproach made her blush, but Dawn knew the man was right. "What about the boyfriend, Tony?"

"I have no evidence against the man. Just the word of a child."

"So you aren't checking him out?"

Sam sighed and put both hands palm down on the tabletop. "I don't have the means," he said. "Pure and simple. All the evidence points to someone at the Well, not an outsider. Jake's ex might be a conspirator, but there's no way she slipped the drug into his IV or into the muffin. Someone at the fort did it."

Dawn could think of no argument.

UPSTAIRS, his heart breaking, Jake listened to Sophie talk. Released at last from the fear and nearness of Joan Dawson, Sophie confessed her own complicity in some of the events. "Mom told me to do what Joan said," she told her father. "I didn't mind at first, 'cause I thought you were bad. Mom told me you were cheating people and that you were stealing money by making them work and not paying them. But after a while, I knew better."

"So even before you came to stay with me this summer, you thought I was bad?" Jake asked, pain and anger mingling in his mind.

"Well, kind of. I really didn't remember you that way, but Mom kept on saying it and saying it, so I guess I finally believed her."

"I understand, honey."

"I was wrong." Sophie sniffed, stifling tears. "I helped Joan with computer stuff, like I said. And... And..."

"Did you help her get the smoke bomb onto the Deep Lab elevator?"

Sophie shook her head vigorously. "No! The only thing I did was set up the electricity thing. But..."

"What is it, Sophie? Please, I really need to know the whole truth."

"I left my identity card out on the kitchen table like Joan told me to. And when I got back, it was gone."

"So someone took your card?"

Sophie nodded.

"When was that?"

"The day before you went to the hospital. Before you broke your arm."

Jake suddenly felt cold. Sophie's card was a copy of his own. That would grant the holder entry to everyplace in the Well. Not even Joan, as security director, had that kind of access. Until now. Joyce had set this up. He still found it hard to believe his ex-wife had so much hatred in her, but the case against her was getting stronger. He had to accept that his near brush with death was by the hand of his child's mother. The pain was sharp and bitter indeed.

And if it hurt him to realize this, what was it likely to do to Sophie? He began to talk to her soothingly, calming her with promises he prayed he could make come true and then telling her a bedtime story that he remembered his own mother telling him.

A few minutes later Jake went to the kitchen to join Dawn and Sam. "She's sleeping," he said. "I think she'll be all right for now." He took a chair and sat down. He put his face in his hands. "I'd give anything if she hadn't been involved in any of this."

"She was manipulated," Dawn said, putting her hand on his arm.

"And the damnable thing is, she knows it. What's this going to do to her?"

"Jake, she's stronger than you may think," Dawn assured him. "After all, she's your daughter. Maybe she'll come to understand that on some level her mother wasn't well—wasn't fully responsible for what she did."

Jake didn't respond. He just stared down at the empty table.

"Get some sleep, Jake," Sam advised. "You look beat to hell."

"I am." He stood up. With a tender look at Dawn, he said, "See you in the morning."

Dawn waited until he had disappeared back upstairs. "Sam, I need to use a phone," she said.

"They're all under surveillance systems."

"Tapped?"

"'Fraid so. Every call is recorded."

She tamped down her frustration. "Okay. It'll wait. I have nothing to hide, but I'd rather not have my conversations taped. Where do I get to sleep?"

Sam didn't crack a smile as she had expected. "There are three bedrooms upstairs. Take whichever one's empty. One shared bathroom right at the top of the stairs. I'm going to crash down here on the sofa. And don't worry. We've got the place covered."

"Good to know it."

"Each room is equipped for an occupant," Sam went on. "You'll find a toothbrush, towels, soap and some nightclothes. Just take what you need."

"Thanks." She said good-night and made her way up the stairs.

The second-floor hallway of the old house was drafty. She found one bedroom with an open door and went inside. The room was small with one double bed and a dresser. The window was closed and shuttered.

So as to present no opportunity for snipers?

Dawn shuddered. She looked in the dresser drawers and found a long flannel nightgown. It was a little big, but it looked warm. She carried it down the hall to the bathroom, took a quick shower, brushed her teeth and put on the gown. The warm flannel felt good against her clean, bare skin. The air in the house had been chilly to start with and it was getting colder. The hem trailed on the floor as she returned to her room.

Jake was waiting for her.

He had been sitting on the bed, but when he saw her, he stood up. His feet were bare, but he still wore an undershirt and jeans. "I need to talk to you," he said. "Now that we're not going to be interrupted."

"Okay." Dawn felt her heart beat faster. She set her clothes down on top of the dresser.

"I didn't respond when you said you loved me."

"I didn't ask you to."

He stood there for a moment, silent, his left arm hanging awkwardly in its cast. "I want to," he said finally. "I want to, but until all this is straightened out, I can't tell you what tomorrow's going to bring, much less make you any promises or pledges."

"I haven't asked for any," she said softly.

He sat back down on the bed. "I'm so damn tired, I can't even think."

She went over and shut the door, turning the key in the lock to give them privacy. "Then lie down and sleep. Here, with me. Just rest. You don't have to think tonight or do anything else."

"I love you," he said.

She wanted to go to him and put her arms around him; instead she moved to the bed and turned down the covers. "Come on. Get out of those jeans," she said gently. "You'll be more comfortable."

"No, this isn't right." He stood up. "I shouldn't stay. I'll go to my room."

"Jake, take off your pants and get in bed!"

He looked a little stunned, then he smiled. "I can't say when I've had a better offer." He unzipped his jeans and stepped out of them.

"It wasn't an offer, it was an order." Dawn switched off the light. "Now, get in bed and go to sleep."

Jake's chuckle in the darkness was low and warm with promise. But he obeyed.

Dawn heard the springs creak as he got on the bed. She slipped in beside him.

His body was warm. The sensation of lying by him stirred her deeply.

But it wasn't time. Not yet.

His hand covered hers. "I wish that we—" he began.

"Hush," she said. "There'll be time. Later. For now, let's take comfort in each other's company."

She heard him take a deep breath and let it out. "I really do love you, Dawn," he said.

"I know," she said softly.

"How? I haven't done anything since we met but get deeper in trouble."

"You trusted me with your daughter and your dreams. If that's not a sign of love, I don't know what it is."

Jake was silent. But his hand squeezed hers hard enough for her to feel the pulse beat in his palm.

A little while later, still lying side by side and only touching hands, they both slept. It was the deepest rest Dawn had enjoyed in a long, long time.

THE NEXT MORNING she woke to find herself alone in her bed. But she could hear Jake and Sophie talking in the hallway. They sounded happy. Smiling, she stretched and got up. Jake loved her, she loved him, and though they hadn't made love yet, they had already bonded in ways that many people never did.

The question was, would they have a chance to enjoy it? She stopped smiling and rummaged through the clean clothing in the drawers until she found a few items she could use to substitute for her own garments.

She went downstairs to find Sam and several other cops gathered at the kitchen table. Sam gave her a nod and indicated the coffeepot. No one else acknowledged her. She saw that Jake and Sophie were out in the living room, eating doughnuts. She got some coffee and joined them.

Jake stood up and greeted her with a light kiss. The look in his eyes told her he'd like to do a lot more. But he smiled and sat back down beside Sophie. "Sleep okay?" he asked.

"Like a log." Dawn grinned and took a doughnut. "You?"

"Best rest I've had in ages. I feel terrific."

Sophie was watching them closely, but said nothing.

"How about you, Sophie?" Dawn asked. "Was your room comfortable?"

"It was okay," Sophie said morosely. "Kind of cold, though." She didn't look at Dawn when she spoke.

Dawn looked questioningly at Jake.

"Soph's still a little put out that she's relegated to the sidelines from now on," Jake explained. "She wants to go back to the Well with you instead of to her grandparents."

"Oh." Dawn put down her coffee mug. "I know how you feel, Sophie."

"No, you don't!" Sophie glared at her. "Nobody does."

Dawn and Jake glanced at each other.

"It's all my fault," Sophie said loudly and angrily. "And you won't let me help fix it."

"Any trouble here?" Sam walked into the room. "Sophie, you're all set to go?"

"Sure," Sophie said sullenly. "I don't have any choice, do I?"

"No, because we're trying to keep you safe, honey," Jake said, putting his arm around her. "But you do have a choice about taking the blame. And I've told you to remember that none of this is your fault. Will you promise me to believe it?"

Sophie didn't reply.

"Promise?" urged her father. "Please?"

"Okay."

Dawn heard rebellion in that word. She only hoped that Sophie would understand after she'd had a chance to think it through. So much had happened so quickly that to absorb it, the child would need time.

Sophie gave Dawn a hug before she left with the policewoman who was to escort her to Fairway. Before she let go, she whispered to Dawn, "Take care of my daddy."

"I will," Dawn whispered back.

The rest of the morning was spent in setting up Sam's cover and Dawn's story. The plan was for Sam and Dawn to return to the Well together. Dawn would introduce Sam as an insurance appraiser she'd met at the hospital and brought back to the Well under Jake's instructions. She was to report that Jake was lingering, but seriously ill and that Sophie had stayed with her father. Since Dawn had been appointed by Jake to be in charge, it was logical for her to help any investigation of the Well operation. The hope was, with Jake in such dire straits, the computer records supposedly destroyed and Dawn's lack of knowledge, the people behind the conspiracy would be less cautious and perhaps do something to reveal their identities as well as their intentions.

Jake would return to the hospital where he would remain, under police protection. He was, in no uncertain terms, bait for an impatient killer or killers. Only when he was dead, Jake reasoned, would the guilty person—or persons—feel safe to go ahead with whatever plans they had for the Well.

As a policeman, Sam was there only as a catalyst. He also cautioned Jake and Dawn to play their roles carefully. Any hint of entrapment and the case against the perpetrators would go right out the window.

"Is everyone clear on this?" he asked when the briefing was finished.

"Yes," Dawn said.

Jake was quiet for a moment. Then he stood up. "Sure," he said. "Let the games begin."

AS SAM AND DAWN JOURNEYED back to the Well, she kept the conversation light and undirected. The sun was out full force, and the roads had cleared enough for most traffic. The countryside was luxuriously draped with snow that sparkled and glittered in the fresh, bright sunlight.

It was a morning to enjoy life.

They reached the gate around noon, and Dawn directed him past it to the back entrance. The going was much rougher there, but they plowed through the soft snow and made it to the fort after about twenty minutes.

"My God," Sam said when he got his first full view of the place. "I feel like we're in a time warp."

"Amazing, isn't it?" Dawn agreed. "Especially with all the snow. You do feel it's the real thing. Like you've gone back in time."

"It's uncanny. Weird."

"And it's going to get weirder. Come on, let's go in."

They played their respective roles for the rest of the day. After showing him one of the guest rooms where he could sleep, Dawn escorted Sam to a room near Jake's office and helped him set up what looked like a preliminary insurance appraisal of the Well. She held a meeting of all the staff, explained Sam's presence and sadly announced that Jake's condition was not looking good. Although it made her feel terrible to lie to so many people she now considered friends, she knew that among them was at least one traitor who was inwardly rejoicing at the news. The lies were necessary.

But it was impossible to tell solely from outward appearance who besides Joan might be a villain. Everyone seemed devastated. Most wept openly. Many asked if there was anything they could do for Jake or Sophie. Dawn made note of those offers with the intent of passing them on to Jake. Even Joan acted deeply stricken by the report. She disappeared after the meeting, and about an hour later, Laurie found Dawn in Jake's office and told her Joan had started drinking again.

"She's not drunk," Laurie said. "But she's got a flask with her, and she's taking slugs from it when she thinks no one's watching."

"There's not much I can do about it, is there?" Dawn said, hating the need to behave as if she didn't care. "I'm just staying until the insurance agent finishes the appraisal. It looks like everyone here's going to be on their own again soon anyway."

"How can you say that? I thought you really liked Jake! I heard your little speech, and I can tell you I don't think much of it. You haven't been here long enough to understand that the power of what Jake did for all of us is lasting." Her voice broke and she started crying.

With difficulty, Dawn held back an offer of comfort. She even tried to change the subject. "Did you and Farley work things out?" she asked.

"That's none of your business," Laurie snapped. "In fact, none of this is any of your business. I'm going to tell everyone I think we ought to take legal action to keep you from running things."

"Laurie, I'm only trying to help."

"How? By putting us out of business?"

"Without Jake—"

"We can do it without Jake," Laurie said. "Where are those disks you copied?"

Dawn froze.

"Come on," Laurie said, standing up. "Hand them over. I know you have them. I was there when you made them. Give them to me or I'll just go out to the cave and make some more."

"Laurie, I can't give them to you. And I can't let you do anything to—"

"You mean you won't!" Laurie interrupted. She was shouting now. "You know what I think? I think you jinxed Jake. He was hurt while he was with you. He trusted you. I think you're—"

A knock on the door stopped her. Sam looked in. "Problem here?" he asked.

Dawn nodded. "I believe so."

Sam came in and shut the door.

"Leave us alone," Laurie declared hotly. "This isn't any of your concern."

"I think it is," Sam said. "Sit down, please, Miss Tanner."

"I will not!"

"Laurie!" Dawn said. "Sam's not an insurance agent."

"Then what...?"

"I'm a cop, Miss Tanner." Sam indicated a chair. "Now, please. Try to calm down and listen to us."

"A cop?" Laurie sat, clearly stunned. "Why are you here?"

Dawn had no idea what to do next. Sam had to lead her on this.

He did. Taking a stance by the window, he calmly explained that Jake's illness had resulted from a deliberate poisoning attempt. Without giving away the fact that Jake was very much alive, he enlisted Laurie's cooperation in the plan to catch the murderer.

"So Dawn's actually helping you?" Laurie asked when Sam was finished. "In order to preserve what Jake built here?"

"That's right."

She turned to Dawn. "I'm sorry," she said contritely. "If I had any idea, I would never have said such terrible things to you."

"I know that. But just please keep this to yourself. Don't tell anyone."

"Not even Farley? You can trust him."

"Until we know for sure who's guilty, I don't trust anyone," Sam said. "Not even Ms. Sutton."

Laurie had no response to that.

Neither did Dawn. Although the statement didn't surprise her.

"You trust her?" Sam asked Dawn after the door was firmly shut behind Laurie.

"To an extent," Dawn answered. "But then, that's the best any of us can say, isn't it?"

Sam had the grace to blush slightly. But he nodded and went back to his office.

Dawn spent the rest of the afternoon and early evening alone. Wrapped in their own grief, the other inhabitants of the Well kept to themselves or went about their daily tasks.

By the time she made her lonely way to Jake's dark cabin, she felt cold and desolate. She regretted her decision to leave the dogs with Johnny, but in fairness, they were better off with the vet at the kennel than they would be with her until some kind of resolution was reached. Besides, taking the dogs back would be an indication that she intended to stand in for Jake, and as Sam had pointed out, that would make her a secondary target.

But it would have been good to have the dogs to greet her when she entered the dark, cold cabin.

It would have been good and it would have been safer. For as soon as she shut the door behind her and reached for the light switch, an iron band clamped around her waist, imprisoning her and a strong hand shut her mouth, silencing her.

CHAPTER FIFTEEN

DAWN STRUGGLED and kicked and screamed behind the muffling hand. She was not about to be subdued easily.

"Shh! It's me," Jake whispered into her ear. His grip on her eased.

She relaxed immediately.

"Sorry," he whispered, still holding her. "I didn't want to scare you, but I didn't want you to turn on the lights or say my name loudly." He took his hand away from her mouth. "The walls of these cabins aren't particularly soundproof, and anyone walking by could hear you."

"You did scare me!" She turned around in his embrace. "Damn it, Jake, you nearly shocked the life out of me! What are you doing here? How did you get here?"

"One of my cousins drove me. Keep your voice down, please."

"Why? You should be back in the hospital, playing sick."

He released her, but put his hand on her shoulder. "To all intents and purposes, I am," he said softly. "But Sam's wrong about the next attack coming at me. It'll be here, and I have too much to do to lie still, acting like a worm on a fish hook, when there's really no reason." He moved his hand to the back of her neck. "So I sneaked out. But don't worry. One of my many cousins is willingly taking my place. Fact is, I'm told, several of them fought over the honor." He laughed, a warm sound in the darkness.

Dawn failed to see any humor in the situation. "Jake, Sam thinks you're there. He'll have a fit!"

"Probably. But Sam won't know. Unless you tell him." His fingers began to caress her. Feathering her skin and hair. Tickling her nape. Trailing down to tease at the edge of her sweater. "My cousin Zeke is my age and looks a lot like me, and he'll fool anyone who doesn't examine him closely. Of course, I had to let Ginny in on the plan. She should be able to stall any questions."

"Jake Barr, you're not helping things by doing this." The sense of intimidation vanished, replaced by the full realization that part of the reason he was here was to make love with her. Dawn felt a current of anticipation charge through her.

"Oh?" He eased her closer. "I thought I was," he said. And he kissed her.

And she forgot about the danger, the sabotage, even Sophie. Holding him close, kissing and being kissed, Dawn *knew* this was where she belonged. In Jake's arms. It was as if everything else in her life had been leading up to this.

After a while, she murmured, "I guess you are helping after all."

"Told you so," he said, smiling.

They continued to kiss slowly and deeply, moving from the cold, dark living room into his bedroom. Clothing fell on the floor as they removed and discarded it. By the time they reached his bed, they were both naked, their skin goosebumped from the chilly air but their bodies hot with need.

Dawn felt her desire for him become all-consuming passion. Fire in her roared through her bloodstream until her entire body seemed to ignite with passion.

"I love you, Jake," she whispered, her lips close to his.

"I love you," he replied, looking into her eyes. "No matter what, remember that!"

A shudder went through her body. "I will," she promised.

And he kissed her again. This time her knees buckled and she fell backward onto the bed.

In a second Jake was on the bed beside her. The sheets were icy against the heat of their skin. The combination of cold and heat continued to play on them as they made love, heightening the erotic sensations they gave to each other.

And sensation built on sensation, until there was no line of separation between them. Their bodies, gripped in passion, moved as one, taking them higher and higher.

At last from a place deep inside, Dawn felt a need uncoil from her center. Slow and exquisite, the sensation made her rise to meet Jake as he entered her, held her, while passion rocked them both.

They lay together for a time afterward, letting the night air cool them. Then Jake reached down and dragged the heavy quilt off the floor where they'd pushed it earlier and put it over them.

"Well," he said softly, holding her close, stroking her hair with his right hand. "Seems to me that was worth the risk."

"You were right. It was." Dawn snuggled against him under the covers. "Okay," she said. "Talk to me. No one can hear us here, even if they try. Aside from the obvious reason, which we've just taken care of, why are you here?"

"After sleeping beside you last night, I couldn't stay away from you," he said.

She moved her hand over his chest. "You must have had another purpose. I can't believe you risked showing up here just to make love."

"Believe it!"

"Jake, come on!"

"Okay. I've been doing some more thinking about this whole thing. While I think Sam really believes someone will make another attempt on my life, I don't. I don't think I'm the primary target. I would never have asked Zeke to stand in for me if I thought he was going to be in any real danger. "

"Who will be then?"

"*What* will be then. Like I said. The Well. Someone wants to destroy the Well."

"Are you sure? I don't know about that."

"Think. After I was hurt, poisoning me became a crime of opportunity. No one could have predicted I would end up sticking my arm in a trap and that my system would be weakened by the loss of blood. But once that happened, the culprit decided getting rid of me would be an easy way to collapse the Well."

Dawn considered his reasoning. "I see your point. But why wouldn't they come after you to finish the job?"

"It is too difficult now. They know my room is being guarded. The opportunity is no longer present."

"So now they'll go back to the first plan. Throw the Well into a state of confusion and mismanagement." Dawn sat up. "You're right. They really won't bother going after you at the hospital, will they?"

"No, they won't. If my suspicions are correct, the long-term aim of whoever's working this scheme is to put the Well out of business so that the market niche I've made is wide open for someone else to enter. They must have immediate plans to set up a similar place, turning out similar products. No, the Well is the target. The motive is economic, I'm sure. They'll strike here." He pulled her down, warming her again. "And this time, I'll be ready."

"How? You're supposed to be very ill?"

"I'll be a ghost, my dearest one. I'll be a ghost," he said.

JAKE REMAINED in his cabin for much of the next day. Using the disks Dawn had copied from the computer in the cave, he set up several programs and worked on Sophie's machine for hours, hunting for anything that would provide a clue to the identity of the saboteur. He had ideas about who it might be, but he needed proof that would stand up in court. Since the person had gone to all the trouble of destroying Jake's records, it made sense there was something hidden that would give his or her identity away.

During the day Dawn brought him food and kept the fireplace filled with logs. To avoid any suspicion, she covered her actions by maintaining an aloof attitude and pretending she wished to be alone as much as possible while the "insurance agent" did his investigative work over in the main building.

Jake enjoyed her fussing over him. Her caring for him warmed his heart. Their lovemaking had restored his energy rather than depleting it, and the trust she showed in him had added incentive to his effort to unravel the schemes of his enemies before they could be carried out.

DAWN PICKED UP the receiver on the second ring. A familiar voice started speaking.

"What's this I hear about Jacob Barr, Dawn?" David Pfaff asked. "He's deathly ill, and you haven't filed a story?"

"Calm down. You run a magazine, David. Not a newspaper," Dawn replied. "You don't need a scoop. Where did you hear about it?"

"Wire service." David's tone softened. "I'm really calling to ask if you're okay. As a friend. So are you okay?"

"No."

"Bail out then. Come home, Dawn. Write what you have and we'll run it. No need to hang on when it looks like the place is cooked. With Barr gone, it'll close down in a few days."

Dawn gripped the receiver. "Who says so?"

"It makes sense. He's the heart and brains of the enterprise. Without him . . ."

"David, this is a unique economic enterprise. Dr. Barr founded it, developed it and set it on the road to success, but it no longer depends solely on him. As long as his people are willing to stay and work . . ."

"Isn't that a problem? I mean, from what I understood, they're all pretty dependent on Barr and it seems to me that they'll all pack up now that he's . . ."

Demanding knocks at the office door kept Dawn from hearing the editor's last few words. "David, I've got to go. I'll call as soon as I have something for you." She hung up. "Come in," she said.

A group of six people led by Laurie and Farley entered the office.

Dawn tensed, not sure what was going to happen.

"We're a delegation," Farley said. "A lot of us just got together over in the auditorium and took a vote."

"We want things to go on," Laurie said. "And we want you to be our new leader."

"What?"

"That's right," Mabel, one of the delegates, declared. "When Jake dies..." She brushed a hand across her eyes. "We all want you to run the Well."

Dawn drew in a breath and blew it out. "I'm stunned, honestly. I thought no one was going to stay."

"Are you kidding?" Laurie said. "We're not going to give up. This is our home now. And it's not just that we prefer it here. Jacob's Well products are our business and our futures."

"A damn good business too!" Larry, the computer technician, said. "So we gotta take care that there is a future. It's...hell, it's what he woulda wanted us to do."

"That's true." Dawn felt a bubble of happiness rising inside. Jake's people were coming through! She yearned to share the truth about him with them, but she reminded herself that until the culprits were exposed, no one was above suspicion. Not even the people gathered here.

"So what do you say?" Farley asked. "Will you stay with us?"

Dawn suppressed a smile. She wouldn't take the job because she didn't need to. Jake would remain in charge once all this was over. "I'll think about it, Farley. That's all I can promise right now."

"Oh." He looked crestfallen. The others also seemed disappointed.

"What I will do, however, is to guide you while the insurance company and the rest of the outside world is nipping at your heels," Dawn said, standing up. "I didn't offer earlier because you had to make up your collective minds about what you wanted for your future. Seems to me you've now done that."

"We have!" Farley stated. "We want this place to go on producing and innovating and inventing."

"We want it to continue to be our home," Laurie said. "And if you can't stay, somehow, we'll find another manager who can. But we really want you. Please?"

"I can stay for now," Dawn said, smiling. "I'll figure out some way to—"

"Hold it, everybody!" Todd shoved his way past the others and entered the office. "I just heard about the meeting and the vote, but I've got some information you need to hear before you let this woman take over our lives."

"We don't need any information from you, Todd," Farley said angrily. "All you've done since the trouble started is to talk doom and gloom. If you had anything important to say, you should have come to the meeting and said it then."

"I didn't know this!" Todd held up an old copy of the *Wilmot Times,* and Dawn cringed inside. "She lied to us all, Jake included. She's a damn reporter," the scientist yelled. "She's here to get all your secrets and put them in a story for the world to read!'' He slammed the magazine down on Jake's desk. ''Her name's even on the masthead. Take a look.''

They did. Laurie looked up from the magazine, tears in her eyes. ''You lied to us and tricked us,'' she said. ''Dawn, how could you?''

''I didn't trick Jake. He knows...knew,'' Dawn said, defending herself. ''He asked me to keep quiet about it, and I—''

''You expect us to believe that?'' Todd asked, sarcasm dripping from his words. ''Jake Barr would never have allowed a reporter into his confidence. He would never have trusted such a person with the inner workings of the Well.''

Others began to murmur agreement angrily.

''But he did,'' Dawn said. ''Do you really think so little of his intelligence that you don't think he knew who I was? Of course he did! I never fooled him for a minute.'' She turned to Laurie. ''Remember when he left me out in the woods and sent you to find me?''

''Yes.''

''He was checking on me then. He hunted me down through the Internet, found my listing at Georgetown and discovered I *also* wrote articles for the *Times*. He let me in knowing all about me.''

''So you say,'' Todd declared. ''I don't believe a word of it myself.''

It was clear from their expressions of confusion and concern, however, that the others weren't so sure.

Dawn plunged on, telling as much of the truth as she could without giving away what was going on now. ''Jake wanted me to keep my reporter's ears and eyes open to see if I could help him track down whoever was responsible for the mysterious happenings around here. He asked me to do that before the smoke bomb went off in the elevator. It became more urgent after that, of course. And once he was hurt, an accident, as you all know, he really needed my assistance. He asked for it himself.''

"You didn't help him," Todd yelled. "You just led him out into a trap."

"Look, Todd. I understand you're upset. Everyone is." Dawn sat down. "But I did not put Jake's arm into that animal trap. How could I? I wasn't even with him when it happened. I didn't ask for this job. He begged me to take it, and now your colleagues are asking me to stay on. I suggest you consider cooling off and figuring out how you can help us all. Unless you want to be part of our pack of problems, that is."

Todd looked around. "What's that supposed to mean?" he asked.

"What do you think, Todd?" Laurie said. "It means that if we're going to get through this time of crisis, we have to work together, not against one another. If Dawn were set to blow the whistle on us, don't you think she would have taken the chance she had to get away? She could easily have left when she went to Francisville. She had no contract, no legal obligation. Instead, she came back here and is willing to help."

Todd scowled but remained silent.

"Come on, Todd," Larry said. "Get with the program. We've got too good a thing here to let it go just because we don't have the guts to fight and work together now that we're on our own. Have you forgotten everything Jake tried to teach you through life here at the Well?"

Dawn smiled. "You know, you've always been on your own, people. Jake just set up symbols so you had a sense of security."

Laurie nodded, clearly understanding. "The fort. His presence. The secrecy of Deep Lab."

"That's right. There's nothing mysterious about this place. Nothing sacred or special. He may be a genius, but he's hardly the only one here. The Well provided a home where you could feel safe. It enabled you to focus and by doing that, you have all managed to overcome whatever it was that drove you here in the first place."

Mabel started to cry. "But Jake built it. We owe it to him now to keep it going."

There were loud comments of consent.

"Dawn, if he trusted you enough to let you be with Sophie like he did, then, by golly, he must have known your heart was in the right place," Larry said. "So I say, even if you are a reporter and do write about us, you're the best person to take Jake's place."

"I can never take his place," Dawn said somberly. "But I can do what I think he'd do now."

"What's that?"

"Get back to the work at hand. With all the trouble and the weather, too much has piled up. I'll ask you all to go on doing your work. Ask you to keep me posted on your projects. And most important, ask you to notify me if you see or hear anything out of the ordinary."

"The troubles aren't over, are they?" Laurie asked.

"No," Dawn replied. "I doubt it. A great deal depends on every single one of us remaining alert. Please, pass the word."

"We will!" came the collective pledge.

"Okay. We've made an agreement. Now I've got to get some work done or all the agreements in the world won't get us back up and running. The snow delayed some of our shipments, and I have a ton of paperwork to deal with."

"Thanks, Dawn," Laurie said. "I speak for all of us."

Dawn shook hands with them all as they filed out of her office. Only Todd passed by with a mere nod. Dawn thought she understood why he was angry. She hadn't been square with them about the magazine until now. Todd had a right to be upset.

But she also had to consider the possibility that he had a different agenda. He might have deliberately intended to get her out of the way in order to keep things upset and nonfunctional until the Well was finally finished as a viable economic unit. Interesting thought. She needed to talk to Jake about this development.

Too many items of business needed her attention immediately, however. Jake might be concerned when she didn't show up for a while. But he would understand once she explained things to him. She stayed at the desk until long after dark. Mabel's kitchen helper brought in some dinner, and Dawn ate part of it, intending to take the rest to Jake when she finally went home.

She was almost ready to pack it in when the phone rang, shrilling, making her jump. She picked up the receiver and started to say hello.

"You've been warned, bitch," the familiar female voice declared. "Now it's too late. You get to die too."

The caller hung up.

Gingerly Dawn replaced the receiver. Tingles of alarm ran through her. She got up and went down the hall to Sam's office.

The door was open. He wasn't there.

Somewhere in the building, a door slammed shut.

Footsteps in the hallway. Behind her.

"Sam?" she said. "Is that you?"

No answer.

She turned in the doorway and looked down the hall. No sign of anyone.

"Hello?" She held her breath, listening.

Nothing.

A growing sense of fear gripped her. She went back out into the hallway and hurried to the main room.

It was empty. No one in the dining room or kitchen either. A low fire burned in the hearth. A few coffee cups and glasses sat around on the tables, some half-full, some empty. As if everyone had left in haste, not bothering to clean up after themselves.

"Hello?" Dawn called out once more. "Anyone here?"

Silence.

She went to the entrance and looked out into the night. People were walking on the paths. Okay, signs of normal life. Her heart was racing, but she was sure she was overreacting. They had all gone out, but not disappeared. She went back to Sam's office and found a note on his desk that she had overlooked. Relief filled her.

He was at a meeting over in the auditorium. The note explained the absence of people here. After visiting Dawn, the delegation, minus Todd, had gone to Sam and requested a meeting with him. Rather than disturb her again, since it had been apparent she was quite busy, Sam had left the note to inform her of the gathering, told her not to worry, but to get home and get some rest.

Good advice. Dawn returned to her office and started to pack up the food for Jake. He'd be hungry by now.

Then she stopped.

Had she left the office door open when she'd gone to find Sam?

Had the plastic container of food been at the same place on her desk?

She remembered the sounds of footsteps. Remembered the poisoned muffin. The telephoned threat. She sniffed the contents of the container. The smell was unwholesome and noxious. She gagged.

The food had been tampered with!

SAM SEALED the box of food and made a few notes on the outside of the wrapper. "Chain of evidence," he explained. "If this stuff has been poisoned, we want clear documentation of who had access to it. My toxicology people will get at it tomorrow."

"If I hadn't been on the alert because of the phone threat and wondering where everyone had gone, I might not have bothered giving it a sniff," Dawn said, still shaken by the close call. They were back in Sam's office. As soon as she'd recovered from the shock, she'd gone to the auditorium to get Sam. The meeting was over, and he'd come immediately when he'd seen the look on her face and heard her say there was a problem.

"Yeah." Sam set the box on his desk. "Tomorrow you're out of here."

"No, I'm not."

"You want to end up in the hospital too? Or on a slab at the morgue?" The cop glared at her. "You're not going to do anyone any good if you're hurt or dead."

"I'll be careful," she said, thinking she had protection he knew nothing about. "Don't worry."

"I'm not worried. I'm telling you..."

"I'll go by the kennel and get Jake's dogs tonight," she said. "No one will get near me with them around."

"Dogs aren't cops with guns," Sam said. "I'll come over and stay in the kid's bedroom."

"No!" Dawn thought quickly. "Really, Sam. I appreciate it, but it'll blow your cover if you do. The dogs will guard me, be certain of it. And I can yell if anything goes wrong. The cabins aren't that far apart that someone won't hear me."

"I don't like it." Sam sat down. "But you're right. People are alert and looking for trouble now. Several of them mentioned hearing odd things today. Seeing shadows and catching glimpses of lurking figures out of the corners of their eyes. They're all jumpy as hell. Good thing no one's armed!"

"True," she replied, thinking of Jake's rifle.

Thinking of Jake. Suddenly the impact of what had happened hit her. She needed to see him and have him hold her tight against the fear she felt.

Needed... needed him!

She hurried to the kennel and found Johnny. The vet was happy to release the Labradors to her care.

"They've been pining," he said. "Without Jake..." He sighed and shook his head. "Dogs know."

"They'll be all right," Dawn assured him. "They're going home."

"It won't be the same," the big man said, clearly upset. "They really loved him."

It took a lot of control not to give Johnny some sort of signal that the dogs would be fine—they were going to see Jake in a just a few minutes. But Dawn kept quiet and led the animals outside. Onyx attached himself to her and limped along, his injured leg not fully functional yet. The other two raced ahead and waited patiently at the door of the cabin for her to arrive and let them in.

Which didn't make any sense. Dawn took the steps up to the porch. If Jake was inside, wouldn't they sense it? Why weren't his pets clawing at the door? Why weren't they barking and yelping in greeting?

She opened the door. The three dogs rushed in and sniffed around, whining deep in their throats.

The cabin was empty.

Jake was gone.

CHAPTER SIXTEEN

"JAKE?" Dawn called his name softly so no one passing by the cabin would hear her. She stepped out the kitchen door, then back out the front door and whispered his name.

Nothing. The dogs whined and trotted around inside then outside, following his scent with their noses to the ground, but stopping a few yards away from the cabin, puzzled and frustrated, obviously having lost the trail.

Pearl raised her muzzle to the moon and howled.

"I know how you feel, girl," Dawn said. Then she called them all back inside. Her worries lasted until she went into Sophie's room and saw that the child's computer had been left on. A screen saver roamed the monitor. It was a design of red hearts that floated on a blue background. Down in the corner was a little flashing icon. She picked up the mouse and clicked on the picture.

A message formed. "Gone to do battle. Plan to win. Will you stay here with me when this is over?"

"Yes," Dawn whispered. "I love you, Jake. Please, please be careful and come back to me."

She slept fitfully that night, her dreams dark and full of foreboding.

THE NEXT DAY it seemed as if the Well would return to normal. As normal as things could be without Jake. Ginny Reynolds came back with the false report that it was only a matter of time before Jake passed away. By now, however, people had come to terms with the loss and were working through their grief. Dawn was uncomfortable being part of the deception, but not as uneasy as Ginny. The doctor met with her shortly after her return. They huddled in Ginny's office and spoke in whispers.

"It's not going to be long before someone figures out that the guy in the hospital bed is not Jake," Ginny declared. "The cops are going to be furious, you know. It was a crazy idea to substitute Zeke Barr. He's enjoying himself far too much and is thinking about chasing the nurses. How long does this charade have to go on?"

"Jake's around here somewhere," Dawn assured her. "He left sometime yesterday and hasn't checked back with me, so I have to believe he's on the trail."

"Hmmph," the doctor said. "He's on something all right. But it isn't good sense, if you ask me. I have a bad feeling about all this."

Dawn tried not to let that bother her. She had enough of her own feelings to deal with.

But that night other things began to happen. Two of the locals who worked as kitchen staff started talking about ghosts, and the rumor spread that a "haint" was visiting the Well. It didn't take long before the restless spirit became Jake's, and three more people swore that they'd seen his shade wandering in the forest just at the edge of the open space of the fort grounds the previous night. Never mind that he wasn't reported dead yet. His spirit was definitely abroad, and people were nervous. Dawn tried to study the others to see if she could tell who was guilty and who was just afraid. But she could come to no conclusions. It was going to be up to Jake to ferret out the traitors at the Well.

No one but Jake owned a gun, but several people had baseball bats, which they'd begun to carry. A watch was set up, and around midnight someone on patrol screamed loud enough to send terror through everyone. Although the screamer turned out to have been started by nothing more supernatural than a wily raccoon on the make for fresh garbage, the incident still left many of the residents extremely shaken and even more nervous.

By morning, Sam Groner, alarmed by the gossip and rumors of phantom sightings, checked with his colleagues in Francisville. They investigated, discovered the switch and made Cousin Zeke's presence known to the cop. Sam cornered Dawn and extracted a confession.

"Where is he? Why did he do this? Our agreement was for him to stay put, to stay safe until I'd done my work here. What the hell is he up to, and, come to think of it, why didn't you tell me?" Sam raged.

"Calm down, Sam. Listen to me. Jake said he couldn't just lie there doing nothing when he was convinced the attack would not be made on him, but would come here instead," she explained to the furious cop. "You didn't buy into his theory about the Well being the next target, so he went to work on his own. There's certainly no ghost out there. It's Jake in the flesh."

"When I get my hands on him again, he'll wish he was a ghost," Sam swore. Then he was off to repair official fences torn down by Jake's actions. He was so angry that he left Dawn to make excuses for his abrupt departure.

She did so, concocting a plausible tale about his having to deal with his superiors at the insurance company. She also told everyone that she was going to make a run to her apartment in Wilmont later in the day to get some necessary personal things, since she intended to stay at the Well for some time.

For far too long, she had been wearing borrowed clothing, and she was more than ready to get back into her own things. The snow was almost gone now, leaving the roads perfectly clear. Temperatures had returned to balmy Indian summer weather, and the countryside was glowing with autumn beauty. That afternoon seemed a perfect time for a drive.

The ground was extremely muddy, thanks to the melted snow. Dawn borrowed waterproof boots from the storeroom and slogged out to her Saab. The sturdy little car's engine turned over the first time she cranked the key.

She drove slowly through the woods out to the dirt road, hoping, unreasonably, that Jake would appear. But she saw no sign of him, and so she made her way to the county road, mud spraying as she went. Once on the harder surface, she sped up, anxious to get her belongings and return to the Well as soon as possible.

It wasn't just because she felt the responsibility to reassure the others either. In a short time, because of Jake, the Well had come to feel more like home than her apartment ever could.

Home. Jake. And Sophie. Would they get through this and have a chance at a life together? She drove a little faster, willing the trip to pass quickly so that she could return to her new home, her new dreams.

The county road led down the mountainside, and on the second hairpin turn, she noticed her brakes were soggy. She tried to slow down, concerned that the accumulation of mud might have caused some trouble. Her foot went almost to the floor when she pressed the brake. The Saab kept gaining speed.

On the next turn, she was sure mud had nothing to do with her problem. The brakes refused to catch at all, and she barely made the turn. Heart pounding and icy sweat running down her sides, Dawn knew she couldn't risk another turn. Her only hope was to force the little car into a complete turnabout. She gripped the steering wheel with all her might, rammed the gearshift down as low as it would go and whipped the Saab in a one-eighty, praying she'd survive.

The tires howled, the gears ground and the car fishtailed on the narrow road. The vehicle slowed, almost stopping, reversed direction and for a glorious second, Dawn thought she'd succeeded.

But then the left rear wheel caught on the softened shoulder. Dawn felt the pull of gravity as the vehicle teetered, threatening to roll backward. She downgeared again, rammed the gas to the floor and prayed even harder. The entire car shook with the strain, the tires dug for purchase and she leaned forward, willing a leap to safety. Willing to defeat gravity.

It didn't happen. Gravity won. The sickening sensation of falling overtook her. The car slowly gave up, slipping backward. She cried out loud in despair.

Then, out of the corner of her eye, she saw a large rock on the side of the road, a few feet behind her. Gritting her teeth, she twisted the steering wheel firmly to the left. The car rolled to the left and came to an abrupt stop, right up against the rock. Dawn was thrown hard against the steering wheel and then back against the headrest. The last conscious thought she had was to wonder why her seat belt hadn't worked.

JAKE STARED at the computer screen and swore. Holed up in the cave during the day, he had managed to rig up the telephone line and modem and to hack into the computer at the Francisville safe house. The task had been relatively easy, since he remembered the phone number there and had spoken to Sophie about the computer system used by the cops. Once in, he had then downloaded the letter Sophie had written to her mother.

There had been a reply. A terrifying one. In no uncertain terms Joyce had ordered Sophie to leave the Well. To get away no matter how she had to do it. Even if she had to walk out by herself. Just get away from the Well and her father. Joyce had told her to go to her grandparents' house. She would meet her there in three days.

Something terrible was going to happen. Something so dangerous that Joyce wanted her daughter far away. And she'd inadvertently given Jake the timetable for disaster. Within three days of when the letter had been written.

Two of those days had passed. That left today.

Another bomb? Possibly. This time not just smoke.

He couldn't take any chances. He had to alert everyone and evacuate the place as soon as possible. Even if that played right into his enemies' hands. A total evacuation would leave the Well unprotected. Showing up in person to give the evacuation order could get him killed.

But it had to be done. He'd called Dawn at his office, but had received no answer. He'd tried calling the police to see if he could reach Sam, only to be treated as if he were a crank. Officially, Dr. Jacob Barr was hospitalized and near death. He hadn't tried again. There wasn't time. For all he knew, the disaster was already in progress.

He shut down the system and stepped outside. Night was coming on. He barely had time to get to the fort before dark. Climbing down the rocks to the trail, he started out first at a fast walk and then at a steady running pace that brought him within sight of the wooden palisades just as twilight settled over the countryside.

The first inhabitants of the Well who saw him barked with delirious joy. The next few screamed in terror.

Jake gasped for breath as his three dogs jumped all over him. While he petted the animals, he waved and smiled at the two men who approached carefully, baseball bats at the ready. "It's really me," he called out. "I'm not sick, not dead, not..."

"Not a ghost?" one of them asked.

"No!" Jake signaled the dogs to follow and made his way into the fort. "Not by a long shot. But we all may be if we don't get out of here. Sound the alarm. I want everyone gathered in the central area immediately. Have them bring pets, any living thing, and wear warm clothes. Nothing else. Don't even try to shut down any projects or production."

The men hastened to obey.

The first person to come running was Farley. "Oh my God!" he cried. "I don't believe it! Yes! Jake, it is you! You are alive! I didn't believe them when they told me you're here and alive."

"Where's Dawn?" Jake asked.

"She went to Wilmont to get her stuff. And that Sam guy took off for—"

"Sam's a cop," Jake said. "We'll call both of them when we get back to the cave."

"This is serious, isn't it?" Farley asked, sobering quickly.

"Dead serious."

"Tell me what to do."

Jake did.

Ten minutes later, eighty-nine Well personnel stood on the muddy ground at the center of the fort and listened to the man they'd thought they'd never see again. Joy mixed with anxiety. Then fear as Jake explained why he had played dead and why he'd returned now.

"I have good reason to believe we're all in grave danger," Jake said, raising his voice so that everyone could hear. "I don't have time to explain anything. But I'm asking you to trust me with your lives."

"We did that a long time ago," Farley shouted. "What do you want us to do?"

"Leave here," Jake replied. "It'll be crowded in the cave, but we can all stay there overnight. There are chambers beyond the one I've used. It won't be comfortable, but it will be dry, relatively warm and safe. In the morning, we can trek to Fairway and..." He paused. "Some of you are missing. Who?"

"Dawn went to her apartment to get her stuff," Laurie said, repeating Farley's information. "We thought she'd be back before dark, but she's the only one who—"

"Joan and Todd aren't here," Johnny said. The vet had his hands full with three horses and a variety of smaller animals. "Fact is, when I think about it, I haven't seen either of 'em for a good while."

Joan and Todd. Jake repeated the names to himself. Could Todd be Joan's accomplice? It made some kind of sick sense. The chemist had never seemed content with the way Jake handled Well business. His ambition and greed had been simmering near the surface for months, now that Jake thought about it.

"I'm sure they're safe," he said, not wanting to make public his suspicions. "Farley, you know the way. Take my dogs and lead everyone to the cave."

"Aren't you coming?"

"Not right away. I have some things to attend to. I want to find out where Dawn is. I'll wait until I know she's aware of what's going on and won't try to return here. Don't worry. I'm not going to be foolhardy or stupid. I'll join you soon."

"What're you going to do?" Laurie asked.

"Shut the fort gate, so that if someone gets over the forest gate, he or she won't wander into the fort without knowing the danger. I'll post a notice on the gate."

"But what about...?"

"We'll deal with all the questions later," Jake said. "For now, I need to know you're all safe. Go!"

When the last person was out of the gate, Jake shut
it from the inside. Then he turned and looked at the
Well. A cold fury rose within him. *The Well*. People
were going to try to destroy it. People who he had
known and trusted. This was his! Damn it all, he'd
built it from the empty forest, and it was his, every log
of it!

How were they planning to take it from him?

More important, how could he prevent them from
succeeding?

"YOU'RE SURE this is where you want me to let you
off, lady?" the old mountaineer asked Dawn as they
pulled up to the back gate. "You had a pretty bad
shock back there, and it's getting dark."

"This is fine," Dawn replied. "I'll walk. In this
heavy truck without front-wheel drive, you'd get
bogged down in the mud in no time. It's not too far."
Her head hurt and her entire body ached from the
impact, but all her instincts screamed at her to get
back to the Well. Her brakes hadn't failed of their own
accord. Someone had tampered with them and with
her seat belt. Someone at the Well.

A passing truck driver had rescued her, opening the
car door and helping her into his pickup. A shot of
moonshine whiskey down her throat had brought her
choking and gasping to full consciousness. Once he'd
seen she didn't have any broken bones or bad cuts—
her injuries were limited to being bruised and shaken
up—the old man had offered to take her wherever she
wanted.

She wanted to go to the Well. But to get there, she
was going to have to trek through the woods in the

dark. She got out of the truck and opened the gate. The effort of moving the wood and metal barrier almost made her pass out.

"Now you look here, young lady," the truck driver said. "You ain't in no kinda shape to be going off in these woods alone. I'm gonna park here and go with you. 'Til you get where you're goin' anyhow. See that you're safe."

"No need. Really. If you'll loan me a flashlight, that'll be enough."

"Dang stubborn wimmin." The driver got out and slammed the pickup door. From the truck bed he retrieved two long objects. One was a flashlight.

The other was a rifle.

"Missy," he said, "you gotta be one o' them young, liberated ladies, thinking you can go trottin' off in the forest alone and unarmed like you are, and after an accident, to boot. But let me tell you, the folks at that fort down there ain't likely to take kindly to any stranger showin' up. They got troubles."

"I know. I'm not a stranger."

The man squinted, studying her from under bushy gray eyebrows. "You ain't? I ain't seen you there."

Dawn regarded him more closely. "And when have you been at the Well, sir? By the way, I didn't get your name."

"Augustus Yeates. At your service. And I, uh, work the land all 'round that there fort. Me'n Jake Barr, we go back a long ways. Knowed his grandpappy, I did."

"You work the land?" Dawn looked in the back of the truck and saw the traps. "You're the poacher!"

Augustus had the grace to look embarrassed. "No, I ain't. Well, I guess I am . . . legally. I heard tell 'bout

Jake gettin' hisself caught in one o' my traps, and I got to tell you I feel right badly 'bout that, I do. But I consider it my right t'make my livin' like my ancestors done. Trappin' for furs and food. Don't mean no harm to nobody by it."

"Well, Mr. Yeates, I can't get angry with you now. You rescued me. Thank you. And I would appreciate your helping me get to the Well. I think the people there are in danger, and I *know* Jake is. Since you owe him, you can help me."

"Why, goodness me." Augustus grinned. "You're his serious woman, ain't you?"

The words sounded good to Dawn. Jake's serious woman. She smiled at the old man. "My name's Dawn Sutton. Come on, Mr. Yeates. Let's go."

"Call me Gus, Miss Sutton," Gus said. "Ever'-body else does."

And with that, they set off for the Well.

AFTER TRYING unsuccessfully to reach Dawn at her apartment, Jake left a message for Sam Groner and then went to Todd's office in the planning building to look for clues. Todd and Joan. He could see the two of them working as a team, although why they had chosen to do so was a mystery to him.

With a little luck, he'd get a chance to ask them.

Todd's office proved to be fertile ground. The door had been locked. Jake kicked it in. No time for niceties. A quick search revealed a number of damning items, including letters from Tony Edwards, schematics of the entire fort layout and two vials of the drug used to poison him. Not smart of Todd. Unless he knew the letters and vials would be destroyed along with everything else in the fort.

Jake sat down and turned on Todd's computer. He started to push aside some scratch paper lying on the desk, but something stopped him. He picked up a piece of paper that lay on the bottom of the pile. He read it.

And his blood seemed to freeze in his veins.

Inscribed on the page was a chemical formula. Underneath was a penciled note that read:

Use this mixture in the main matrix, Todd. *Do not* change the catalyst, or the potion will become deadly instead of just toxic. Once you load it into the processor, get yourself and Joan out of there. We'll get Sophie. You know where to meet us. You'll receive your payment then. I don't want my child to be harmed, and I don't want you two to get caught. All I want is what's due me.

No signature.

Jake didn't need one. This was Joyce's handwriting.

But the marks made on the side of the page weren't Joyce's. Jake studied the figures.

He grew colder.

They'd altered the original formula just enough. Who had done this? Someone with a more scientific mind than either Joyce or Todd. Tony? Whatever was cooking somewhere on the grounds of the Well was an evil brew of death and destruction!

He had to find it. Had to stop it. If enough of it was being used, it would produce enough toxic gas to kill every living thing within a radius of several miles.

It would destroy the people sheltering in the cave.

Jake stared at the piece of paper. There *had* to be a way to neutralize the brew. He pushed back the chair and stood up, thinking hard. There was a possibility—a long shot, admittedly. But maybe if one added . . . Jake heard a sound behind him; he turned around.

And looked at the business end of a handgun.

"Hello, Jake," his ex-wife said. "Hope you're not in a hurry. I have only one question to ask you. Where's Sophie?"

DAWN AND GUS reached the fort just as the moon rose over the tops of the pine trees. Dawn had trouble keeping up with the old man's surprisingly fast pace. Her head and chest hurt. But she was determined. Too much depended on their reaching the Well quickly for her to allow herself to falter.

But the moon showed her something odd. "The entrance gate's closed," she said. "That's unusual. Most of the time it stays open in case anyone wants to take a walk in the woods."

"Don't want no visitors tonight maybe," Gus said. "Let's knock."

They started across the open space.

"No." Dawn put out her arm, stopping him. "Let's not get too close yet. Listen."

Gus halted and was quiet. "Don't hear nothin'," he said after a minute.

"That's right." Dawn sniffed the night air. "And do you smell that?"

Gus snorted. "Smell the pine trees. The mud. That's about all."

"There's something else. Something... Gus, there's always a little noise coming from the Well. People slamming doors, moving around, talking, dogs barking, the machinery in the back. I don't hear a thing. And that smell..." She sniffed again. "It's *wrong*."

"So you don't wanna knock?"

"I don't know what I want. I just know things aren't right." She hesitated. "But we have to go in and see."

"There's a back way."

"No there's not."

"Yep. Ain't a real entrance, but you kin get in if you wanna."

She regarded him. "Okay, Gus. Take me to this secret entrance of yours."

"This here's serious business, this thing you're worryin' about? Harmful stuff?"

"Yes, it is."

"Okay, miss. Come on." He turned away from the front gate and led her along the side of the fort, keeping to the shadow cast by the palisades. After a while he came to a place where the logs didn't quite join. The gap was narrow, but passable. "Skinny in," he said. "You're a little woman. You kin make it."

"Come here often, do you?" Dawn asked as she squeezed through.

"Now 'n then," Gus confessed. "Don't do nothin'. Just look 'round when I'm runnin' my trap lines."

"I see."

"Kinda outta habit, I guess," he added, moving through the opening with ease. "See, 'fore young Jake built this here place, the land was mine to roam. So I figure even though he put up this stockade, the ground's still mine."

Dawn had no reply to that sort of logic.

Instead, she looked around. The fort seemed deserted.

"Ain't nobody here," Gus declared.

"I think you're right," Dawn said. "And I'm very much afraid that's a bad sign." She sniffed the air again. The smell was stronger and nearer.

"Think we oughta leave," Gus said.

"Let's just look around a little first."

"Don't think that's such a good idear."

"Then you leave." Dawn moved away from the palisades wall. She sniffed again and began to follow the smell.

"Dang stubborn wimmin," Gus repeated. He hesitated, then set out after her.

Not surprisingly, the odor led Dawn to the production building. She was about to open the door when movement from across the way caught her eye. Obeying an instinct deeper than thought, she shrank back into the shadows. Behind her, Gus did the same.

Two people walked out of the planning building and made their way along the walkway toward the production building. The moonlight spotted them.

It was Jake and a strange woman. He walked in front with his right hand in the air. His left arm was still in a sling and cast.

The woman had a gun.

Dawn tensed. She heard Gus's intake of breath and the click of metal as he moved his rifle. She turned and mouthed, "Wait." Gus nodded.

The pair came closer, and Dawn saw that the woman had been crying. Jake looked grim.

"All you have to do is tell me where you hid her and I'll let you go," Dawn heard the woman say. "I don't want to hurt you." She seemed to be still struggling against tears.

Dawn suppressed a gasp of shock. It was the voice on the telephone. Joyce Barr!

"I didn't hide her. I don't know where she is," Jake replied, his tone and manner also indicating great distress. "I told you! She was at my folks'. Why she left or where she is, is as much a mystery to me as it is to you. And if you had any sense, Joyce, you'd let me go so I can find her!" He turned and faced his ex-wife. "Why won't you listen? I can't believe you'd let yourself get involved with murder. Joyce, we once loved each other. Don't you remember?"

Joyce lost control. "Shut up! Shut up, or I swear I'll shoot you where you stand, you bastard!" She started crying and the gun in her hand pointed right at Jake's heart.

"Think of Sophie, Joyce. Listen to me . . ."

"Shut up!" she screamed, sobbing, the gun wobbling in her grip.

Dawn realized that the woman was seconds from shooting Jake.

A hand touched Dawn's shoulder.

Dawn looked back at Gus. He lifted his rifle and raised one eyebrow, asking permission.

Dawn shook her head.

Gus nodded. He stooped and set the rifle down. Then he picked up a fist-size stone.

Taking careful aim, Gus threw the rock.

Joyce screamed. The missile hit the target and the gun flew out of her hand. She stumbled, falling off the walkway and sprawling in the mud. Jake kicked the gun away, then turned to face the shadows, ready to fight. "Who's there?" he demanded.

"Us, Jake." Dawn stepped out into the moonlight.

"Dawn!" Jake's expression softened. "What're you...?" He started to reach out for her. Then he saw the old man and drew back. "Hello, Gus Yeates," he said dryly. "It's been a long time."

"'Deed it has, young Jake Barr," Gus declared. "Got you a bit o' wimmin trouble, seems t'me."

"Hell of a lot more than that," Jake said. "Gus, thank you for saving my life." He indicated Joyce, who still lay, sobbing, on the wet ground. "Would you please keep that woman under guard. I have to deal with an emergency inside this building." He pointed to production.

"Is it what I'm smelling?" Dawn asked.

"It smells?"

Dawn was puzzled until she recalled that most people who worked here had lost their sense of smell. "Yes," she told Jake. "Something awful."

"Come with me," Jake said. "I need you."

They went inside, and Dawn started to gag and choke. Jake's nose wrinkled, but it didn't bother him as much. "Can you tell where it is?" he asked.

"I don't know." Dawn covered her face with her hands. "It's too pervasive!"

"It's also extremely deadly," Jake said. "I've got to find it and neutralize it. Or we're all going to die."

Dawn took her hands away from her nose and began to hunt. She found the source of the odor quickly.

The poison was in a huge vat set directly under a ventilating shaft. Her nasal passages burning and her eyes streaming tears, she helped Jake uncover the mess and stood to one side as he gingerly added a series of chemical ingredients taken from a storage cabinet nearby. That done, he signaled her to his side.

"I'm going to mix it now," he said, his voice rasping in his throat from the fumes. "If I've miscalculated..."

"Just do it," she said. "I love you."

He looked at her then, and his eyes told her everything she needed to know. No kiss, just a touch of his lips to hers.

Then Jake pushed a button set on the side of the vat, and machinery started moving.

CHAPTER SEVENTEEN

NOTHING HAPPENED. If anything, the odor got worse. Dawn sneezed vigorously and ran over to the wall where the gas masks were hung. She grabbed two.

Jake stood by the vat, staring at the churning, smoldering contents, his face a picture of consternation and anger. "I put in all the correct ingredients. It should have shut down the process," he said. "I don't know what to do now."

Dawn handed him a mask. "Put this on," she said, gasping. She slid hers over her face.

Jake held the mask. He didn't put it on. "I just can't figure it out. What else needs . . ."

The door opened, and Gus entered, pulling Joyce with him. "Wooeee," the old man declared. "Smells like a polecat died in here!"

"Gus, get out," Jake said. "Get out and run as fast as you can. This stuff's toxic."

"I know that," Gus said, pushing Joyce forward. "Lady here says she knows how t'make it quit."

Dawn slipped off her mask. "Do you?" she asked. "Mrs. Barr, if you'll do that, I know things will go much easier for you with the police."

"They made me do it." Joyce started to sob. Words tumbled from her. "Tony made me. He and Todd Beckman were old classmates and they schemed together to go beyond anything I'd planned. I just wanted to ruin Jake's business. To get even for his being so successful after leaving me. I hate him for that, but not enough for murder. Tony changed the formula. It was his idea to kill people. I never wanted to hurt anyone.''

''Then help us, Joyce,'' Dawn said firmly. ''They can't make you do anything now.''

''Joyce...'' Jake spoke slowly as if to a child. ''Listen to me carefully. We don't know where Sophie is. If this matrix goes gaseous, which I think it will in a few minutes, not only are we all dead, but Sophie may be in the path of the toxic cloud. The gas will be sucked right out into the night by the ventilating system. I don't have time to shut it down, and even if I did, I don't know if it would stop the gas from escaping and spreading. From here, it could cover the entire county. No telling how many could die. Come on. Help me. What did I leave out?''

''What did you put in?'' Joyce seemed to pull herself together.

Jake told her. Joyce nodded and began to recite a list of chemical compounds. As she spoke, Jake's expression took on a look of understanding. He went to a cupboard and took out more containers. Opening them, he began to measure and dump ingredients into the odoriferous stew. Once more he pressed the button for the mixing system to start.

Dawn held her breath, crossed her fingers and prayed.

Five minutes later the acrid smell was much weaker and a pleasant, floral fragrance was beginning to replace it. Jake had succeeded!

Joyce stood still, expressionless, like a person in a trance.

Gus grinned. "Looks like you done the job, Jake Barr," he said. "Smells right purty in here."

Jake put his arm around Dawn's shoulders. "We're safe now," he said. "The process has to continue for a while, but it's stable. In an hour it'll be nothing more dangerous than a vatful of baby oil. Let's go outside."

The night air was clean and cold. Joyce started to shiver, her body shaking and her eyes blank. Dawn could see the woman needed medical attention. "Has everyone left?" Dawn asked Jake. "Including Ginny?"

"They all went to shelter in the cave," Jake said. He slipped off his jacket and put it around Joyce's shoulders. He held the woman's face and looked into her blank eyes. He waved his good hand in front of her, but she didn't even blink. "Let's take her over to the infirmary. From there we can contact Ginny on the cellular phone. With her help maybe we can get Joyce back to normal and get some sense out of her. I have to know if she has any idea where Sophie might have—"

A ratcheting, roaring noise from the sky above cut him off. Dawn looked up to see a helicopter angling over the fort, moving lower, easing down to land in the central area. The overhead blades made a *whup-whupping* sound as the machine settled on the muddy ground.

Sam Groner got out. Ducking his head, he ran through the mud until he reached them. "Here you are! You had an accident. Your car was found squeezed against a rock like a concertina,'' he yelled at Dawn. ''When we looked, there was no body, so we figured you crawled out and walked for help. What the hell were you thinking of, coming back here?''

''Jake, of course,'' Dawn shouted in reply. ''And I'm fine except for a headache. Someone tampered with my brakes.'' She indicated Gus. ''This gentleman came along and rescued me.''

''What's this? Tampered with your brakes? An accident?'' Jake asked, astonished. He encircled Dawn with his uninjured arm. ''You didn't say anything about your car! Or about Gus's rescuing you!''

''There wasn't exactly time,'' she replied. ''I'll tell you all about it later.''

''Who's this?'' Sam asked, indicating the now-catatonic Joyce. ''Something going on I ought to know about?''

''Did you check on Sophie?'' Jake yelled. ''Joyce says she's not at my folks' place.''

''Well, like father, like daughter, I suppose. You weren't in the hospital like you were supposed to be! And you were supposed to have stayed here,'' Sam declared, turning to Dawn. ''Don't any of you people do what you're told to?''

''Sophie was supposed to wait for Joyce in Fairway,'' Jake persisted, ignoring Sam's belligerent attitude. ''She's not there, Joyce says. Joyce and Tony were to pick her up, then meet Joan and Todd for their getaway. But Sophie wasn't there so Tony went on to find the other two, and Joyce came back, hoping Sophie had come here. She took a terrible risk herself, and she helped us stop a disaster.''

''What kind of disaster?'' Sam looked skeptical.

"Sam, listen to him!" Dawn entreated. "Jake and Mrs. Barr just saved all our lives by putting a stop to a plan to cause a poisonous gas to escape from one of the vats in the production building. And now three of her coconspirators are missing. If Sophie's gone, she might be with them."

Sam stared. "Poison gas?"

"Yes. And if they'd succeeded, the countryside for miles around could have been affected."

Sam swore.

"Exactly," Jake said.

"Where the hell's everyone else?" Sam asked.

"They're in a natural cave a few miles from here." Jake explained. "Dawn knows where it is. You can land that helicopter on a flat area nearby. Tell the Well residents it's all right to come home. And you'd better have Ginny take a look at Joyce. She seems to be in shock." He looked at Dawn. "I don't believe there's much hope of it, but if she does come around, ask her what she knows about Sophie, please."

"What about you?" Dawn asked.

"I'm going to find Joan, Todd and Tony. And I'm going to find Sophie if she's out in the woods. I can follow the track Joan and Todd left." Jake looked at Gus. "How about it, old-timer? Care to join me in a hunting party?"

Gus grinned widely. "I'd surely like that, young'un. Make up fer some o' the trouble I caused you."

"We'll be doing some talking about that," Jake warned, lifting his injured arm. "The poaching's got to stop, Gus. But tonight I would appreciate your help."

"You got it," Gus replied.

"I don't understand," Sam said. "What's going on?"

Dawn indicated the helicopter. "Let's go for a ride, Sam," she said. "I think I can bring you up to speed in a few minutes." She turned to Jake. "I'll take charge of Joyce. Get her to Ginny," she said. "You find Sophie!"

"I will," he said. Then he pulled her in for a tight embrace.

No other words needed to be spoken between them.

AS THE HELICOPTER rose into the night sky, Jake turned to Gus. "I don't know where Joyce's boyfriend is, but the two people from here must have left the fort before I ordered the mass exodus. Tony might have been with them. They knew the poison gas was going to cover this area within a few hours, so they'd have been in a hurry to get to safety."

"Easy t'reckon," Gus said. "You plannin' t'go out unarmed?"

"No."

"Git your gear, then, young 'un. I'll wait."

A few minutes later, the two men emerged from the fort, dark shadows against the palisade walls. Both carried long rifles. Both moved so silently, they seemed more like ghosts than living men.

They walked slowly around the log walls, searching for signs. Soon they discovered the tracks of the prey they hunted. They set off, moving quickly across the moonlit landscape, rifles held ready. Jake managed with great effort to suppress his anger at the betrayal and his fear for Sophie and to settle himself into tracking and hunting mode. His emotions sank into cold purpose. All he knew now was the trail before him.

And the prey at the end of it.

Gus was an ideal companion, surprisingly. Without speech, they communicated, following the trail for several miles over a low range of hills then through open fields, stubbled with the remains of summer's harvest. The fleeing pair clearly intended trying to head for the nearest highway, Jake realized. But not knowing the country very well, they had accidently taken the wrong direction and were travelling deeper into Appalacia.

Toward the mountain pass that led to Fairway.

"I'M ALL RIGHT," Dawn said, waving Ginny away when the doctor tried to insist on examining her. "Take care of Joyce, Ginny. I've got to help Jake."

Ginny muttered something about stubborn people, shook her head and departed from the office.

"How the hell do you plan to do that?" Sam asked angrily. "He's out there in the woods somewhere, playing the Lone Ranger with old Gus as his sidekick."

"You and I have to go to Fairway," Dawn explained. "Find out who saw Sophie last and where she was. We can trace her from the town while Jake's out in the country."

"How? Neither one of us is any kind of tracker."

"No. But I've got Pearl and Jasper, ready to go, and I'm willing to bet some of Jake's relatives are more than a little competent in the woods."

Sam considered that. "Good point. Okay, let's see if you're right." he said, sounding less annoyed now.

She was.

She, the two older dogs and Sam arrived in Fairway thirty minutes later by police helicopter and were soon talking to Jake's parents in the Barr home. Sophie had apparently just walked away from safety there, and no one knew where she was. Mr. and Mrs. Barr were taut with concern about their granddaughter. They clearly blamed themselves for her being missing.

"She left the house about three hours ago," Joe Barr said. "Said she was going for a little walk to do some thinking. Not unusual for her to do that. Didn't start to worry till she'd been gone a full hour."

"She's a strong-minded child," Emily Barr explained. "We let her go out by herself because she asked to be alone. No one dreamed she'd be in any danger here. She promised she wouldn't go far."

"She wasn't in danger here," Sam reassured them. "But it looks like she took it into her head to go back to the Well and try to help her father." He didn't want to alarm the elderly couple more than necessary so he didn't elaborate.

"We must go after her. Is there someone here who could help us?" Dawn asked. "And we'll need something of Sophie's for Jake's dogs."

Emily fetched a sweater of Sophie's. Joe stood up and went over to the front door. "I was getting a search party up when you people showed," he said. "My brother, Lemuel, and I are the best trackers in the county. We were just about to set out." He opened the door and let out a piercing whistle. Dogs barked and howled. A tall lean older man jogged out of the darkness into the light, leading a pair of bloodhounds.

Once the four dogs established themselves with one another, the party set out into the night. Dawn wondered whether she should stay behind, thinking she might slow down the experienced trackers, but Joe insisted she join them.

"Jake's dogs know and trust you," he said. "And they'll be more likely to find Sophie than Lem's hounds, because they're motivated by loyalty and love. So you come along." For the first time that night Joe smiled. "I understand you're very important to my boy, so it's fitting you help find his child."

Dawn smiled at him in return, not quite certain how to reply. But she agreed to go. They set out into the night, the dogs straining at their leashes.

The trail was easy to follow, since Sophie wasn't trying to hide. She had set out on a direct line for the Well, moving over territory that must have been as familiar to her as the back of her hand, even in the darkness.

The silver moonlight gave some illumination to the path. Dawn felt her headache easing as they moved through the woods. The air was clean and fresh, the temperature relatively warm, and she was doing something that mattered greatly. She felt part of a team. It was a good feeling, even if the mission they were on was a desperate one.

In a short time the dogs all began to whine loudly.

"We're getting pretty close to her by the sound of 'em," Lemuel explained after telling his animals to hush up. "Ordinary thing to do would be set the dogs loose. But I don't want 'em running up to her and scaring her."

"Or alerting anyone else," Sam said darkly. He spoke softly so only Dawn could hear.

Dawn felt sick. "You really think Tony Edwards has her?"

"No way to tell until we find her and him," Sam said. "But the fact is we haven't located Edwards yet, so there's that chance."

"She's used to the wilderness, and she's small," Dawn said. "Maybe she could hide from him."

"Unless he indicated he had her father. He might lie to trick her into going with him."

Dawn felt worse. Sam was right. Sophie would take any chance to help her dad. They had to find her quickly. She ordered Pearl and Jasper to be silent, and they obeyed, although she could see the hair rising along their backbones. They knew their quarry was close.

The track led to the top of the low mountain to the south of Fairway. Then it passed over the rise and descended into a series of hills and meadows. The moon provided enough light for them to see clearly for a good distance. Suddenly Joe let out a soft gasp of dismay. Dawn stared and froze in her tracks.

Sophie was standing in the center of the wide meadow. She was not alone. A man Dawn did not recognize had a grip on her arm.

He also held a handgun, which he aimed casually at Sophie's small head.

Two other people were moving across the meadow toward them. Todd Beckman and Joan Dawson.

Pearl stared to growl deep in her chest. Jasper joined the menacing chorus. Dawn whispered them to silence. The Labs were quiet at her command. The two bloodhounds snuffled and chuffed with their noses, but didn't make another sound.

"Get down," Joe commanded. "They don't know we're up here."

The four crouched. Lem made a motion with his hand, and his dogs lay flat, ears forward, eyes on the scene below. Silent.

The slope of the hillside acted as a sound amplifier, allowing them to hear what was being said. Dawn watched as Todd and Joan hurried toward the man and child. Ignoring Sophie, they greeted the stranger effusively. Their voices and gestures indicated that they were frightened.

"We got lost," Todd said, panting for breath. "Took a wrong turn somewhere. We've all got to get out of here. That cloud from the Well will be slow, since there's no wind, but it's going to cover this ground eventually."

"Do you have our money?" Joan asked, her voice harsh on the night air, raspy as if she'd been drinking on the way.

"Where's Joyce?" the man asked.

"We don't know," Todd replied. "We left on schedule. Thought she was going to Fairway to join up with you."

"She did. But the kid was gone. Joyce got frantic and started looking all over town. I circled the woods and found Sophie walking toward you two idiots! Now I want to know where Joyce is."

"She's probably in jail," Sophie said, speaking with a firm tone. "Even if Daddy said—"

The stranger shook the little girl roughly. "Your daddy's dead, kid. Now shut up."

"He might not be," Joan said, her words slurred. "Some people said they saw him around the fort last night. Don't believe in ghosts, myself."

"But you heard the news. You gave him that poison. You—"

The man's words were cut off as Sophie launched herself at Joan. "You did it!" she screamed. "You put the stuff in the muffin I gave him!"

Joan batted her to the ground where she lay, stunned.

Dawn rose.

Sam grabbed her. "Don't!" he whispered urgently.

Pearl and Jasper stood up, watching Dawn and the action below, their dark heads turning, their eyes pleading for the order to attack.

The man pointed his gun at Joan. "Don't hurt her yet," he warned. "She's the key." He leaned over and helped Sophie to her feet. "Okay, kid. Time to tell the truth. Where's your mom, and is your dad really ready to kick the bucket?"

Sophie was silent.

The man shook her again. "Come on, Sophie. I'm not feeling patient tonight. I want the truth and I want it now."

"Go jump off a cliff!" Sophie told him. "And take these two creeps with you!"

The man lifted his left hand, ready to strike the child.

Dawn unhooked the dogs' leashes. They waited for her command. She could hear Sam swearing softly in frustration and anger. Lem loosened his dogs, but kept them at his feet. Joe raised his rifle.

"I mean it, Sophie," the man said. He hefted his gun. "One more chance or I'll—"

"Hey, Tony!" Jake's voice rang out across the moonlit meadow. "Antony Edwards! Here I am! Pick on someone your own size for a change."

Dawn looked. At the edge of the forest stood Jake and Gus. Much too far away to reach Sophie in time to save her from either a fist or a bullet. She didn't think Jake could shoot well anyway with his left arm still in the cast. He held his rifle awkwardly in his right hand, the butt resting against his hip.

But Gus, the poacher, stood behind Jake with the barrel of his long rifle resting on Jake's shoulder.

The three criminals said nothing. They seemed too startled by Jake's sudden appearance to react. Sophie didn't move, but Dawn could see the girl was tensed for action.

"Put the gun down, Tony," Jake yelled. "Game's over. Joyce helped me stop your poison brew. It's neutralized. You and your plans are finished. Give it up! Now!"

Tony didn't move. But he kept the gun pointed at Sophie. "I don't believe you, Barr. And I've got your kid, so you'd better—"

"Sophie! Hit the dirt!" Jake shouted. His rifle spoke.

Dawn saw Sophie fall to the ground and cover her head with her arms. The gun flew out of Tony's hand. He screamed with pain and rage and dug frantically in his jacket pocket with his uninjured hand.

Sophie didn't stir.

Tony drew out another gun and pointed it at her. Gus fired. At the same time, Joe's rifle banged. Lem's echoed it. Sam's pistol barked.

And Tony Edwards fell.

Joan and Todd screamed and started sprinting for the far side of the meadow. Dawn touched Pearl and Jasper on their flanks. "Get them!" she commanded. The Labradors took off, followed closely by the baying bloodhounds. In moments the four dogs had the pair down and were circling them, growling and snarling. Joan and Todd wisely remained motionless.

Sam, the smoking police pistol still clutched in his hands, stood up and gazed at the scene below. "Oh my God," he said softly. "We got them, but we're going to have a hell of time sorting this one out."

Dawn glanced at him. He was smiling. She gave him a grin in reply and started running down the slope to Jake and Sophie. When she reached the girl, Sophie was getting to her feet, and Jake was on his knees, embracing her tightly.

Jake held out his hand for Dawn. She looked into his green eyes and saw all the magic that had first drawn her to him. It was still as strong as it had been that first moment, but now the magic had become reality. She entered the circle of their arms and shared his embrace with Sophie. Dawn started to cry then, and her body ached all over.

She had never in her life felt so good!

AS SAM HAD PREDICTED, it took a while to sort everything out.

Dawn's Saab was towed into town, and police investigation showed clearly that the brakes had been deliberately set for failure. And the seat belt had been tampered with as well. She had been lucky to find a rock big enough to withstand the onslaught.

After some official pressure was brought to bear, Joan Dawson confessed to rigging the brakes and the seat belt. A second count of attempted murder was added to the ex-cop's indictment sheet. She had also been responsible for adding the poison to Jake's system, first through his IV, then in the innocent-looking muffin. Joan was going down, and going down hard.

Todd Beckman confessed to setting the smoke bomb in the elevator as well as a variety of sabotages involving the computers. It had been his fine hand at work, destroying all the data on Jake's computer. He had also aided Tony in adjusting Joyce's relatively harmless—if very unpleasant—formula into a toxic brew.

Sophie had been used as a pawn by her mother and Tony. She had been sent to the Well under orders to obey Joan Dawson. Joyce had poisoned her daughter's mind against her ex-husband by telling her stories about Jake's supposed illegal actions and his intentions of using the Well for insurance fraud. Sophie had been torn by dual loyalties as she rediscovered her love for her father. By the time Joan began to demand her services and help, Sophie was an emotional mess. Only Joyce's regular e-mail admonitions kept her in line.

Joyce had suffered a deep mental breakdown as a result of her encounter with Jake and the reality of what Tony had intended. For the time being, she was under the best care Jake's money could provide, but she would eventually have to answer for her part in the crimes.

Sophie had recovered from her traumatic encounter with Tony with the resilience of youth. While she genuinely grieved for her mother, she was able to accept the situation.

After all, as she pointed out, she was going to get to stay at the Well with Dawn and Jake. She didn't have to go to school with "geeky" kids, and she was able to bask in her fame as a heroine. Because she'd had the sense to follow Jake's command when she'd been in danger of being shot by Tony, she was seen by the locals as a child worthy of the Barr family lineage. She was given respect and a sense of belonging that she had never enjoyed before.

Sophie Barr was truly happy for perhaps the first time in her young life.

It was obvious that Farley Wold and Laurie Tanner were also happy. "Things are going really well between us," Laurie confided in Dawn. "We've talked for hours and hours."

Dawn smiled at the happiness in Laurie's voice. She could say the same about Jake and herself. That terrible night, kneeling on the cold ground in the high meadow, held against Jake's body by his strong arm, her emotions still ablaze over the brush with death they had all suffered, she *knew* without a shadow of a doubt that this was where she belonged. Everything else she had done was only preparation for this: her love and her future with Jake Barr.

It was almost two years later when the book *Alive and Well* by Dawn Sutton-Barr hit the *New York Times* bestseller list.

The back-cover blurb about the author read:

Dr. Dawn Sutton received her Ph.D. in 1996 after defending her thesis on ''Innovative Ways to Link Business and Community.'' She is married to Dr. Jacob Barr, founder of the highly successful enterprise, Jacob's Well, on which this book is based.

The couple make their home at the Well, deep in the West Virginian woods, with their thirteen-year-old daughter, Sophie, and infant son, Camden.

HARLEQUIN SUPERROMANCE®

WOMEN WHO DARE
They take chances, make changes
and follow their hearts!

The Father Factor
by Kathryn Shay

Amanda Carson has helped many parents in her job as
guidance counsellor but never has she come across one who
challenges her as much as Nick DiMarco. The single father of
two is determined to prove he can handle everything—even
his difficult teenager. Fiercely proud, he wants no help from
"outsiders." But the DiMarco kids—and their stubborn
father—have found a special place in Amanda's heart. Now
all she has to do is convince Nick to let her into his.

**Watch for *The Father Factor*
by Kathryn Shay**

**Available in September 1995 wherever
Harlequin books are sold.**

HARLEQUIN SUPERROMANCE®

**He's sexy, he's single...and he's a father.
Can any woman resist?**

JACOB'S GIRLS
by Tara Taylor Quinn

Girl trouble. Jacob Ryan has it in triplicate. Seven-year-old Allie
is organizing her teacher to death. Seven-year-old Jessie is crying
in class. Seven-year-old Meggie is becoming almost reclusive.
Jacob's told that what the triplets need is a woman in their lives—
and maybe they do. But that's the last thing *Jacob* needs.

Woman trouble. He's gone that route before. All it did was get his
daughters' hopes up—*his* hopes up—and then the lady left.
Maybe the answer is to enlist the help of a friend, someone like
his partner, Michelle....

**Watch for *JACOB'S GIRLS* by Tara Taylor Quinn.
Available in September 1995,
wherever Harlequin books are sold.**

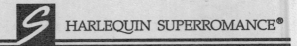

Pregnant...and on her own!

THREE FOR THE ROAD
by Shannon Waverly

Mary Elizabeth Drummond: She's a sheltered "good girl" with a pedigree a mile long. She's three months pregnant. She has no intention of marrying her baby's father. She's lost her credit cards, her driver's license and her money. She's on her own for the first time in her life.

Then she meets Pete Mitchell—tough, sexy, a confirmed bachelor.

Things are looking up.

Watch for *Three for the Road* by Shannon Waverly.
Available in September 1995,
wherever Harlequin books are sold.

NML-4

The Dunleavy Legacy
by Janis Flores

For more than a century, the Dunleavy name stood behind
the winners of horseracing's most prestigious prizes. The
family's wealth and fame was recognized in the most
powerful circles.

But times are different now, and the new generation of
Dunleavys is about to claim its legacy. Meet the three
grandchildren of Octavia Dunleavy, matriarch of the
family, as they deal with old feuds and jealousies, with
family pride and betrayal, in their struggle to restore the
Dunleavy dynasty to its former glory.

Follow the fortunes of Carla, Nan and Seth
in three dramatic, involving love stories.

#654 DONE DRIFTIN' (August 1995)
#658 DONE CRYIN' (September 1995)
#662 NEVER DONE DREAMIN' (October 1995)

This eagerly awaited trilogy by critically acclaimed
writer Janis Flores—a veteran author of both mainstream
and romance novels—is available wherever Harlequin
books are sold.

DLL-1

PRIZE SURPRISE SWEEPSTAKES!

This month's prize:

BEAUTIFUL WEDGWOOD CHINA!

This month, as a special surprise, we're giving away a bone china dinner service for eight by Wedgwood**, one of England's most prestigious manufacturers!

Think how beautiful your table will look, set with lovely Wedgwood china in the casual Countryware pattern! Each five-piece place setting includes dinner plate, salad plate, soup bowl and cup and saucer.

The facing page contains two Entry Coupons (as does every book you received this shipment). Complete and return *all* the entry coupons; **the more times you enter, the better your chances of winning!**

Then keep your fingers crossed, because you'll find out by September 15, 1995 if you're the winner!

Remember: The more times you enter, the better your chances of winning!*

*NO PURCHASE OR OBLIGATION TO CONTINUE BEING A SUBSCRIBER NECESSARY TO ENTER. SEE THE REVERSE SIDE OF ANY ENTRY COUPON FOR ALTERNATE MEANS OF ENTRY.

**THE PROPRIETORS OF THE TRADEMARK ARE NOT ASSOCIATED WITH THIS PROMOTION.

PWW KAL